Lily and the Ghost of Michael Thorne

NP Haley

Edited by Ron Vincent

Lily and the Ghost of Michael Thorne

Copyright 2014

All rights reserved. No part of this publication may be reproduced, stored in a retrieval system or transmitted in any form by any means, electronic, mechanical, photocopy, recording or otherwise without the prior permission of the publisher except as provided by USA copyright law.

ISBN-13: 978-0-9891276-1-5

Layout and interior design:
Infinity Graphics
Okemos, Michigan
www.mycoverdesign.com

Printer:
Infinity Graphics
Okemos, Michigan
www.infinitygraphics.com

Published by:
All 50!-Publications

*This book was written in loving memory
of my Mother and Father*

Rev. Arthur C Pruiett
*My good-looking father who, as a child
growing up in Caruthersville
and surrounding areas,
was called "Bugpappy"*

&

Catherine Patterson-Pruiett
*My beautiful American Indian mother
who was born in Malden, MO*

"Except for the fact that my father was called "Bugpappy" as a child, and the town of Caruthersville, MO being an actual town, *Lily and the Ghost of Michael Thorne* is entirely fiction. This book evolved from my Dad's stories of his life along the Mississippi River."

NP Haley

Acknowledgements

THIS BOOK IS DEDICATED TO RON HALEY; you are a unbelievably wonderful husband and supporter of my efforts. Without you I would have given up. You are the wind beneath my wings. My beautiful daughter Kathy; you are the precious gift God gave me when I needed something good in my life. And to Ronnie Vincent; you will never know how much you help and inspire me. Not only in the writing of this book, but in so many other aspects of life. I love you all.

To Steve Martin; you opened the door of my dream and made it a possibility.

All of you are a wonderful part of my life

> *"In everyone's life, at some time, our inner fire goes out. It is then burst into flames again by an encounter with another human being. We should all be thankful for those people we call friends who rekindle the inner spirit."*
>
> - Albert Schweitzer -

Lily and the Ghost of Michael Thorne

Glossary

For those of you who may not be familiar with some of the words used in the south during the late 1800's

fracas	a noisy scramble of people or proceedings
consumption	a word used to describe any disease a doctor could not identify
vittles	"food"
hit	"it"
frippery	something showy, frivolous or unnecessary
tinny piano	a cheap, well-used, out-of-tune piano (sounding like a tin can)
levee	a man-made embankment built to prevent flooding
haint	"ghost"
jest	"just"
privy	outhouse, outside bathroom
thar' or thur'	"there" or "their"
fur or fer	"for"
shanty	a very small abandoned shack or shed

x   *Lily and the Ghost of Michael Thorne*

CHAPTER ONE

The Levee

Sweat dripped down her back and soaked through her shirt as she squatted in the pickle barrel. The sickening-sweet smell of vinegar and pickling spices made her stomach churn as if trying to expel its contents. She was quite certain she would lose the little bit of food she had in her stomach if she didn't breathe through her mouth.

So there she sat, holding her nose and listening to rats scurrying around the barrel in their frantic search for food. They were scratching and squealing at one another as if one of them had found a pot full of pickle pieces. She knew if she pushed the top of the barrel up, she would see rats scurrying around and squealing as they fought for food.

She could also hear the two river drunks stumbling and knocking over empty barrels as they yelled for her to come out and show herself.

"Boy…ya betta' come on outta thar from whur ya be a'hidin." One of them yelled in a drunken slur.

"Come on boy, get on out here."

The other drunk belched loudly as he tried to yell, but the burp overpowered his words making the entire sentence came out as one long disgusting belch.

Again he belched long and loud; ending the episode with a loud, drawn out fart — he may have filled his drawers!

"Ahhh," he signed "I'm a'feelin mighty fine now. All that thar a'runnin with a belly full of whiskey and slop, that thar say-loon calls food, jest ain't a'settin' too rightly in my belly."

"We jest want to talk to ya, boy." the first drunk called out. "We jest want to talk to ya and see if ya be cold or hungry. We done got some vittles here fur ya, boy."

"Whad'ja say that fur, Pug?" the second drunk yelled, "We ain't got no vittles. And if'fen we did, I'd be a'eatin em fur sure."

"I know'd it. I'm just a'tryin' to coax him on outa his hidey-hole. I'm a'thinkin he's hungry. He must be. He's skinny as this here stick I'm a'carrying."

"So, they think I'm a boy!" Lily thought to herself, "well, good. If they find out I am a girl, they will never give up looking for me,"

She had been up on the river road, looking for Benny and Tessa when the two drunks spotted her and quickly started stumble-running towards her. She had begun running and was well ahead of them when she got a stitch in her side.

"Chicken poo," she had gasped as she stopped to catch her breath.

She had put her hands on her knees and hung her head down, trying to catch her breath and get rid of the pain in her side.

That was when the strangest thing happened; it was as if a dark cloak was placed around her shoulders and engulfed her entire body. It swept her along a lot faster than she normally ran.

But once she reached the dock, on the river side of the levee, which was full of empty pickle barrels waiting to be refilled and shipped down the river to New Orleans, the cloak had vanished, and there she was standing next to all the empty wooden pickle barrels.

The pounding of her heart had jumped up into her ears; it had felt as if her heart was trying to jump out of her chest and take off running on its own.

Quickly and quietly she had moved into the crowd of barrels; selected one close to the levee wall she dove inside, and pulled the lid into place as she went.

And now, here she sat, shaking uncontrollably, breathing though her mouth with her stomach rolling and churning from the smell of pickle brine.

"What the holy Hannah was with that darkness?" she whispered to herself. When the darkness had first wrapped itself around her, she thought it was because she was going to faint. But here she was — she hadn't fainted. In fact, the darkness had felt warm and comforting.

She was quite certain that all her blood had, by now, drained into her feet. She felt light-headed and her brain seemed to be as fuzzy as a baby chick's down. The thoughts of the darkness and the thick smells of pickle brine were almost too much for her.

Maybe she had just imagined the whole thing. She didn't know what that darkness had been or where it had come from and at the moment she didn't care. Even if it was all in her mind it sure had helped her move faster!

The fear she had felt when those drunks started yelling at her was enough to make her sprout wings and fly.

They had just kept on stumble-running after her, all the while yelling for her to "Stop, we jest want ta talk ta ya, young'un!"

She knew they didn't want to "just talk to her", especially once they found out she was a girl. If she was caught, within minutes she would have been on a riverboat heading down to New Orleans to be secretly sold to the highest bidder and taken away to unknown places.

All who live along the Mississippi River knows the stories of the illegal child slave-trade and how rampant it is in New Orleans and other port cities along the Gulf. It didn't matter what color or age; a kidnapped child will put a bag of gold into the kidnapper's pockets. It is something that is only whispered about in polite society, but everyone in the south knows about this evil business; but very little has been done to put an end to it.

"Whur the heck is that thar' brat?" one drunk called out. "Dang it all to Hades and back, I know'ed he were a'runnin down onta this here riverboat dock. I see'd him with my own eyeballs."

The two drunks stopped walking and looked around as they continued talking to each other. "I bet'ja he slipped inta that thar river and swimmed away," one said.

"That thar's jest what he done did! Stupid young'un!" the other replied.

"Let 'em drown! That thar' water's too cold to go in a'swimmin. I ain't a'goin in thar' ta fish 'em out."

"Dammed if I know'd whur he is. I cain't see 'em a'floatin' in the river. He's done gone and drowned his own self!"

"Well, ya won't see 'em yet cuz he ain't done a'drownin' yet. Hit's body has ta fill all the way up ta hit's neck fur him to start in a'floatin'."

"I ain't knowin' about that thar! Let me tell ya bout a feller I once't knowed that up and got snatched inta this here ole river — right here. We was out on one of them thar boats that take ya across the river and hit was a'taken us cross to Ten-see when all of a sudden-like, that thar feller was gone! Hit was jest like a water haint jest reached right up and grabbed a'holt of him and snatched him right off'en our boat! And that feller was the meanest one of us all. He would sell his own granny fur a chicken leg. Hit was like God himself come'd right on up out'a that thar river and drow't him in this here water. I'm a'thinkin' — that thar feller is right now a'sitting down in that thar farrie' furnace. Prob'ly jest a'wonderin what happened."

The drunk was telling his story with gusto and Lily was certain his arms were flapping around as he acted out the whole story.

"Now, I gotta tell ya, Pug, I weren't a lookin' at the feller when hit happened, but some of the other fellers was. They swear'd on thar mama's grave that a haint hand came right on up outta that thar water and latched right onta that feller. Hit were a big ol' haints hand.

That thar haints hand were as big as the boat we was a'ridin in, so they said. Hit was plum scary, I tell ya, plum scary. Hit was like maybe a water haint was in thar for that one par-tic-lar man and and hit only wanted jest that feller. Maybe like — the good Lord sent in his water haint to snatch him right off'en that thar boat!

And he weren't in that thar river but fer one shake and all of a sudden-like his body pops right back up outa that thar water like a cannon. He was dead I tell ya. His belly was already as big as a punkin and his face was a'lookin like hit was about to explode. We took on out of thar a'for that thar body came back down to the water. We got on land and never looked back. All's we heard behind us were this here big ol' ker-plunk! And I ain't never been back inta this here river, and I ain't never gonna go back inta this here river. Hit could be full of water haints jest a'lookin fur me, I tell ya, and I ain's the best living feller around! Nope. Ya ain't never gonna citch me a'goin inta this here river. Ain't a'gonna do hit and — hit ain't a'gonna take very long fur that'un to fill up either. He ain't nothin' but a stick."

"Well ya didn't see him with yur own two eyeballs a'tall, Jug. Ya only got jest one eyeball, ya pea brain," the other drunk stated.

"Well, I done did see 'em with my one eyeball and anyways, we sure be a'needin to find 'em."

"Yeah, I know'ed it," replied Pug, "We be a'gettin a pretty dang big ol' poke of gold fur that'un. He be mighty scrawny fur a young'un, but, he'll be a'fillin out plenty when he gets his full grow a'goin and all."

"I bet we could get a hun'erd dollars in gold dust fur that'un."

"Well, hits a'lookin' like he done got away from us. Let's go on back ta that thar say-loon an have another look-see tomor'ee. I be so winded I cain't hardly take a breath." Pug panted. "So if'n yur' a'wantin' to keep on a'lookin', go right on ahead. I'm a'going on back ta wet my whistle. He done gone and jumped inta that thar river and is purt near fish bait by now."

"Good idee'," Jug glumly replied. "But I be about all out of money jest like you be. So I'm a'keepin' my eyeball open fur that thar little critter. How he got so fur ahead of us so fast, I'll not be a'knowing.. Hit weren't normal I tell ya. Hit jest weren't normal."

"Yeah, I think I'm a'wantin to get on out of here too. Thinking about them thar river haints and all gets me a mite spooked. Let's get on out of here."

Well, we'll citch him. Maybe not tonight, but there's always tomor'ee."

"Maybe somebody's a'knowin' who he is and whur his hidey-hole is."

Lily sat perfectly still as she tried to breathe quietly. She squeezed her eyes shut and lifted her head toward heaven.

"Dear Lord in heaven, I ask you to please send them away." Lily whispered. "They are dirty rotten flap-eared, egg-sucking, stinking pole-cats, and I need to find Benny and Tessa. Sorry God, I know I shouldn't be calling them names while I'm asking for help, but you know they are the most low-down, stinking piles of pig-poop on this earth. Pardon me again, God, I know you already know that."

She heard the drunks scrambling around as they tried to get away from the dock and the haints as fast as their drunken legs could carry them.

After quite a bit of huffing, puffing, farting, burping and cussing, they managed to stumble back out onto Waterfront Street; all the while crying about the bag of gold that just jumped in the river and "swimmed" away.

Thump…thump…thump… she could hear the huge paddle steam-wheeler boats bumping and rubbing against the sides of the docks as the river currents pushed and pulled them against the wooden framework. Every time the one of the boats hit the framework, Lily's heart jumped into her throat. That sound was enough to scare the skin off her body!

The steam-wheelers loomed high above the landing, their towering smoke stacks swaying back and forth with the rhythm of the river. Some of the boats had four levels and three smoke stacks. The smoke stacks were so tall they could be seen from the other side of the levee.

As they sat majestically on the river, these steam-wheelers were a grand sight to see. Every day, people near the river could hear the look-out pilots calling out, "nooo bottom" or "marrrk twain" as he measured the depth of the river while passing by the small towns. Hearing the look-out pilot calling out the depth of the mighty river always put a longing in Lily to board one of these steam-wheelers and travel the world.

These huge boats reminded Lily of the pictures she had seen, as a small child, of the queens in Europe. Like most of the queens, the passenger steamers were always bedecked in a lot of frippery. Ruffled lattice work winding around each deck railing made them look like squatty, chubby queens floating down the river. In her mind's eye, Lily always imagined little short, chubby, queenly legs floating along underneath the steamers as they chugged up and down the Mississippi.

The most magnificent steam-wheeler of all was the New Orleans Sirene. When the Sirene came up or down the Mississippi, all the people living along the river's edge would go out and watch her pass. She never had the need to stop at a small town like Caruthersville, Missouri, but the passengers from Natchez or New Orleans paid a large amount of money to ride the New Orleans Siren, did so because they wanted to preen and display their wealth along the way.

The majority of the passengers were quite wealthy, so when life in New Orleans grew boring, when they became tired of parties and teas, they paid outrageous fares to ride the Siren all the way up north to the mouth of the Missouri River and all the way back down. A trip on the Sirene took longer than usual; what with the passengers demanding that the captain move slowly so everyone on shore would be able to have a grand look at them and their finery.

Most of the passengers were not going anywhere in particular. They just delighted in showing off their wealth to the river folk — or so it was told in the New Orleans mansions where servants passed the gossip along to the commoners.

So every time the Sirene passed, people lined up on the river bank to watch her pass by. She was the high point of all the farmers along the river. It was the dream of most families along the river to one day be able to ride the Sirene. She was a beauty!

Musicians lining the Sirene's upper level always played the music of New Orleans as she passed by, with all the ladies on board patiently walking back and forth along the upper deck as they waited for an audience. The single young ladies would bunch together as they leaned over the railings, laughing and waving at the small-town folks. They twirled their parasols and daintily waved their lacy white-gloved hands; all the while throwing kisses to everyone admiring them. Quite often they would throw small pieces of tatted lace into the water so they could watch the young farm boys swim out and grab them. The children on board were dressed as miniature replicas of their parents. The little girls pranced up and down the decks as they twirled their parasols and waved their little girl handkerchiefs. The small boys wore suits and top hats and carried miniature canes. Their shoes were just as finely made and polished as their papas' were, and their little short walking canes were exactly like their papas'.

The Sirene was midnight black with bright red, white and gold trim. All the smoke stacks were painted a shiny black with the words "New Orleans Sirene" painted in gold down either side so it could be seen by viewers on both sides of the river. The top of the smoke stacks were capped with over-sized gold crowns which gleamed and sparkled when the sun hit them. Below the third level railing "New Orleans Sirene" was painted in bright red against a solid white background.

There were times when Lily had watched as the finely dressed female passengers walked back into their cabins with faces black from the thick smoke from the smoke stacks as it settled on the slow moving boat. But to the New Orleans ladies, it was all worthwhile because they had been able to show the river people just how beautiful and wealthy they were.

"The Sirene sure is the queen of the river," Lily thought as she sat in the pickle barrel peeking out through the crack between the barrel lip and the lid.

Shaking herself, Lily came back to her present problem.

During the day, the dock was not a safe place for any child, but at night it was downright dangerous and scary. Drunken sailors staggered on and off the boats while beggars and thieves wandered along the levee looking for anyone who may be an easy victim.

Lily pushed the lid of the barrel up and took a quick look-see around. The moon was peeking around the clouds and the moonlight glistened off the riggings that stretched between each smoke stack. The ropes were heavy with the night moisture and the moonlight glistening off the ropes made them look like giant, silver spider webs. The swaying shadows of the spider webs, mixed with the shadows of the boats moving with the rhythm of the river, appeared to be hiding evil spirits and creatures of the night. The moonlight played tricks on Lily's eyes as she peeked out onto the landings. The shadowy forms of the ropes and pulleys shifted from looking like glistening dewy spider webs to creatures skulking along the tops of the boats and jumping from the boats onto the landing. All the shadows seemed to be dancing a devil's dance on the wooden planks of the wet shimmering dock.

Lily could hear the slapping of the water around the huge paddle wheels as the boat rose and fell with the rough Mississippi. The river seemed to be in turmoil as the wind slapped the waves and knocked them against the steam boats. The sounds of the wooden docks being pushed and pulled by the movement of the water caused fear to swell up in Lily's stomach.

Lily pulled her old hat down lower on her head and tried to tighten her coat. Since she had worn a pair of Gran-pappy's old woolen socks, her feet weren't too cold. It was a good thing no one had thrown out Gran-pappy's things when he died.

Lily wrinkled her nose as she slowly pushed the top of the empty barrel further up and was quite sure she would never eat another pickle again for the rest of her life.

Thank goodness the two drunks had been too drunk, or too stupid, to realize all the barrels had been emptied and were waiting to be refilled and shipped out on the next pickle boat going down river. For some reason, probably drunkenness, they had not checked every barrel.

She peeked out to see if anyone was watching from the landing. Nothing moved.

The only thing she could hear was the movement of the paddleboats rubbing against the landing docks and the mumbling of voices coming from the top levels of the boats. The steam engines were quiet. It wouldn't become loud and noisy until just before dawn when the steam started building up in the engines.

The men standing on the top levels of the boats were guards in case someone tried to climb aboard their particular boat without permission. All of the boats, even the cargo boats, had gambling rooms, so some of those standing on the upper levels were probably gamblers taking a break from losing all their money. Since all the winning gamblers never took a break, it was obvious that these men were either losers or guards.

The guards did not care about bums and drunks walking along the docks, so they sure wouldn't care if they saw a skinny boy (or so they thought) snooping around.

"All the sailors must be in the saloons," Lily thought to herself as she pushed the top of the pickle barrel completely off. The wooden lid clunked loudly and rattled as it fell onto the wooden planks of the dock. Lily froze. Immediately, she ducked back down into the barrel for a few more minutes, and then slowly she stood up and slipped over the rim and stepped out onto the landing.

Benny's pants fit snuggly beneath Lily's shabby brown coat. Maybe she should have worn Gran-pappy's old pants, she thought to herself, she would have had to use a string to hold them up, but at least they were more comfortable than Benny's.

Out in the river, she could see more paddle steamers. The Mississippi was almost a mile wide here in Caruthersville, so the boats would drop anchor and wait to pull up to the landings just as the first rays of sunlight slipped their fingers across the river and the boats which were already docked began to leave.

As soon as the captains could see where to dock, they would be starting up the steam and slowly move toward the docks.

Because of the large number of cotton growers near Caruthersville, all the cargo paddle-steamers stopped and loaded up before heading up or down the river.

Each boat, anchored out on the river, was lit up brightly with their gas lamps gleaming from every window, making sure any night rafters or smaller boats would be able see them and avoid ramming their hulls. Against the dark sky, the big boats sparkled with light as the lanterns swayed with the rhythm of the water. But up close these very boats could be filled with evil. Some of these boats were used to take children from their families and never return them.

Yet every one of the steamers compelled the young boys of every town along the river. It was every young boy's dream to be a riverboat captain of a steam-wheeler.

"Benny!" Lily whispered loudly as she crouched over and scurried out onto the landing.

Trying not to alert anyone, Lily leaned over the side of the planks to get a closer look. The wooden planks were soaked and dripping with cold river water.

She lay on her stomach, feeling the water seep through her coat and shirt as she hung her head further over the side. She lifted one hand to hold her hat, and leaned over a little further.

"Benny!" Lily called a little louder. "Are you and Tessa down there? It's me, Lily!"

She could see the entire wooden framework underneath the landing. The moonlight made eerie glistening shadows within the intricate weave of the wooden planks. The planks crossed each other so many times it looked like spindly spider patch work. Under the docks, a person could easily hide from unwanted eyes. The whole structure creaked and groaned loudly with the pressure from the water coming in and going out, and the boats rubbing against its sides.

"Benny, it's me, Lily, if you're down there, answer me. We have to get out of here before someone sees us or Aunt Birdie sends ole Elmer down here to find us." Lily paused for a second, and then said once more, "Benny, come on, answer me!"

Then a small squeaky voice called out from under the dock, "Lily!" Lily could hear a lot of mumbling, then Benny spoke loudly.

"Tessa! If you will just keep you voice down and do what I tell you to do, I can get us out of here. Lily, we're coming out on the right side of the dock. There are some wood planks we can use as a ladder. Reach out and grab Tessa's hand before she yells out again or falls in the river."

Lily scurried over to the other side of the dock and looked under. Finally she saw them. Benny had a tight hold on Tessa's waistband and was almost dragging her through the wet slippery wooden framework.

Lily held her breath and watched as Tessa's feet kept sliding off the planks and Benny had to drag her back up by her waistband.

As Benny and Tessa inched along the planks, Lily could barely breathe. The waves were splashing against the wooden planks; at times nearly covering both Benny and Tessa. If Tessa lost her footing with both feet, Benny may not be able to keep her upright. The water was extremely deep and rough here and she doubted Benny could save Tessa.

Neither Lily nor Tessa knew how to swim very well, and Benny couldn't save a frantic Tessa.

Lily held her breath until they were within reaching distance then quickly stretched down and grabbed Tessa's hand to pull her up onto the dock.

Tessa was shivering, her lips were blue, and all her clothes were dripping with water. Both she and Benny were soaked from the river water.

Tessa's wet clothes made her look incredibly thin and she looked as if she would crumble onto the landing at any moment. Lily took her own coat off and wrapped it around Tessa's small body.

Lily started to worry. If Tessa got sick how would she and Benny be able to help her? "Come on Benny, hurry up. Tessa is so cold her lips are blue." Lily whispered loudly.

"I'm coming as fast as I can, Lily!" Benny snapped. As he reached to pull himself up, Lily took his hand and helped him. His hands were as cold as Tessa's were.

"What were you two doing down there? You had me worried sick!" Lily said.

"Well," Benny started saying — then he looked at Tessa. "Ah, let's go get Tessa warm and then I'll tell you about it."

The three of them hurried along the dock and up onto the path leading to Waterfront Street. They ran as fast as they possibly could, Lily and Benny each holding one of Tessa's arms they helped her hurry along. They ducked down behind barrels and boxes whenever someone came their way. Lily couldn't help but wonder what had happened.

As they approached the Waterfront St saloons, all three of them bunched closer together so they could wedge Tessa between them. Farm hands, stevedores, longshoremen, drunks and ladies of the night were everywhere. The clank of the tinny, out of tune, saloon pianos were loud; each of them trying to out-play the next. Drunken men wandered the streets as they kept a keen eye open for any opportunity to snatch up a child, no matter the color, and sell them to the slavers who, in return, would sell them to profiteers who would

CHAPTER ONE: THE LEVEE

turn around and sell them to the underground slave market. The sailors were mean, ugly men. Most of them had lost all their teeth and their faces were so dirty it was hard to determine what they really looked like.

If one of them got within ten feet of a blind person, he or she would know they were from the boats anchored on the river. Their smell always gave them away. The smell of whiskey, sweat, urine and filth surrounded the water front businesses as it left a lingering odor floating around the inhabitants who walked the streets. Lily had seen men from the boats urinating on themselves because they were too drunk or stupid to realize what they were doing. They were disgusting evil men.

"Hey, boys!" A drunk shouted, as he sat on a woodpile outside one of the saloons. "Wanna sell that thar little girlie ya got with ya?" Lily heard Tessa's gasp as she tightened her grasp on Lily's hand.

They started running, Lily and Benny pretty much dragging Tessa along with them.

They all knew stories of parents who would sell their children to these men in order to feed the rest of their children.

"They probably didn't want their children in the first place." Lily thought to herself. "They probably have children just to sell to the slavers and make more money." Lily knew one thing for sure: she and Benny had to get themselves and Tessa away as soon as they possibly could.

There were times when Lily would see proper ladies coming off the passenger boats with handkerchiefs covering their noses and not touching anything until they were handed into their carriages which awaited them at the end of the dock. The carriages whisk the ladies away as quickly as they could.

"Come on, come on!" Lily whispered loudly. "If we're caught, we'll all be in a fine mess." As the three passed each saloon, they hunkered down so no one inside could see them through the windows or open holes where the windows had once been (before it had been shattered by something, or someone, being thrown through it). Some of the saloons had boards nailed across the openings. The owners had grown tired of purchasing glass and having it shattered every Saturday night. At least planks kept out all the four and two legged animals.

When the three of them passed the Ruby Slipper Saloon they turned right and went into the back alley. Quietly they slipped into the small shanty behind the Ruby Slipper.

"Okay," Lily said, as she lit the lantern and the small potbellied stove. "Tell me what happened."

"Well," Benny whispered a little louder as Lily sat Tessa down and took Tessa's wet shoes and stockings off, "just as me and Tessa came out of the back of the bake shop, Aunt Birdie walked past and saw us."

"She started yelling and trying to catch us." Tessa whispered, wide-eyed with fear. Then Benny continued, "I was so scared she would get Tessa, my heart was pounding right out of my chest. We ran as fast as we could until we got to the docks. I knew if we hid underneath them Aunt Hogs-waddle would never find us. I sure was glad you came along when you did Lily, I thought for sure she would go home and get that old man, Elmer, and send him back to find us. That's why we were down at the far end of the landing once you got there. I don't think Aunt Hogs-waddle realized we could squeeze under the planks down on that side."

"Her name isn't Aunt Hogs-waddle, Benny, it's Aunt Birdie." Lily replied softly.

"Well" Benny said, "She looks just like a hog waddling to me, I don't understand why Pappy H called her Birdie. She's too wide for a bird and she couldn't fly if she had a whole flock of eagles holding onto her arms. She looks just like that ol' hog of Mr. Pruiett's waddling down the path though the field!" Benny mimicked a waddling hog as he told his story, "She waddles so much she could knock a grown-up man down to the ground; or even out into the street if she hit him with her behind! And her face, I swear by the bottom of my britches, looks just like a hog! In fact our ol' hog Sully looks prettier than she does, and Sully is much nicer! Sully really is a nice hog. If a hog can be nice," Benny laughed.

"Aunt Hog's eyes are smaller than Sully's are and Sully's nose is much prettier. Sully is a pretty smart hog. I've even taught her to roll over and come to me when I call her. Well, she will if I have the slop bucket with me." Benny laughed loudly,

"Ha, I'd like to see Aunt Waddles roll in the mud and come running for the slop bucket. Wouldn't that be funny, Lily?" he grinned as he continued; "I can see it now, Aunt Waddle just a-sloppin' in the slop-bucket trying to eat her supper."

"Benny" Lily answered sharply, "Aunt Birdie is not fat or wide or ugly. You just think that because she is not a nice person. She is skinnier than mama was but she's not nice, that's the whole problem. She's not a good person. But you really shouldn't be talking like this in front of Tessa."

"Lily, I already know she looks like a hog waddling from the back." Tessa giggled and her big green eyes widened and her eyebrows arched higher than usual.

"And her face really does looks like a hog. I think when she was born, Pappy and Granny H got her mixed up with someone else's baby. Somebody must have crawled into Granny H's window during the night and switched babies. Probably because her real mama took one look at her baby and keeled right over onto the floor in a faint and then wouldn't get up until she had a baby that was human." Tessa laughed out loudly.

Benny laughed so hard he started coughing.

"That's it!" Benny exclaimed, "Her name has to be 'Birdie Anne Hog-jaws' and I bet you a goldurn good nickel she really isn't our aunt. She can't be Pa's sister; she's just too mean spirited! I just don't think she is our aunt! Pa would have warned us about her meanness. What we have to do here is to find a family with the last name of

"Hog-jaws" and they'll have our real Aunt Birdie!" Benny laughed as he kept on talking.

"We can just take their kin back to them, and take our real Aunt Birdie home with us! We get the good aunt, and they get the bad aunt along with her bad spirit. Hmm... But they may like our real aunt and not want this mean one we have. Maybe we can sneak in their house during the night and make the switch. They probably live up there in the Ozarks, so maybe they'll be happy to finally find their own kin. They won't really know how mean she is until it's too late and we'll be home already and too bad for them. They won't be able to do a goldurn thing! What do you think Lily?"

"I think you better stop cussing right now. We have to be serious about this." Lily scolded.

"I am being serious, me love," Benny said with a twinkle in his eyes as he used one of Pa's favorite endearments, "Aunt Birdie Hog-jaws is seriously ugly and seriously mean. I was scared serious. What was Aunt Birdie Hog-jaws doing at the bakeshop after dark? She never goes to town when it's dark, or even when it's close to dark as far as that goes. Ah-ha! I know! Maybe she stopped to get some hog feed and forgot the time of day" Benny smirked. "Or maybe, just maybe, she needed a new 'hog-trough' for her supper plate". He grinned wider, giving Tessa a wink as Tessa started giggling.

"I really don't know." Lily said. "But I bet I could guess," she thought to herself. "She was up to no good, that's for sure."

"You think she has some of those young'uns from over in Burl and is trying to sell them to the slavers?" Benny whispered, once again in a very serious voice.

Burl is a small settlement outside of town that is full of freed slaves and their families. They are now free men and women and they work the land for their food just like all the rest of the farmers along the river. Some of them fish for a living and bring their fish into town to sell. A few of them always stop at the farms along the way into town to sell some of their fish. Most years, Granny Tomason hires some of the young men folk to help work her farm; the same as their Pa had done during harvest season.

Tessa's eyes grew huge as she spoke in a whisper; "I saw her with two of Mrs. Sophie's girls the day before we left our house, they were crying for their mama, and Aunt Birdie told them if they stopped crying she would take them on a nice boat ride with a big picnic basket. The little one, Sylvie, stopped crying but then her older sister, Lizzy, jerked her arm away from Aunt Birdie, grabbed little Sylvie's hand and took off running as fast as she could out across the field towards her own house. All the while yelling at Aunt Birdie that her mama had told them that they were not to go anywhere with anyone and that her and her little sister wasn't going anywhere anyway with a mean old woman like Aunt Birdie.

Well, Aunt Birdie yelled something about getting the law after her for being sassy, but Lizzy just kept right on running. I was in the berry patch and I could see and hear the whole thing." Tessa's eyes were wide as she stretched out her arms and made a big circle.

"Later on that same day, Aunt Birdie started asking me about those squatters down in the river bottom. You know, Lily, the ones with those three little girls who all look alike. They are little like me and they never have to go to school. They're so lucky! Lily, you know what else, Lily. Their names are Molly, Polly, and Dolly, isn't that funny? I like them. They have wonderful names! And they all have real white hair and their eyes are the color of my eyes! Isn't that something, Lily?"

Tessa giggled and kept chattering on. "Our names should be, uh, Tessa, Bessa, and Lessa. And Caitlin could be Messa. Because of the big mess she is in. They even told me that they all have the same birthday. Isn't that funny?" Tessa's eyes were huge again. Every time she got excited about something, her eyes reacted.

"They're called triplets, Tessa," Lily told her. "They were all born on the same day."

"Really? Wow! Well that's a mighty fine thing!" Tessa smiled. "Well, anyway, Aunt Birdie Hog-jaws asked me all kinds of questions about them, but I didn't tell her a single thing. I just kept my lips shut tight and acted like I didn't even know who she was asking about."

"I don't like her." Tessa whispered as she frowned, making her eyebrows almost touch. "She would sell her own baby, if she had one. But she's too mean to have a baby. No man would want to put a baby in her belly. She's too scary." Tessa said.

"Tessa, you have to stop talking like that! That isn't the way a lady should talk!" Lily scolded. "But we do have to stay away from her until we can find Caitlin. I think Aunt Birdie could be dangerous."

Tessa's eyes filled with tears and she looked at Lily hopefully. "What happened to our Caitlin, Lily? Did she really just leave us here with Aunt Birdie and run away with a lover?" Tessa asked.

"No sweetheart. Aunt Birdie lied to us. She would like to snatch us up and tell everybody that Caitlin left us and now she has to take care of us. And she would say that she is doing the best Christian thing and that she dearly loves us but all the while she would be planning on selling us and say we ran away." Lily spoke sternly. "Just stay away from her. If you ever see her again, run."

"Here, Benny, you and Tessa share these sweet buns Mr. Johnston gave me. He said he would have to throw them out since they didn't look the way he wanted them to look. I thought they looked fine, but he said 'no one would buy them', so I accepted them. I'll go out and see if Granny Tomason's mulch cow will give me some milk for the morning."

As Lily put Gran-pappy's old hat and coat on, she watched Benny take Tessa over to the pile of old rags by the stove. He helped her take off her wet coat then turned around so she could have some privacy while putting on her long-johns and a dry dress.

The pot-bellied stove had warmed the shanty enough to keep them warm for the night.

Just in case someone stumbled along the alley and decided to check out the light coming from the shanty, Lily blew out the lantern, but they had to leave the fire burning in the old rusty pot-belly stove or it would get too cold for Tessa.

The weather was still cold at nights, but during the day it was growing warmer and warmer. Spring had arrived and the grass and trees were already turning green. The early spring flowers were now in full bloom. During the day the open fields and forest clearings were evolving into colorful paintings as an abundance of flowers displayed their petals of vivid color.

Lily was worried about Tessa. Tessa was only five, and small for her age. The good thing was that her mind was way beyond five. She could say some things that surprised the rest of them. She had a quick mind and a quicker mouth.

Lily's mind drifted to her brother and sisters. Tessa looked just like their mama, with her red-blonde hair and green eyes. When Lily thought of her mama, sometimes she pictured her with very light red hair and other times with light golden blonde hair. It was as if God could not make up his mind whether to give her and Tessa red hair or blonde hair. Occasionally Pa would refer to them as his jewels and say that their hair was part ruby red and part spun gold. When it came to eye color, Mama and Tessa's eyes could look as green as the leaves on the oak trees, and other times they looked like the green leaves of the lily-pads that grew in the pond behind Granny's house. They both had fair skin, with a sprinkling of freckle across their noses, and expressive dark brown eyebrows that moved up and down with their thoughts and moods.

Benny looked like Pappy H with his dark red hair and blue eyes. Mama had told them that Pappy H had freckles until the day he died, so Lily was sure Benny's freckles were on his face to stay as well. His arms and legs seemed to belong to a much taller person. Granny Tomason said Benny's body would one day catch up with his arms and legs. Lily sure hoped so, because he looked rather funny at the moment.

Caitlin and Lily looked like their Pa — dark black hair, amber gold eyes, with black eyebrows and long black lashes surrounding their eyes. Whenever Mama was worried about the crops coming in during harvest or anything else that went along with the cost of raising a family, Pa would laugh, give her a hug and tell her they had enough gold in the eyes of their two oldest daughters to last the two of them a lifetime and all he had to do was talk both girls into giving him their eyeballs and he and Mama could run away from their rascally wild offspring and live forever on a tropical island. At which time he would jump toward the girls and chase them out of and around the house, yelling at the top of his booming voice, "Give me ye gold ye pirating wench's!"

Caitlin and Lily would be running and screaming as if the demons of hell were after them. They would run off into the woods and Pa would act as if they had escaped him and go back to the house to tell Mama that the gold had slipped through his fingers, but that he would try again another day.

Mama would laugh at his foolishness and once again be in a good mood. What a happy man Pa had been. He had been the best father a person could ever want.

Thank goodness Benny had Pa's personality; he was very dependable and responsible. Instead of just running away when Caitlin disappeared, he had stayed by Lily and Tessa and helped get them all out of the house. Without Benny, she would have had to take Tessa with her every time she left the shanty.

"Where is Caitlin?" Lily wondered. "Had Aunt Birdie talked old Elmer into carrying her off to the boats?"

Elmer was a scary old man, and looked just as mean as Aunt Birdie. He was as tall as Pa had been, but he looked mean. He had crooked, dirty, greenish teeth and smelled like one of the sailors from the docks. His hair was always dirty, slicked back and tied at the nape of his neck with a piece of rawhide. It was black as coal and hung straight down his back, almost to his waist. Sometimes he wore it in a long braid which almost touched the top of his britches. His skin had a red darkness to it which made him look Indian. Or at least part Indian. His face was leathered from working in the outdoors so many years. He had the high cheekbones of an Indian, but his eyes were not the coal black of a true Indian, but they had a touch of green to them. He also had a piercing stare. If Elmer stared at a dead body, it would probably roll away. He was also without eyebrows. Instead, in their place, there were scars. It looked as if his eyebrows had, a one time, been sliced off with a knife, probably in a saloon fight Lily always thought. Oft times Lily wanted to ask him what had happened to his eyebrows, but she was too afraid of him to bother asking.

He had huge hands and massive muscles. He could probably carry away a full grown man without even breathing heavy. Sometimes Lily wondered why Aunt Birdie and Elmer had not gotten married since Aunt Birdie claimed Elmer had been her handyman for a long, long time.

Maybe Elmer just stayed around because he had a warm place in the barn to sleep and Aunt Birdie gave him plenty of food to eat. All he had to do was the small amount of work around the farm, which Benny helped him with. Aunt Birdie must be giving him money for his whiskey. Lily and her siblings had never figured out where Aunt Birdie got her money.

When Mama and Pa died, Caitlin had promised to take care of Benny, Lily and Tessa. She had also told them that since she was twenty-three, no one could take them away from her. Surely that included Aunt Birdie! Aunt Birdie and Elmer had arrived the day after Mama and Pa's funeral. Aunt birdie said they were already on their way for a visit when they got the sad news about the accident.

A little at a time Aunt Birdie took over everything in the house as she started cooking and cleaning as if it were her own house. She gradually moved Mama and Pa's things out of the house and into the barn. She told them it just made her too sad to look at things that reminded her of her beloved Daniel.

Every time she moved something out of the house and into the barn, Caitlin would move it back into her own bedroom. If Caitlin had not moved into Mama and Pa's bedroom the night after their funeral, Lily was sure Aunt Birdie would have gone straight into their room and stayed.

As it was, Aunt Birdie had told Lily and Tessa they would have to share the same room so she could have the room Lily and Caitlin had originally shared.

She started telling everyone what to do and when to do it. Caitlin tried to stop her by telling her that there was no need for her to work so hard since all four of them lived there and it really was their house. But Aunt Birdie had smiled and said stiffly, "Oh mercy me dear, I do realize that, I surely do. But I am sure your dear sweet mother and my sweet Daniel would surely want me to stay and take care of you children to the best of my ability. This will all work out for the best, yes indeed it will."

When Caitlin disappeared, Aunt Birdie told everyone in town that the house was now hers; now that Caitlin had run off with a lover and left all the children for her to take care of.

Lily's stomach grew tight and an ache rose up in her chest just thinking about all of it. Caitlin would never leave them. Even if she had run off with a "lover", which she did not do, she sure wouldn't leave her younger sisters and brother here with Aunt Birdie and old Elmer. Something had happened to her.

Lily and the Ghost of Michael Thorne

CHAPTER TWO

The Fog

LILY HURRIED along the dark alleyway. She really didn't want to leave Benny and Tessa alone for any length of time, but she had no choice. It was safer for Tessa if Benny stayed with her, and Tessa shouldn't be out in the cold after getting so wet. So that left Lily to go alone to Granny Tomason's house.

The flickering rays of light coming from the windows of the building along the alley would soon be gone and Lily would be in total darkness. The night air was cold and crisp and the fog was tumbling in from the river as it slipped its misty fingers into town. The hungry misty tentacles of fog curled around every obstacle in its path and swirled upward, all the while pulling everything, no matter what the size, into its shroud. Trees, buildings, and shrubs were becoming heavily veiled within the fog. It reminded Lily of an animal trying to devour its food before it was taken away.

Tree shadows moved and shifted in the night breeze like imaginary creatures as the fog swirled its way up their trunks, totally blocking out small leaves and pale spring blossoms. Then, just as quickly, the breeze blew the fog away, bringing trees, shrubs and houses back into focus, then with a rush, it swept in again, once again creeping up the surrounding building, trees and shrubs.

Lily found herself holding her breath as she looked down and realized the fog was swirling around her feet as it crept up her legs in an effort to blanket her in its wispy fingers. Goose bumps on her arms started tingling with cold as the mist slowly crept its way up her body.

She tried to brush it away, but it clung to her hands and made little puffs of fog when she shook it off. A slight breeze from the river pushed the fog all the way up to her waist in a quick rush.

Lily felt fear slide up her back and into her brain. Her mind envisioned herself being carried down the alley and into the river by these wispy fingers of fog. Frantically she began swinging her arms up and down her body as she tried to push the clinging fog away. "Okay Lily-girl," she said loudly, "Stop it. It's just fog."

The sounds from the saloons became fainter as she quickly walked away from the waterfront, her feet pushing the fog into puffs around her ankles like dry powdery dust.

She heard the yipping of a dog in the distance.

As it continued to yip, she could tell it was coming closer. She stood still as she tried to listen, the hound burst through the fog running directly towards her. Frozen in fear, Lily watched the hound sprint right by her, passing her without bothering to give her a glance. It was as if the dog had never seen her, even though it had brushed her pant leg as it passed. Wherever it was going, it was in a hurry. The hound left billows of fog tumbling behind him as he raced down the road and he kept glancing back as if he expected to see something or someone chasing him. It looked as if the fog was trying to keep up with the hound but was having a difficult time doing so. The fog eventually enveloped the hound, hiding him from Lily's sight and once again leaving only the fading yips.

Lily heard the hooting of the night owls and crickets as she continued to hurry along the road. The sounds of the night always seemed eerie to Lily, even back in her own home with the rest of her family. Tonight though, the fog rolling into the dark alley made the sounds downright spooky.

As she continued, the tinny sounds of the saloon pianos grew too faint to hear, and the sounds of the night became quiet. No owls were calling, and the bullfrogs and cricket had stopped their singing. The breeze was picking up and the fog was rolling along the road like giant tumble weeds being blown across the prairies. It quickly swirled, twisted and danced to the tune of the winds. It was eerily captivating.

Then, in a moment's time, the fog became thick and dense. The river seemed to have flung out a strong arm and given the fog a sharp push into Lily's path. Her view was completely blocked. Her vision was limited to a few short feet in front of her. She slowed down until she was walking in a shuffle, displacing the misty fog with every step. She felt claustrophobic, as if she were being encircled in a small closet surrounded by a white blanket.

There was no way she could see the road.

She had to stop — she couldn't breathe. She couldn't even move without fear of running into something.

Panic rose in her throat and terror swelled up within her.

Then, just as quickly as it had appeared, the fog and the winds were gone, leaving only a soft breeze to settle the mist and once again render the roads visible. The breeze actually felt warmer, like a gentle summer wind.

With the swirling fog settling to the ground, Lily's mind wandered back to the tales she had heard from her Pa about the dark evils that happen in the Black Forest of Germany when the moon and stars were covered and the fog was thick. She remembered stories of how wolves would come out at night to hunt for human flesh and howl, sometimes surrounding cabins built deep in the heart of the forest, as they called for someone to come out.

In those dark tales of the Black Forest, the occupants would swear the wolves could speak to them in a language they understood. The wolves would tell them of all the gold and silver they would give to anyone who would risk opening their doors. They would promise not to harm the humans if someone would just bring food out for them. The stories told of fools who believed the lies and opened the doors only to disappear forever.

It was told that the inhabitants of the cabins would have to put boards across their windows and doors to keep the wolves out. They had to put cotton in their ears to block out the soothing words of the wolves. Supposedly the wolves were so wise (and the men so foolish) that if any man, woman or child heard their soothing convincing lies, they would heed their call. On windowsills and behind closed doors, candles would burn brightly throughout the night to keep the evil whispers from slipping through the cracks like mist. The inhabitants had to keep a fire going in the fireplace, even in the hot summer nights, or words of the wolves would creep into the homes through the chimney.

Lily also thought of the tales Pa told about bad ghosts and leprechauns from Ireland — tales of how night evils would come when the fog was thick and the nights were black. He told of times when the moon and stars would hide themselves, as if afraid, behind heavy black clouds, and evil winds were heard echoing off the rolling green hills. A man, alone on the dark cobblestone streets of Dublin, would feel the clinch of fear as something, or someone, brushed its hand across the back of his neck, making goose bumps rise along their arms and legs. Hovering orbs of yellow light – the light of streetlamps obscured by the chilly fog – were the only source of light. The fog seemed to try to conceal the light, pushing it back into the lamps as far as possible.

This fog would ride in on great gusts of wind from the ocean, thick enough to stick to the sides of buildings and creep up the walls to the roof tops. It was called the devil's fog.

All the people of Ireland knew of the devil's fog, and believed that it truly could take your soul — or parts of your body — and leave behind an empty hole where your spirit had once lived.

When the devil's fog rolled in, the villagers would rush into their homes, shut and lock the shutters, turn the locks on the doors and not look out until the next morning. If a poor soul was caught in this sinister fog, they would rush to the nearest house, begging the residents to let them stay the night. There were many, many tales of what happened to poor souls who could not find a safe haven for the night. Some would be found the next morning, their arms and legs gone, or maybe with all their blood drained from their bodies. Worse yet, their life may have been spared, but at the cost of their soul, which was taken by the inhabitants of the devil's fog. From then on, night after night they would walk the streets of the village hunting for their lost souls. They were like the zombies in the African tales, never eating or sleeping, just trying to fill the empty hole where their souls had once lived.

Just in case the "devil's fog" came upon the village unawares, most of the shops on the village streets kept cots in the back where their workers could sleep for the night. Each shop had extra bedding for strangers who might rush to their doors during the fog's sudden appearance.

When Pa told his tall tales of ghouls and goblins, his voice would get low and he would speak slowly, leaning over his children as they sat on the floor staring up at him with eyes wide and mouths open. It was as if speaking any louder would conjure up vile creatures that would suddenly appear right behind them. Lily would scoot as close to Pa as possible and wrap her arm around his leg, keeping Benny behind her just in case the creatures tried to sneak in. Benny would try to laugh and Pa would look at him and say in a low rhythmic Irish lilt, "Don't believe it do ya now, laddie?" Pa would be grinning the whole time. "Let us all wait and see into the future, me boy. You'll come to see your dear ole Pa and be a-telling me the fearsome things ya had seen and heard as a wee laddie and be asking for me knowledge on how to be telling it to your own wee lads and lass's."

Mama would scold Pa, saying, "hush you're scaring me own wee-ones with such foolish tales, Daniel Henry Quinn. Don't ya believe his foolish tales, me wee ducks. Come on over here and I'll be telling ya tales of good leprechauns who give all good children, like yourselves, sweets and hugs."

"No Mama!" they would all say together, "we want to hear more of Pa's foolish tales!" Pa would laugh, wink at Mama, and start another.

On those nights, so long ago, Lily, Caitlin and Tessa would all sleep in the same bed. Even though Tessa was just a little infant and unable to understand any of the tales, having her in bed with them made Lily and Caitlin feel safer.

As Lily strained to see through the swirling fog, she spotted a lone shadow leaning against the side of a building. She stopped, swallowed and blinked her eyes to get a better look. Was it a leprechaun? Her heart was in her throat, the hair on the back of her neck stood up and once again bumps popped up on her arms and legs as the blood in her veins turned to ice. The shadow didn't move, but Lily could feel him watching her. She could not see the shadows eyes as he waved his arm beckoning to her.

Lily didn't move.

The shadow once again motioned for her to come closer.

"Run, Lily-girl, run!" she yelled in her mind.

She tried to start running, but her legs refused to move. They were not reacting to her brain's commands. Fear had her frozen. "Come on, come on!" she thought to herself.

The shadow moved, as if to come toward her, but stopped when a shutter on a second-floor window above him banged open. A woman stuck her head out the window and looked around.

"Well, Jack, me man, it could be God's own boots a'stomping right outside our window, but this fog is so thick we couldn't see him even if he was a'wearing candles on his boot straps," she yelled to someone behind her.

"It's as thick as river mud, this fog is. Get out there yourself, man, if you want to be a'seein' what the noise is, I'm not going out in this fine mess." The woman yelled again.

Lily had not heard the noise the woman was talking about. All she could see was the shadow. Lily squinted again to get a better look, but she could only make out the form — a person with a military hat and uniform.

"Whoa!" she muttered. "Who in the hind-leg-of-a-hound dog is that?"

The man was in a full soldier uniform! He started walking toward her. The man's hat was pulled down over his face, preventing Lily from making out his identity. He had a full beard and mustache with a slight smile; Lily didn't know if she should feel relief or fear.

As he got closer, Lily could see he was holding something out, as if he wanted her to take it. She couldn't make out what it was, but it lay in his open, outstretched palm.

"Lily-Beth," the shadow called to her in a low voice, "Lily-Beth, come here. Please. I need to talk to ya."

Lily thought her heart may have stopped for a moment. The only person who had ever called her by that name was Michael Thorne.

But Michael Thorne was dead!

The shadow was not quite into the alley when the fog suddenly tumbled back in with a quick, audible 'whoosh' and totally covered the man as it pulled him into its thickness. The upstairs window slammed shut and Lily's muscles woke up. She began to run as fast as she possibly could, fully expecting at any time to feel death's icy hands grab her ankles and pull her back into the fog.

Lily ran for what seemed like forever, her chest burning from breathing so hard, tears wanting to fly out of her eyes. She ran and ran, all the while quietly singing under her breath, interrupted by loud gasps for air, one of Pa's merry Irish tunes about the washerwoman; hoping it would calm her nerves:

When I was at home, I was merry and frisky.
My pa kept a pig, but my mother sold whiskey.
My uncle was rich, but ne'er could be easy
Till I was enlisted by Corporal Casey.

She ran and sang until she was out of breath and had to stop so she could breathe.

Finally — she was able to make out the light in Granny Tomason's window. Glancing over her shoulder, she saw no one following. No one was within sight. But that didn't mean they weren't back there somewhere. Still breathing heavily, she bent over and rested her hands on her knees trying to catch her breath. Lifting her head, she peered back down the road again. No one followed.

Straightening up, she knew she had to keep moving, in case the shadow had taken a different route to follow her. The tension in her body eased as she turned toward Granny's house and started to hurry along the path.

"Thank you, good Lord in heaven!" Lily sighed. "I sure hope I got away from whomever that was."

Granny Tomason's small farm was in the middle of a field of wild flowers and oak trees. Some of the wildflowers had already bloomed and the oak trees were full of lush green leaves. The wide path going up to Granny's gate was free of weeds.

Granny's house was a double shotgun house. Reason being, if you were to shoot a shotgun through the front door, the shot would go straight out the back door. Granny's house was larger than most shotgun houses, though. When you opened the front door, you immediately entered a straight hallway which enabled you to see the door to the back porch. There were four bedrooms off the left side of the hall and a parlor, dining room and very large kitchen off the right side of the hall. Granny's kitchen took up half of the right side of the house. It had a large walk-in pantry and a big eating table in the center of the room. A huge wood-burning cook stove stood along the back wall of the kitchen with wood piled as high as Lily's head on one side and the water pump in the dry sink on the other side. Granny said that was so she didn't have to tote water all the way across the room just to heat it.

The best thing about Granny's house was that it was covered with white and blue Morning Glory vines in the summer. The vines grew all the way up to the roof top and covered her roof. During the heat of the Missouri summers there were flowers all over her house.

Mama once told all of them that Granny and her husband had wanted a lot of children when they first married, but it never happened, so now Granny had a big beautiful home but no children to fill it. Granny said that the good Lord knew what was best and she was fine with his decision. When the topic of children came up, Granny always said, "The good Lord always knows what he's doing".

Most days Granny paid Benny or one of the boys from town to come out and chop wood and do her heavy chores. She either gave the boys cash or food for their families. The boys worked hard for her and kept her farm in good condition.

As she walked up to the house, Lily could hear the rustle of small animals among the wildflowers that grew tall and thick across the meadow in front of the house. During the summer months, a variety of flowers — Blue Bonnets, Clementine's, Coneflowers and particularly wild red rose bushes — painted the meadow with color.

Granny Tomason was not really their granny, but she had known Mama and Pa for a long time. She was the Quinn children's best friend, and a good friend at that — she would help them out with anything they needed. She had once told Lily that she was some distant relative, but Lily could not remember which side of the family Granny said she came from.

34 *Lily and the Ghost of Michael Thorne*

CHAPTER THREE

Granny's House

LILY APPROACHED Granny Tomason's house through the front gate as Pie Eater, Granny Tomason's dog, stood up on the porch and started barking. His tail was wagging so hard his whole backside and back legs were moving with it. He had red fur and was as big as a small mama bear.

But Pie Eater wouldn't hurt a flea. All he wanted was a free handout of food and as much belly-scratching as he could beg off a person.

"Hi, Pie Eater!" Lily called out. Pie Eater had gotten that particular name because he always ate Granny's pies as they sat on her windowsill cooling after coming out of the oven.

Pie Eater loped down the steps and jumped on Lily as she came in through the gate. She smiled and scratched his head.

The door to the house opened and Granny's face peeked out.

"Well, Lily Quinn, hurry up child and get on in here. It's too cold to be out in this kind of weather. What are you doing coming all the way out here this time of the night? What's happening at your house? Something I should know about? You children need some help?"

With a sigh of relief Lily replied, "Yes, Granny, we do. Caitlin's disappeared and we left our house because Aunt Birdie slapped me. We just need a little milk until Benny and I can find Caitlin. Mr.

Johnston, the baker, is giving us some of his sweet buns at the end of each day, so we have something to eat, but I'm worried about Tessa." Lily blinked and swallowed, afraid she would start crying.

Lily decided she wouldn't tell Granny about the shadow she encountered on the way out. Granny might make her stay the night and Lily couldn't leave Benny and Tessa alone in the shanty for that long.

"Whoa, hold on there girl. Come on in here where it's warm and have a set-down at the table. So Caitlin's missing? What in tarnation is going on here? What is wrong with little Tessa and where is Tessa and Benny? She pulled out a chair and motioned for Lily to sit down.

Granny put some wood into her cook stove and stoked the fire. She bustled around getting Lily something to eat as she waved her hand at Lily as if to say "start in talking". Lily told Granny all about what had happened and where they were staying. She told her about the drunken sailors at the levee, getting sweet rolls from Mr. Johnston and not being able to find decent food for the three of them. She assured Granny that they would pay her back if she could manage to help them out with food.

"Lily girl, don't you be worrying about paying me back for anything I give you young'uns. But," she paused, "I don't think this will work out too well. Might be that old aunt of yours has done her dirty work again, I'm afraid. Maybe she had our Caitlin carried off. I think you three children better come out and stay with me. I have plenty of rooms for sleeping and food for eating. You can all help work this farm and we'll be just fine and dandy. Come on; come on, Lily-girl. Eat some of these here warm biscuits. And put some of that warm honey on them, Warm honey is good for the body and the soul. I have more than I will ever be able to use up. You take plenty of these biscuits and honey on back to little Tessa and Benny. Go on out to the barn and get some milk from Bells, and you children hurry on back here as soon as you can. If you want to come back tonight, that's quite alright. If not, just be sure and be here first thing before daylight. You don't want anyone seeing all of you leaving and coming out my way. We'll keep your whereabouts a secret for a while."

Granny Tomason always seemed to have the right solution to any problem. She also had plenty of food and never wanted for anything. She lived very comfortably, but didn't sell much from her farm. She owned a few heads of cattle, a mulch cow, and chickens for eggs and eating. The garden she planted every year was big enough for her and maybe the whole confederate army. The overabundance of vegetables from her summer garden was often cheerfully given away to families in need. All she asked in return was for someone from the needy family to come out and help with such things as planting, hoeing, harvesting and canning. Granny always has money for anyone who was in need, and food for anyone who was hungry. Any available eggs she sells to the baker in town; sometimes she sold a few head of cattle to other people, but that wasn't really enough to live on.

Lily didn't know where she got her money, but she did know that Granny Tomason had once been married to a very mysterious man from Europe who came home only for a few weeks each year.

Lily remembered seeing him a few times in her life. Granny and her husband Mr. Frederick Tom-a-son (that was the way he introduced himself), would come over and visit with Mama and Pa. He was a big man with twinkling blue eyes, a pirate's mustache, pirate boots and a loud, blustery voice which seemed to fill the room with laughter. Sometimes he walked with a limp as if he, at one time, had been on the receiving end of a leg injury. And for some reason he always smelled of rum and cinnamon. Mama once told the children that Mr. Frederick Tomason was a gentleman and a scholar. He had been educated in Europe and was the smartest man Mama had ever met. And since Mama's father and grandfather had been very well educated in Europe, she would be the one to know.

Mr. Frederick seemed to always have his arm around Granny's shoulder and Lily remembered staring at him and watching him give

Granny a kiss on the check whenever he said something funny and let out a loud laugh. Granny would gaze up at him and smile. Granny had explained to them that Mr. Freddy, as she called him, had many, many business dealings in England and India and could not come home often. Most people in town thought "Mr. Freddy" was a pirate and was too afraid of Americans to live here.

A short while before Mama and Pa died in the carriage accident, Granny had came over and told the family that her Mr. Freddy had gone down with one of his ships off the coast of Madagascar. She was heart-broken and cried the entire time she was doing the telling. Mama insisted that Granny stay with them for a few days so she could have people about and not be so alone.

Pa said that Granny had gotten a large sum of money from Mr. Frederick's holdings; Lily was sure that was the reason Granny was able to help so many people. The town gossips said that Granny inherited all of Mr. Freddy's evil-gotten treasures from his pirating days. "A pirate?" Lily would mumble whenever she heard someone say something about Mr. Frederick's acts of piracy. "There are no pirates in this modern age."

Lily's mind came back to the present and she looked at Granny. "Oh, Granny, thank you so much. But, if Aunt Birdie finds out we are staying here, she will take us back. What would we do if she took it into her head to give Tessa, Benny or me to one of those slaver boats?" Lily said.

"Oh pooh on your Aunt Birdie," Granny said, "don't you be worrying about her. You just get those other two young-uns out here just as soon as you wake up in the morning. I'm sure I'll be able to prove I'm a better person and maybe even a closer relative than that ol' Bird."

Lily looked at Granny as if for the first time. Granny was a tiny little woman, full of energy and quite pretty for a granny. She still had dark red hair and eyes the color of the blue sky over the blue Mediterranean Sea.. That was what Mr. Freddy always told her when he was home – he called her his "blue-eyed beauty with the hair of a hot fire". A ready smile was always on her lips and she kept herself neat and clean. She had the energy of a much younger woman and was always flying around like a humming bird as she did chores.

When Mama and Pa died, Granny had wept like they were her own children. She tried to talk Caitlin into bringing them all out to her house to live, but Caitlin said it would be best if the four of them stayed where Pa had built them a home. Granny said she supposed that was the best, but if need be, she would move in with them. Caitlin assured Granny that that was not necessary but Granny had stayed with them until Aunt Birdie arrived. Granny then said it would be best if she moved back to her own house.

"Don't you be worrying about anything right now except getting the three of you out here as soon as possible, Lily girl!" Granny's voice brought Lily back to her present problem. "Let's just worry about that for right now. The three of you need to get out here so you can stay warm and start eating something that will stick to your ribs. Let me think on this problem we have and maybe I can come up with a solution.

Since Birdie is supposedly your Pa's sister, I guess she has the right to try and take you away. But, if it comes to that, we'll just give her a fine race in the courts over that. I don't like the thought of you three living in that shanty and begging for your food. It isn't right. Your mama and Pa would certainly not approve and Caitlin is old enough to take care of all of you. Let me help you try and find her. I'll start asking around and keeping my eyes and ears open. Everyone in Caruthersville thinks I'm too old and don't understand much, but I understand every word I hear and every look I see in that town. Why, just the other day I heard someone say, "Those three would be worth a pot of gold". Don't know what or who they were talking about, but as sure as I'm standing here, they were up to no good. Those men at the docks would sell their souls to the devil for gold."

Lily thought to herself, "They may have been talking about the three little girls down in the river bottom, or maybe even Tessa, Benny and me. I need to let the triplets' ma and pa know." She then asked, "Granny, do you know the squatters that live down in the shoot?"

"Well, not real well, Lily, but Mr. Peterson does work for me once in a while. He seems to be a right nice fellow. He never has brought his wife or kids along so I really can't say I know them. Why do you ask?"

"Well, Tessa told Benny and me that Aunt Birdie was asking her a lot of questions about them before we got out of her — rather, our — house. I wonder if she might be thinking of snatching those three little girls from their ma and pa and selling them down the river."

"Don't you worry about them Lily girl, I'll take care of that. I'll go down there tomorrow and let their ma and pa know to keep an eye out for anyone coming along. I'm sure their pa has a shotgun and won't hesitate to use it if he thinks someone is trying to get his girls. Now you get on out there and get some milk for you and those other young'uns and don't be worrying about something you can't control."

"Thanks Granny, I'll talk to Benny and see if we can't figure out a way to come out here with you. At least you won't be by yourself and Benny and I can help you out."

"Well get going Lily girl. Bring that milk back in and I'll put some in a jug for you all."

"I love you Granny," Lily said as she jumped up and gave Granny a hug and kiss. "I'll be right back in."

The back door squeaked as Lily stepped out into the darkness and walked to the barn. Pie Eater came around and followed her out; Granny's cow turned and gave a soft lowing sound as Lily walked into the stall and started petting Bells head.

"Hello Bells," Lily said, "It will just take a minute and then I'll leave you alone."

Pie Eater sat right down beside Bells as he waited to see if he could beg some milk off Lily. His tongue was hanging out and his eyes were fixed on the milk bucket.

Lily laughed as she looked at Pie Eater. Every so often she would spurt some mile towards Pie Eater and he would catch it and lick his lips. As she milked Bells, she began thinking about how she and Benny could find Caitlin. What could have happened to her? Lily's thoughts went back to the night Caitlin disappeared. Lily had been woken up by sounds coming from the outside of the house. It sounded like brush rubbing against the window and something thumping against the house. Then she heard a man whispering to someone else. As Lily lay there listening, she had thought it was Elmer and his old drinking buddies again, since they were snickering and breathing heavy.

"That's it," Lily thought, "I bet they were carrying Caitlin away! They must have gotten into her room and pulled her through the window!"

The next morning was when Aunt Birdie had informed them that Caitlin ran off during the night with a lover and left them because they were too much trouble and Caitlin wanted a life of her own.

Lily had looked directly into Aunt Birdie's eyes and said, "That's a lie! Caitlin would never ever leave us!" That was when Aunt Birdie slapped her across the face. "Don't you ever call me a liar again, girl!" Aunt Birdie screamed. "You try that again and all of you will be sorry!" Lily, Benny and Tessa were so shocked; they just sat there and said nothing. They didn't finish eating until Aunt Birdie left the room.

Benny then went out to the barn and Lily and Tessa started cleaning up the kitchen. As soon as Lily and Tessa cleaned up the cook stove and the dishes, they went out and found Benny and they all decided that they had to leave — there was no telling what Aunt Birdie would do next. It had been easy to get a few things together and get away. Aunt Birdie was always too busy digging around in the attic to pay much attention to the three of them. Lily had taken their mama's small amount of jewelry and Pa's smoke pipe. After Tessa and Benny got their things together and Aunt Birdie was out of sight, Benny had checked to make sure Elmer wasn't around, and then the three of them walked through the woods into Caruthersville. Once they got into town, they had found the old abandoned shanty behind the Ruby Slipper Saloon, and that's where they had been ever since. It had been three days since Caitlin disappeared, and Lily was getting more worried as each day passed.

What would they do if they never found Caitlin? Maybe they should try to get on one of those wagon trains going west. Maybe that was where someone had taken Caitlin. She and Benny could work until Tessa was big enough to help. Maybe they could sneak aboard one of those boats going down the river to New Orleans and find some work. But, Benny was only fourteen and she was only thirteen. Maybe she could get a job in one of the bakeries. Mama had taught her how to bake all types of cakes, pies and tarts.

Lily sat back on the milk stool and put her face on her knees. "What are we going to do?" she sighed.

Lily finished milking Bells and took the milk back inside to Granny so she could pour some into a jug for Lily to take back to the shanty.

The fog was gone now so Lily was able to walk quickly, all the while trying to keep the milk from spilling out of the jug, but fast enough to get back quickly. She could hear the hoot owls and the rustling of small animals again. Her eyes darted behind each tree and down each path as she hurried along the deserted road to town. When she got to the place where she had seen the shadowy soldier, she crossed to the opposite side of the alley and walked a little faster.

She was still a bit jumpy. Every cat or dog she saw made her jump, and any voices coming from the homes and buildings made her heart beat a little faster. If given the choice, she would rather run into a wild animal, large or small, than a shadowy person!

Once she got close to the shanty, the fog was again thick, but it didn't remind her of the devil's fog, as it had done earlier. No breeze made the fog come alive, and no strange shadows — male, female, military or non-military — lurked among the houses and buildings. When she was close enough to hear the saloon pianos, she was relieved. Her heart slowed to its normal pace and she felt a little more secure.

"Who could that have been, and what did they want from me?" she wondered to herself. Lily hadn't seen a soldier in full uniform in a long time. A lot of ex-soldiers still wore their jackets or just their military pants, but not the whole uniform. And she was sure she would not be able to help any of them with anything. She was only thirteen, and the only reason a stray soldier would want to speak to a thirteen year old girl was if he was up to no good.

What gave her pause was that he had called her "Lily-Beth". Now, that was certainly strange! How had he known that was the name Michael had called her? Maybe he had been a friend of Michael's during the war and was now a little off in the head from living through that terrible time.

That whole experience had been a downright scary encounter; that was for sure. She was thankful to the good Lord on high for stomping outside that woman's window and to the woman herself for slamming the shutters open. That may have prevented the shadow from reaching her before she could talk her legs into getting her out of there. Lily wondered what would have happened if that woman had not banged open her shutters. She shivered at the thought. "Well, I don't really want to find out, that's for sure." she muttered.

Her mind kept going back to the shadow. For some reason the man had seemed familiar to her. It couldn't be Michael. Unless he had been lying sick for all this time since the war ended. But, if that was the reason he had not come home, why didn't he just come on into town and talk to everyone? It sure was a strange thing. That was for sure.

As she slipped back into the shanty, Lily kept thinking about it. Why would a man in a soldier's uniform approach her? What could he have possibly wanted?

She wondered who his family was — maybe he was just a renegade soldier, wandering from town to town. Maybe in his mind, he really didn't know where he wanted to go or, even worse, who he really was.

Even though she was afraid, she had felt he had not meant her any harm. Why was that? He was out in the thick fog beckoning for her to come toward him. Of course he meant her harm! The question was — what was wrong with her own head in thinking maybe it was a nice ghost wanting to chat? "Well, I'm just glad I got away," she once again mumbled to herself.

When she got inside the shanty, Tessa was asleep on the pile of rags and Benny was snoring loud enough to wake the dead. "So?" Benny said, as he woke up with a start. "What did Granny Tomason have to say?"

"She wants us to go out to her house in the morning and stay there until we find Caitlin and are able to return to our house. What do you think, Benny? Think it's a good idea?"

"Well," he yawned, "It's not a bad idea. At least we would have a decent place to sleep. And Granny would let us work for food to eat. Why don't we give it a try? If anything happens and Aunt Birdie finds us, we can always go out to one of the caves on Granny's back acres."

"Okay, Benny, sounds like a good idea to me too. Let's try and get some sleep. In the morning we'll take off for Granny's house."

After they settled down for the night, Lily decided to tell Benny about the shadow soldier. When she came to the end and stopped speaking, Benny sat up and looked at her for a while.

"Lily, you can't go out alone at night any more. It's too dangerous and there are too many renegade soldiers about. He could have gone after you and had you within minutes. What if he was the one who has Caitlin and is just waiting to catch each of us alone? No, Lily, you cannot do that again."

"Benny, it was the strangest thing I ever have experienced. For some reason I had the feeling that he meant no harm and that maybe he was, like," She paused, looking him in the eyes, trying to get him to believe her, "I know it sounds crazy, but maybe like he was from someplace else. Like maybe he was a confederate soldier's spirit or something. I know that sounds unreal, but that's the feeling I got as I was standing there looking at him. There was nothing scary about him himself. The scary part was just the whole situation put together. It was the sudden stop of the hoot owls, the fog blowing in with a gust just before he appeared and then the slamming of the window shutters from the person on the second floor of the building. I felt as if he wanted to say something to me, but something else didn't want him to. The thick fog tumbled in towards him and he just disappeared into it, almost like it had swept him away. When I think about it, I think he was holding something in his hands. Not a gun or anything dangerous, just something he wanted me to see. It was just the strangest thing ever."

Benny and Lily both lay back down and within minutes they were both sound asleep. Neither of them heard anything when something was laid just outside the door of the shanty.

Lily and the Ghost of Michael Thorne

CHAPTER FOUR

Sheriff Beaumont

THE NEXT MORNING, before the sun was up, Lily, Benny and Tessa gathered up the few pieces of clothing they had and walked out of the shanty to go to Granny Tomason's house.

"Hey, Lily, Benny, look what I found. It was right in front of the shanty door! Look Lily," Tessa said with a puzzled look on her face, "This looks like one of Caitlin's hair combs. Did you bring one with you from our house, Lily?"

"No," Lily replied, peering down at the hair comb.

"I didn't either. Did you, Benny?" Tessa said, looking at her brother questionably.

"No, I didn't," Benny said, looking at the hair comb. "Maybe this didn't belong to Caitlin at all. It was probably dropped by one of the saloon girls who came out here last night."

"No," Lily replied, holding the hair comb in the palm of her hand, "This is Caitlin's hair comb all right. See the design on the edges. Pa carved it for Caitlin on her fifth birthday. We weren't even born yet but one time when I wanted to wear these hair combs, Caitlin told me about Pa making them for her. She had given one to Michael when he went off to the war, and she kept one for herself. She told

Michael she wanted him to have a part of her with him and for him to carry it at all times until he came home to be with her again. After Mama and Pa were killed, she said she would never wear hers again since she didn't want it to break. That's strange." Lily said as she slipped the hair comb into her pocket, "Who would have taken this from Caitlin's room? Maybe Aunt Birdie is selling our things off for money."

"Aunt Birdie is going too far. This has to stop! I wonder what else she's sold off, and who dropped Caitlin's hair comb in front of the shanty." Lily then thought to herself, "If it was one of those low-down saloon girls, I'm going to scratch her eyes out."

As they started out to Granny's house, Tessa chattered on about everything along the way, she stopped to check out the ants as they marched along single file, and bugs or flowers, or to just pick up a rock, but Lily and Benny were too lost in their own thoughts to talk with her. When they got to the gate in front of Granny's house, Benny called out, "hello the house", and they opened the gate as Pie Eater came bounding around the corner of the house. They could smell bacon and biscuits cooking. Granny called them on in, and when they entered, the house felt warm and smelled wonderful. Rubbing their hands together to get them warm, they made their way into the big kitchen, they smiled when Granny once again called out to them from one of the bedrooms.

"Have a seat, children, and I'll be with you in just a moment. I want to put more blankets on this bed for Benny." Lily, Benny and Tessa smiled at each other as they felt the fire warming their cold feet and hands. "This kitchen smells sooo nice," Tessa said as she looked around. "I want to stay at Granny's forever. Or at least until we find our Caitlin."

"I think Granny will let us." Lily replied. "Or at least until Aunt Birdie finds out we're here and tries her best to take us back." Tessa's eyes grew huge again and Lily was sorry she had said anything about Aunt Birdie. "Don't worry Tessa," Lily said as she put her arms around her little sister, "Aunt Birdie won't find us." Lily hid her concern from her Tessa.

"You children sit down and eat up, eat up." Granny said, as she hurried back into the kitchen.

The food was on the table and looked wonderful. Eggs, bacon, hot biscuits, milk gravy, fresh butter, fried apple pie and fried potatoes with fresh cold milk from Bells.

"It's cold out there and you need something to warm your bellies," Granny said. "Eat up!"

They all sat down, including Granny, and started eating. After surviving for three days on leftover sweet rolls from the bake shop, Granny's food was delicious!

All of a sudden they heard Pie Eater start barking loudly. All three children's forks stopped in midair and they stared at Granny. They seemed to be frozen in time. Granny looked up, with just as much surprise as the three children, and said; "Now I wonder who that could be this time of the morning?"

"You children stay right here and don't come out of this kitchen. I'm going to see who it is and if it's anyone it shouldn't be, I'll get rid of them. In fact, I'll get rid of them no matter who or what it is."

The pounding on the door came as soon as Granny walked out of the kitchen. Whoever it was waited for a few seconds and started pounding again.

"Lily, I'm really scared, I think it's Aunt Birdie or ol' Elmer." Tessa whispered.

"Open up Granny, this is Sheriff Beaumont. Ah walked the whole way out he'ah and it's dam cold out."

Sheriff Beaumont's family was from way down around the Louisiana swamps, and even though he was raised in Missouri, sometimes his words slipped into his parents' slow, Cajun "New Orleeeen's" drawl. He had a low, melodic voice with words which seemed to flow like warm molasses whenever he spoke. His voice made a person feel all warm and cozy inside like the comfort of a thick warm blanket on a cold winter night. He was the main target for every mother with a daughter who was of marrying age.

The sheriff was probably six foot three inches tall. He had black, curly hair which fell onto his forehead and a thick mustache. His eyes were as black as pitch, with lashes that were too long and thick for a man. His teeth seemed to shine in his mouth when he smiled. With his black mustache and tan skin, he looked like he should be sitting on a river boat in the New Orleans harbor, making money at the gambling tables or riding the gambling boats up and down the Mississippi fleecing all the wealthy men as they came aboard to gamble at each port. His shoulders almost touched the sides of Granny's door frame. It was said that his pa had come over from France and his mother was a beautiful full-blood Indian. His pa's name was Pierre Michel Beaumont; his ma's name was Cathereen "Mourning Dove". She had been taken away from her Indian village and put into one of the Indian schools outside New Orleans where they changed her name from Morning Dove to Cathereen, and taught her the ways of the white world. After she married Pierre, she started using her Indian name again. Pierre Beaumont had loved his Indian wife and called her "Dovey". Whatever the case, Sheriff Beaumont was quite the handsome man in most ladies' eyes.

"I'm coming, I'm coming Sheriff! Hold your taters and I'll be there in a second. And I don't want to hear another cuss word out of you again, young man." As Granny opened the door a crack, Sheriff Beaumont grinned broadly and pushed it open a little further.

"Ah'm coming on in Granny, it's too dam cold to stand outside — and that's the last cuss word ah'll say today, ma'am." He drawled, as he continued to smile at Granny.

"Well, Sheriff, I surely hope so, and I guess I don't have a choice if you come in or not, seeing as how you're already inside. What do you want coming all the way out here to call on me this early in the morning anyway? I don't have much coffee made or I'd offer you some. All I have is some warm biscuits and honey."

"Well, ah'm looking for those three Quinn kids, Granny. Their auntie is worried about them and ah thought maybe ya had seen them around he'ah. Have ya?"

"Why would you be looking for the Quinn children out here Andre? You know they have a home of their own. Why would they be here with me?"

Andre Beaumont looked Granny straight in the eyes and said, "They've been gone from their'ah Auntie's house for nye on three days now and she wants them back. Granny, if yor'ah hidin' them, it's against the law and ah will have to take them back to Birdie Quinn's house and arrest you for kidnapping. You know that don't ya?"

"Well, of course I know that, Andre Beaumont." Granny had her hands on her hips and was tapping her foot. "Do you think I was born yesterday? And for your information young man, that house is not Birdie's house. It belongs to Benny, Lily, Tessa and Caitlin. Birdie just decided to take it over, and no one has bothered to correct her. It's about time you set her straight, Andre. You should be more worried about finding that little Caitlin than worrying about me and if I have those three young'uns. Caitlin's been gone for three days now and no one is looking for her. Maybe you should check with all those sailors and dock drunks to see if they saw her about the time she disappeared. If I see those children, I'll make sure and do the right thing for them. I'm a law-abiding person; and you very well know that, Andre Beaumont. Now wait right here young man, and I'll get you a warm biscuit to take with you on your way back to town."

"Ah'll just come with ya Granny." Sheriff Beaumont drawled.

Well then, come on into the kitchen, Sheriff." Granny said a little louder than usual.

"Granny, word is that Caitlin ran off with her lov'ah."

CHAPTER FOUR: SHERIFF BEAUMONT   51

"Oh, poot!" Granny snorted and just kept on stomping back toward the kitchen with Sheriff Beaumont right behind her. When she got to the kitchen door Granny glanced around and continued walking in. The table was clean as a whistle and all the food, except for the biscuits, was gone.

"Here you go, Andre," Granny said, reaching over and wrapping four warm biscuits in a cloth. "Now hurry on back to town and start looking for that little Caitlin. She didn't run off with a lover, Andre Beaumont, and as a matter of fact, she doesn't even have a lover. The only one she loved was Michael Thorne and, as you know, he died in the war."

Sheriff Beaumont sighed and rolled his eyes upward.

"Granny, thanks for the warm biscuits, but ya sure do cook a lot for just one. A body might would think ya were havin' company. It sure smells like bacon in he'ah, and maybe some eggs. Ya sure ya haven't seen those Quinn kids, Granny?" he asked, looking closely into her eyes. Sheriff Beaumont had to lean over to look into Granny's eyes. "Ah sure don't want to arrest a granny, but maybe it would be a fine thing because then ya could cook for me. That might just be a good idea." He drawled softly.

"Get on out of here, you young whipper-snapper. And mind your manners! I have a farm to take care of and you have plenty of women to cook for you. And don't you be snooping around my farm. My old dog will let me know if someone's around and that shotgun over my door can't see too well in the night and just might go off and blow someone's leg off, not knowing who is out there sneaking around and all."

Sheriff Beaumont laughed and patted Granny on the head. Granny slapped his hand away and started walking towards the front door.

"Ya're an old softy Granny" he said, "But ah do swear'ah, ah will arrest ya if ah have to. Ah'll be on my way and ah'll stop by and tell Miss Birdie that ah guess those young'uns aren't around he'ah after all. Maybe they took off in one of those wagon trains going west. That would be the exact place ah would go if ah were a kid and wanted to get out of Caruthersville. So long Granny, and make sure'ah ya have some pie and coffee the next time ah come out to see ya, ya he'ah."

"I'll do that Andre, and you be careful out in the dark of night doing your sheriffin'. Bye now, and tell your Miss Tidbury hello for me." Miss Tidbury was Sheriff Beaumont's old widow woman landlady and the town gossip.

"Ah'll be sure and do that." Sheriff Beaumont replied as he sauntered out the front door and shut it behind him.

"Dam, it's cold out today," Andre thought. "That Granny, she thought she could pull the wool over my eyes. They might have gotten away with it too, if one of those kids hadn't sniffed as they sat in the pantry. They must have taken every crumb of food except the biscuits in ther'ah with them. I sure could have used a warm plate of eggs and bacon."

Maybe he should look for that little Caitlin Quinn. Andre thought to himself. She sure was a pretty thing. Twenty-three and considered an old maid. She kept to herself, taking care of her brother and sisters. If he remembered right, she had had a beau before the war and the fella had gone off and gotten himself killed. She was the same age his sister Renée would be — if she were still alive.

An ache pressed against his chest as he thought of Renée. She had been the light in his bleak life. After their mother died, Andre had pretty much raised Renée on his own, since his pa had given up on everything the day of his Dovey's funeral. One would never have guessed that Pierre Beaumont had two children of his own. All he did was sit in the rocking chair in front of the window and watch the world pass him by as he held the one and only picture of his "Dovey".

Andre and Renée tried to get him to talk, but no conversation could be coaxed out of him. The only time he spoke at all was after he finished his meals and said a soft "thank you, sweetheart" to Renée or a "thank you, son" to Andre.

The only time he got up from his rocking chair was to eat, go to the privy or to bed. That was it. He hadn't taken a daily wash and never again did he shave or work. Not a single day, for the rest of his life, did Pierre Beaumont step a foot away from their property.

Andre had tried to keep food on the table by doing odd jobs in Caruthersville, and Renée cleaned the house, washed their clothes and did what cooking she could. Renée was only nine, and Andre was thirteen at the time of their mother's death. Those days were difficult for Andre and Renée. Not only had they lost their mother to the jaws of death, but they had also lost their father. Pierre Beaumont's spirit and soul had been buried with Dovey.

Three years later on the same exact day, Pierre Beaumont died; Andre had gotten home and found him in his chair with his picture of Dovey clutched to his chest and a soft relaxed look on his face. His father had not only taken a bath, but he had shaved. It was if he knew he was going to die and had gotten ready to see his Dovey. Andre had felt relief for his father, knowing death was what he really wanted. For in dying, Pierre was sure he would be with his wife.

After that, Andre and Renée moved into a very small, one bedroom shanty outside of Caruthersville and by that time, Andre had grown into a big muscled boy and was able to take on jobs that paid more money. Renée was twelve and went to work at the local bakery, helping out with the early morning baking. She told Andre she loved her job and wanted to someday open her own bake shop. Mr. Johnston, the baker, had told her that she had a great talent for baking and he would help her in any way he could.

But one morning, as she walked to the bakery in the early morning light, she was grabbed by a drunken sailor. When she tried to fight him off, he hit her on the head with his fist, hoping to just knock her out, but she had not survived the blow. The owner of the Ruby Slipper Saloon had found her lying in the back alley where whoever had hit her decided to dump her body. Andre went a little crazy. He really didn't remember what happened after the sheriff came to get him from the docks. All he remembered was staring down at Renée, thinking how small she looked lying on that doctor's table in her pretty blue dress, with her dark hair curled around her face. The doctor had fixed her hair so as to hide the mark from the man's fist, but Andre had been able to see the broken skin. The doc had closed her eyes and washed the dirt and mud away from her face and clothes. She looked the same as she did when she was sleeping.

He remembered thinking, "Ah can't do this, Ah just can't bury her in that cold ground. She's all ah have and ah'm all she has. She will be so afraid all bi herself in that graveyard. Ah can't do it." He must have spoken out loud because the sheriff had put his arm around Andre's shoulders and said, "She won't be alone son. Your ma and pa will be with her. She was a beautiful young girl and a wonderful sister to you, Andre. Let her go now. At least that river scum didn't have time to get her on that boat. Let her go, son. We'll find who did this if it takes us the rest of our natural life."

So Andre buried Renée next to his ma and pa. It had been the worst day of his sixteen years. He went back to work the next day, vowing to find the person who had killed her.

So when Andre turned eighteen, he applied for the position of deputy sheriff in the sleepy little river town of Tennemo, Tennessee, and got the job. Tennemo was a little town with few problems or crimes. Andre enjoyed the work in Tennemo, but he returned to Caruthersville when he was twenty-five and heard that the position of sheriff was available. Andre stepped into the position with ease, seeing that the retiring Sheriff was the same one who had been there when Andre was younger. The older sheriff helped Andre in his hunt to find Renée's killer and until the day he died, the old sheriff continued to search for information about Renée's death; but to no avail.

"Will it ev'ah stop hurting," Andre wondered. "No, God, don't let it stop. I want to always remember Renée and what that person or persons did. They ended a young girl's life before it had even started. They viciously ripped her out of this world and into the cold ground. I will nev'ah stop trying to find them."

As the image of Renée came back into Andre's mind, the pressure in his chest seemed to well up into his throat and he had to keep swallowing and blinking his eyes to keep from crying.

"Ah wonder if maybe the same thing has happened to the Quinn girl, Caitlin?" Andre puzzled over in his mind.

Slowly he walked down the path to the road leading into town. It was cold and he was in a foul mood. "What the hell is going on with these Quinn kids? Where is their'ah sister and why are they at Granny Tomason's house instead of their'ah own house?" The thought of one of those slimy sailors getting a hold on Caitlin Quinn made Andre sick to his stomach.

"Ah guess ah'm going to have to start somewhere'ah," Andre thought, "It might as well be at their'ah own home. What an old biddy that Birdie Quinn is. She is just a mean old woman who has nev'ah been married and probably nev'ah will be. What man could live with that old woman? Maybe that fella Elm'ah would, but no one else would even give it a second thought." Andre concluded.

When he got down the road a short distance from Granny's house, he turned right onto a narrow field path and started walking up to the Quinn's house. The Quinn's farm had been a nice farm once upon a time. Andre could remember Mr. Quinn working hard every day trying to keep the farm going. Andre had worked for him during a few heavy harvest seasons. Nice guy. Always had a smile on his face and a laugh to share about something. And Mrs. Quinn was a looker. She seemed to love her husband and kids, but she sure was good-looking, even to a kid of sixteen. She was definitely Irish. With that red-gold hair, fair skin and eyes of a soft green leaf, she was one handsome woman. It sure was sad when they both died in that carriage accident. Sometimes it seemed as if bad things happen to good people and the bad people have very few problems. Maybe it should have been that old Birdie and Elmer in that accident.

As Andre got closer to the Quinn's house, he could hear Birdie yelling at someone.

"You should have been there and made sure it all went right! Now look what happened. What's wrong with you old man? My money is the money that feeds you and keeps you out of the weather. Maybe you should strike out on your own and see how you like it!"

"Wonder what she's talking about," Andre thought.

"Maybe you should do the dirty work from now on, Bird!" Elmer yelled back. "There are a few things in life I won't do and tak-"

As Andre stepped up onto the porch, Birdie and Elmer's voices quickly quieted. Andre heard low whispering, but couldn't make out what they were saying.

Birdie turned around and appeared at the front door. Her apron was spotless white and her hair perfectly slicked back into a tight bun at the back of her neck. Not a hair or piece of clothing was out of place. Birdie was a big woman. She wasn't what one would call fat, but very well endowed on the top and her hips were very broad. She looked the perfect matronly woman. But everyone knew she was not a nice person.

Elmer was standing a few feet behind her with a big grin on his face. Elmer looked the part of a rascal. With dirty, slicked back hair, his clothes were rumpled as if he had slept with the horses for days on end.

"Well hello, Sheriff." Elmer spoke up with the big grin still spread across his face. "Come in, come in and have a cup of hot coffee. Birdie, run on into the kitchen and get the sheriff a cup of coffee. It's pretty cold out this morning, isn't it Sheriff?" Birdie gave Elmer a look that would have killed him dead, if possible.

"Yes," Birdie said turning back to the sheriff and smiling sweetly, "and come on in out of the chill, Sheriff. Have a seat in the parlor and I'll get us all some coffee and sweet biscuits."

Andre could tell Birdie did not really want to let him in, but Elmer had put her on the spot and she had to ask him in.

As Andre looked at Miss Birdie's handyman, Elmer just kept right on grinning, and when Miss Birdie turned around Andre saw the reason why — Birdie's skirt and petticoats were tucked into the waistband of her drawers. Skirt, petticoats and all were tucked up. Her whole backside was exposed. There was a large hole torn in her bloomers and her derrière was shining through like a big jagged round sun. The hole was perfectly rounded; it was as if maybe a mouse had gotten into her under drawers drawer and eaten a belly full of cotton. Her stockings came up to her knees and six inches above them her bloomers started. Her bloomers were black and the "sunshine" hole was right in the middle of her left cheek.

Elmer started laughing right out loud and Miss Birdie whirled around and gave him a stern look, as if to ask, "What are you laughing at?"

Andre had a hard time keeping his smile to himself as Miss Birdie turned and walked back toward the kitchen, her hips started swaying and the hole started moving around her backside. First it moved to the right, than it moved to the left, back to the right, and back to the left. As the hole moved back to the right, part of it got caught in the crack of her behind and stayed there. The hole just stuck and the crack stayed in view. Andre squeezed his eyes shut, and when he opened them back up, she had stopped and bent over to pick up something off the floor. The hole stretched further down her derrière. Andre was sure he felt his eyes bug right out of their sockets.

"Holy Moses," Elmer croaked quietly, "I ain't never seen anything this funny a'fore."

"Get out of he'ah quick boy," Andre told himself, "Pick up your feet and get them movin' quick before it's too late."

Elmer sat down hard on the chair in the foyer; hung his head and was quietly laughing so hard, tears ran down his face as he looked at Birdie than back to Andre.

"Sheriff, if that don't look like the light of the high noon sun, I'll eat my hat. Makes a feller just want to snatch her up and kiss her all over, don't it sheriff?" Elmer gasped.

It was the funniest sight Andre had seen in a long time. He guessed it was mainly because Miss Birdie considered herself so prim and proper. "Holy Hannah!" Andre thought. "How am ah gonna talk to this he'ah woman without laughing right out loud?"

Andre finally went over and pulled Elmer up off the chair and dragged him into the parlor. Not a word was said between them. They just sat there. Andre knew if he looked at Elmer, he would start laughing and not be able to stop. Every few seconds Elmer would snort out a laugh and Andre would give him a glare.

Elmer had his dirty handkerchief out and was wiping his eyes and blowing his nose. "If this fella doesn't stop laughing," Andre thought, "ah'm not gonna be able to stay he'ah."

"Just as sweet looking as sugar biscuits on a Sunday morning, ain't she sheriff?" Elmer croaked out. They could hear Miss Birdie coming down the hall and both men looked at the door and tried not to look at each other.

"Here we go Sheriff Beaumont, have some nice hot coffee and sweet biscuits. I just took them out of the warmer and they're still nice and fluffy."

Well, you had to hand it to Miss Birdie Quinn; she was one of the best cooks and cleanest women in Caruthersville. She could charm the feathers off a blue jay if she wanted to. But then again she usually shrieked at anyone who annoyed her.

"Thank you kindly, ma'am, ah believe ah will" Andre said, not looking at Miss Birdie's face. "These biscuits sure'ah look tasty. Ya are a mighty fine cook, ma'am."

"Why thank you sheriff. I do try. The Lord in heaven knows I try to be the best living soul I can be. I live my life the way the good book says." Birdie looked over at Elmer. "Don't I, Mr. Elmer? Why, Mr.

CHAPTER FOUR: SHERIFF BEAUMONT

Elmer has been my handyman for many years and I don't think he can think of a single time when I haven't done my Christian duty for every soul I come in contact with. Isn't that so, Mr. Elmer?"

Elmer looked like he was going to choke on the biscuit he had in his mouth. He was having a problem talking, grinning and keeping the food in his mouth at the same time.

"Why, Sheriff Beaumont," Elmer finally managed to say, "Sometimes Miss Birdie gets up early, early in the morning to cook for the needy. That's right, Sheriff Beaumont, at the crack of dawn she gets up and cooks; trying to bake for all the needy in town. Yes sir, Sheriff, at the crack of dawn," Elmer muttered with a snicker.

With that statement Elmer took on another choking spell and had to suck down some of his hot coffee.

"Here, Elm'ah, please, help yor'ah self to my share." Andre passed the plate to Elmer, thinking if he could keep Elmer's mouth full of biscuits, maybe he would stop laughing.

"Thank you Sheriff and yes, Miss Quinn you surely, surely are a good cook. You are one good Christian woman, a wonderful Christian woman. That's exactly what you are ma'am. You surely are one big," he paused, "… hearted woman. You are certainly a ray of sunshine for Caruthersville!"

Elmer started choking on his biscuit again and had to take another big gulp of hot coffee to make it go down. As he brought the cup away from his mouth he said in a very solemn preacher type voice, "Yes ma'am, you are one big hearted woman. Without you there would be a big hole in all our hearts." With that said, Elmer looked at Andre and grinned from ear to ear.

Andre didn't think he was going to be able to get through this conversation with these two characters. "Okay Andre," he told himself. "Don't think about anything but the missing girl."

"Well, Sheriff," Miss Birdie asked, "Have you seen those-" she stopped to correct herself, "- my children? I miss those three, ah, four children so much. First Caitlin runs off with her lover and leaves them with me, and then those three little ones come up missing. Have you found them or heard anything about them? I'm just worried sick. Their Pa, who was my dear brother, you know, God rest his soul, would be so worried about them. When he passed on, God rest his soul, I promised God and myself that I would make sure those children grew up to be God-fearing. Now I've already failed with that Caitlin. My brother, God rest his soul, would be so upset at that girl."

"Well ma'am," Andre replied, "Ah don't rightly know for sure'ah where they are, but ah'm sure'ah they are fine. Ah thought ah saw them at the oth'ah end of the street, down from the sheriff's office, last night, but ah couldn't get there fast enough to make sure'ah. Where ever'ah they're staying, Ah'm sure'ah they will be okay."

"And just how do you know they will be alright?" Miss Birdie voice got a bit demanding. "Do you know where they are and you just aren't telling me? If that's it, Sheriff, I will personally send for the governor. You not telling me where those children are would be breaking the law, as you well know!

Did you check over at that old Mrs. Tomason's house like I told you?" Miss Birdie continued. "That old woman is nothing but trouble. She's an evil old woman, and I'm worried about my children and what she might do to them. Her husband was a pirate, you know, and no telling what on God's green earth she has influenced them to do. She probably has a house full of stolen treasure from her husband's pirating days. He was an evil man, I hear. Just ask some of the good Christian folks in town. She says she's some kind of a relative to their mother, but I don't believe it. I am truly Daniel Quinn's sister, and I never heard tell of her in all my born days! I want those three children back and I want them back today!"

"Now calm down, Miss Birdie, I am not a liah," Andre's voice got a little louder, "and ah went to Granny Tomason's house this morning, and no, ah didn't see them ther'ah at all. Granny has a hard enough time, as it is, running her farm without havin' to take care of three children. Ah'm sure'ah Granny will let me know if she hear'ahs anythin' about the children. What about their'ah older sista, Caitlin? Have ya heard anythin' about her?" Andre asked, looking at Elmer.

Elmer's face went straight and immediately flushed; he quickly looked away from Andre.

"No, Sheriff" Miss Birdie spoke up for Elmer, "Mr. Elmer and I haven't seen hide nor hair from that Caitlin. I tell you, she ran off with some lover and we won't hear from her again. It's better that way really since I wouldn't want her bad reputation to ruin those two young sisters of hers. Yes, it is better that she stays away and never comes back."

"How about you, Elm'ah?" Andre looked him directly in the eyes. "Ah'd like to hear'ah it straight from your own mouth. Have ya heard anythin' about Caitlin and this person she supposedly ran off with?"

Elmer looked back at Andre. "No sir, I haven't. But if I do, I'll be sure and let you know right away."

"That's strange," Andre thought. Elmer sounds like he is pretty sincere about this.

"Well, folks, thanks for the coffee and biscuits. Ah appreciate yor'ah time and ah'll be back here'ah if I hear'ah anythin." Andre stood up and walked to the front door.

Miss Birdie and Elmer followed him to the door. She had returned to her sugar sweet attitude once again as she spoke. "Thank you so very much for helping us Sheriff, and don't you be worrying about that Caitlin. She's done made her bed, let her sleep in it," Birdie said to his back.

She waited until Andre was out and down the steps before she turned to Elmer and started hissing at him. Andre could hear Elmer's laughter coming from the house, and Birdie's stomping feet as she walked back down the hall. Elmer must have told her about her drawers and the "sunshine hole."

CHAPTER FIVE

The Hunt Begins

LILY, BENNY AND TESSA tumbled out of the pantry. "Whew, that was a close one." Benny said.

"I can't believe we got away with that, Granny." Lily said, smiling over at her.

"Yeah," Tessa whispered. "I was so scared I almost wet myself when I heard him stomp into the kitchen with you, Granny."

"Well, I don't know if we really fooled him or not. Sheriff Beaumont is a smart fella, and one of the best and nicest sheriffs we've had. I'm sure-a-shootin' that he heard the sniffle. That Andre is a good boy. If he thinks you young-uns are better off with me, instead of that Aunt Birdie of yours, he won't be a-telling anyone about you being here."

"Do you trust him, Granny?" Benny asked.

"With my own babies, if I had any, Benny-boy," Granny replied.

"What will he tell Aunt Birdie if she asked him?" Lily asked.

"Well," Granny said, "I'm thinking he's a right smart fella and will be able to cover whatever he knows and still not have to tell her a lie."

Tessa smiled broadly. "Just like you did, huh Granny?"

"You don't have to worry about me telling a lie to anyone, little sweet gal. I know how to protect those I love and slip right on by the

63

old devil before he can catch a hold on my arm." She smiled. "I didn't tell any lies today and don't plan on doing it in the future." Granny put her arm around Tessa and gave her a squeeze.

"I really, really love you, Granny" Tessa said softly as she put her arms around Granny's neck. "Me, Benny and Lily will stay here and help you with your farm. We used to help Pa on our own farm. Benny is very strong and so is Lily. But Lily is a girl and really should not be as strong as Benny. He's my big brother and I know he will take care of of us. Won't you Benny?"

Benny's face lit up like a candle in the dark. "I sure will Tessa. You, Granny and Lily can depend on me. I can do anything a grown man can do to make sure we all stay safe."

Lily looked at her brother for a minute and smiled. At times he had to poke his eyes back into his head from gawking at the girls, but he was a good brother.

Benny was a lot taller than Lily and one could already see the muscles developing in his arms and legs. Mama said Benny acted like Pa, though. Always easy to get along with, full of mischief and always taking care of anything he possibly could. Even when their parents were alive, Benny was always busy helping out whenever he wasn't in school. He would come home from school and immediately start in working on the farm with their Pa. Many times he said he loved working the soil more than anything else. Benny was a good person and Lily was proud to call him her brother.

Lily also knew Caitlin did not have a lover, or anyone else she would have left them for. Caitlin still loved Michael Thorne. Not that it would do her any good — Michael had not returned home after the war ended. Caitlin had finally realized he must have died in the field during some battle and was probably buried in a makeshift graveyard together with so many other young soldiers. Along with his parents, Caitlin had planned a funeral for him. There was not a body in the grave, but having an actual funeral and a headstone on that empty grave gave the missing soldier's family and loved ones a little closure.

Many families had done the same thing after the war ended when their loved ones never returned to them. Lily guessed the funeral and the burying of an empty casket must soften the sorrow of their loss.

Although some families had gotten a wonderful surprise, when after a very long time their son or husband wandered home. Some of the soldiers had been too sick to let their families know where they were and others couldn't remember who they were until sometime later. But Michael Thorne never returned.

Caitlin had waited and watched. She would walk into town most every day around the time of the train arrival, using one excuse or another, but Lily knew she was watching for Michael to come in on the train. No one found his body or any of his belongings. And if they had, they didn't bother with sending them to his family.

So many boys were buried in unmarked graves back East and most of the dead soldiers had no type of identification left on their bodies after the opposing side stripped them of all their personal belongings. Every type of identification was carried back to a commanding officer to be collected and checked for any evidence of fallen officers. That was the way each side knew if there were groups of enemy soldiers still fighting without an officer to lead them. Those groups would become easy targets.

At other times injured soldiers crawled off into the surrounding woods, thinking they would recover while hiding in the thick woods, and be able to return and fight again. But instead of recovering, they died alone. Some soldiers were buried in the thick woods, never to be found by their families. Their fellow soldiers buried them in places where enemy soldiers could not dig up their remains and steal their personal belongings. Other times, fellow soldiers took all the personal belongings off the fallen soldiers; thinking they would be able to send them to the soldiers family, but in the melee and confusion of battle, they themselves perished. The battles were too intense for any living soldiers to carry the dead back to their camps – many times the injured were not taken back to their camps.

Caitlin told Lily she guessed the soldiers had done the best they could, seeing that they were fighting in very hot weather and there was absolutely no place to put the dead except in the ground. For quite some time Caitlin had cried every time she spoke about Michael.

She said Michael probably wouldn't want to come home injured like some of his friends had done, so maybe it was best that he didn't come home at all. But as she was saying that, tears were rolling down her face and Lily knew Caitlin would have taken him back — no matter how injured he had been.

It sure was a sad time for all of America, Lily thought, and the north and south had both lost so many of their sons and husbands.

"Maybe when Caitlin comes home, she will find a nice beau like Michael and she can be happy again. When she gets home, maybe Benny and I will go out and help find her a new beau." Lily thought "Maybe Caitlin would like that Sheriff Beaumont."

"We will have to see if he is worthy of being with Caitlin. If Granny Tomason thinks he is so nice, we'll just have to see." Lily thought.

"Benny," Lily said when they finally finished eating and had the kitchen back in order, "let's go into town and see if we can find any clues as to what might have happened to Caitlin. While we're there, we can see if the baker needs any of Granny's eggs today. Would you like us to do that for you Granny?"

"That would be just wonderful, Lily; it would save me a trip into town and I'm sure Mr. Johnston is about ready for some more eggs. But you two be very careful about who you run into and make sure you stay away from that river landing."

"Is it okay if Tessa stays here with you Granny? Or do you want us to take her along? Whatever you want us to do will be okay."

"Of course Tessa can stay here with me. I haven't had the company of a sweet little gal in a long time. The first thing Tessa and I will do is take a ride down to the Peterson's house in the river bottom and tell Mr. and Mrs. Peterson to be on the lookout for anyone coming around their little gals, and then we can make some chicken and dumplings for supper, and maybe some gingerbread cookies to go along with it. What do you say, Tessa girl? Is that a good idea?"

"Oh yes, Granny." Tessa said excitingly, "That's just what me and Mama used to do. Let's get started right now. What do you want me to do first?"

"Well, let's see your sister and brother off first, and then we'll start out for our visit and after that we'll come back and start in cooking. But before we leave for our visit, we can fix up a big basket to take along with us. That way we can have a nice lunch with Mr. and Mrs. Peterson and those three little gals. How does that sound?"

"Yippee! We are going on a picnic and I can play with Molly, Polly and Dolly!"

"Benny, you and Lily stay together and be very watchful in town, and keep an eye out for that Elmer and your Aunt Birdie. You stay away from those saloons. I hear Elmer is down around the riverfront most every day. Your Aunt Birdie goes into the mercantile pretty much every other day, and she also goes down to the boat landing. I really don't know why she goes to the docks. I hear tell she says she gets fresh fish, but I don't really think so. You two young'uns keep an eye open and don't speak to anyone you don't know, and stay together. Now give me a hug and get out of here. Tessa and I'll be watching for you before dark comes on."

"Thanks, Granny, and I'll make sure Lily stays safe and we will be sure and stay together," Benny replied. "Both of us can out-run that old Elmer or Aunt Birdie if they see us and give chase."

"Yeah," Lily spoke up, "Unless Elmer catches us from behind he won't be able to catch either one of us. Aunt Birdie can't run fast enough to catch a turtle, much less one of us."

After they collected Granny's eggs, Lily and Benny started down the path to town. Lily pulled her hat low and buttoned her coat all the up to her neck. Granny had given her some mittens to keep her fingers warm until the morning chill burned off and she pulled them up as far as they could go. The mittens were too big, but they were better than nothing at all.

Benny had on an old hat he had pulled low over his ears and he buttoned up his fairly new coat. Benny's pant legs were a little too short; so his socks were pulled up to cover the space between his pant legs and his shoes.

But at least they weren't hungry and Granny had given them everything she could find to help keep them warm this early in the morning. The wind blew softly — not enough to bother them much, but it was still cold.

"Benny, we have to find Caitlin." Lily stated firmly, as soon as they were clear of the house. "She has to be on one of those boats waiting to go down the river, or on a wagon train going out west. But I think she's on one of those boats down at the boat landing and tied up in one of the rooms. If someone put her on one of the wagons going west, she would have screamed louder than a mountain cat and people would have helped her get away. Let's go down to the boat landing and see if we hear or see anything."

"I thought maybe you wanted to do just that very thing." Benny replied, "That mean-hearted Aunt Waddle has gotten her last bag of gold. She shouldn't have been so greedy as to take away her own niece. We'll get her back, Lily, you can count on that."

As the two walked toward town, they remained quiet; each of them lost in their own thoughts about how they were going to find Caitlin. Benny was pretty sure he could sneak onto some of the boats and hid among all the barrels until he could manage to slip around and see if Caitlin was being held in one of the cabins. Maybe if he acted like he was interested in being an errand boy, or something on the boat, they would let him on board. But he would have to make sure they didn't lie to him — just to get him on board — and then tie him up and not let him go until they were down around New Orleans and he had no chance of getting back home.

Quite often, the slavers would use black walnut juice to darken a person's skin so as to make it easier to sell them; luckily, his red hair made that option unlikely.

Benny thought about seeing if there were any wagon trains going west before he tried to get on board one of the river boats. He hadn't heard of any coming though lately, but since it was now spring, the wagon trains would soon be coming through more frequently. But he had not noticed any wagon trains coming through in the last few days, so the likelihood of Caitlin being taken west was small.

Whenever a wagon train came though the river towns, everyone who could would go out to visit with the travelers and ask hundreds of questions. Some of the town people were always thinking about taking off for the West with each wagon train that came along. Other people swore they were going to join up with the next one passing through.

Few of them actually did. Most of the people just dreamed about going — it was an exciting thing to think about. Everyone wanted to know why the people on the wagon trains were going and how they would make a living once they arrived. Addresses were often exchanged and promises were made to keep in touch with each other.

Very seldom did the townspeople hear from any of the travelers. And only a few travelers kept their promises. One family in particular, the Fitzpatrick's, had turned around before the wagon train made it to the great desert and returned to Caruthersville to open a general store. The things they told about their trip were thrilling and scary. They told of being attacked by hostile Indians and renegades so many times that the first chance they got to return east, they took it. There were tales of attacks by grizzly bears, mountain lions and deaths from Cholera. Most Indians had been friendly, but the renegade groups of ex-soldiers and thieves were fearsome. Mrs. Fitzpatrick had kept a diary and in it she told of how many graves they passed each day. Not a day went by, she said, in which they did not pass at least seven to ten graves.

CHAPTER FIVE: THE HUNT BEGINS

The wagon trains were all going to California or Oregon. Some of the pioneers wanted to start a business or a farm. Quite a few of the single men were going to strike it rich in the gold fields. They had their wagons full of necessities: food, water, guns, cooking utensils for cooking outdoors, and a bare minimum of furniture. The travelers were always filled with excitement.

Some of the trains were fifty wagons long. All the children would be whooping and hollering when the day came for them to continue their journey west. It sure had been tempting to Benny after his ma and Pa died, but he felt responsible for his sisters. Going to California on a wagon train sure would be one grand adventure, though.

Wait!

A train!

That might be it. It's probably the railroad train, not the wagon trains! Why hadn't they thought of that earlier?

"Lily!" Benny cried. "The train – Caitlin could be in one of those cars waiting at the train depot! Maybe Caitlin has been put on the train. Whoever took her might have put her in one of the train cars waiting for the train to come through and hook up with it. They could take her down to New Orleans on a train faster than they could a boat, once they were hooked up to the engine."

Lily stopped and looked at Benny with her mouth and eyes wide open. "Jumping Jehoshaphat, you're right! I didn't think of that. You're probably right Benny! Let's get on over to the train depot!

Let's go and ask Pete, the ticket master, if he's seen Caitlin or anyone who seems suspicious. Maybe Pete really doesn't sleep while he's sitting there at the ticket window as much as people think. Maybe he caught something with his half-closed eyes that no one else saw."

CHAPTER SIX

The Depot

LILY AND BENNY TOOK OFF RUNNING toward the train depot. It didn't take them long to get there, and just as they were running up the platform steps, the morning train was blowing its whistle; signaling its departure in thirty minutes. The trains stopping in Caruthersville were a mixture of different types of cars. First, of course, was the engine and hooked up to the engine was four passenger cars and then there was the baggage/cargo car and then the stock car was next with the caboose bringing up the end.

Local passengers were hugging their relatives and getting onboard. Most of the passengers were going down river to visit relatives, but some were going to New Orleans on business. Porters were loading baggage into the baggage car at the same time two cowboys were trying to coax their stubborn horses into the stock car. The porters were yelling at the cowboys to get out of the way and the cowboys were yelling at the porters to shut-up. All the while, the horses were bucking and trying to kick anyone who came within reach. On the platform, vendors were loudly yelling out the types of food they were selling. Food, water and whiskey were being quickly exchanged for money through the open windows of the train.

People were leaning out the train windows shouting at the vendors. The passengers were all trying to buy from the overwhelmed vendors, who in turn were yelling at each other in their attempt to satisfy all the customers. The stop in Caruthersville wasn't long enough for anyone to get off the train and go into a local café, so the cafés and saloons came to the trains. The noise coming from the sound of feet stomping and the multitude of voices yelling was almost as loud as the train itself. Black smoke was billowing out from the coal engine and the breeze pushed it onto the platform; but no one seemed to be bothered by the black smoke, all their attention was on the vendors and what they were selling.

Vendors were slapping food into bowls and filling whiskey cups as fast as jackrabbits. The returned bowls were refilled for the next customer without being wiped clean, even if the bowl still had food left in it the vendor just dipped it back into the pot and filled the bowl full. The same spoons were used for all the customers and no one seemed to mind. They were snatching and grabbing food just as fast as the vendors were snatching and grabbing their money. Money was changing hands so fast a person couldn't keep track even if he had wanted to. All the passengers must have brought along the correct amount of money because no change was being given to anyone. It was complete bedlam.

"Fried chicken and taters!" A vendor yelled out.

"Beef stew and biscuits!" Yelled another, as he waved his arms.

"Fluffy hot biscuits! Just as light as goose feathers and covered with gravy!" Still another shouted.

A young, very bored, boy was standing beside the fried chicken vendor and was holding up a large haphazard sign advertising the meal.

The busiest vendors were selling whiskey from the local saloons. There were three boys running up and down the platform selling whiskey as fast as they could dip it out of the barrel. Before the train even arrived, the saloons had their whisky barrels waiting on the platform. As fast as a passenger gulped down the whiskey, the boys snatched the cup back, dipped into the barrel for a refill and scurried away to hand it to the next paying passenger. Some of the men on the train gulped down their whiskey and threw the tin cup back out the window. The whiskey vendors would have to run and grab the cup before a street bum standing on the platform snatched it up and tried to get a free gulp of whiskey from one of the barrels. Vendors scrambled quickly over to the empty cups and snatched them away from the non-paying intruder.

Lily and Benny stood still with their mouths wide open. "They have all gone loco," Lily said to Benny.

"Crackers and crawfish!" Benny said, laughing. "Every time I see this I am amazed!"

"Son, if ya don't close yor'ah mouth, yor'ah gonna catch a fly and choke on it," came a husky voice from behind them.

Lily and Benny whirled around and stared into the face peering down at them.

"Oh hello, Sheriff Beaumont," Lily gasped.

She wanted to grab Benny and run for the hills as fast as they could to get away from the sheriff. She was sure he was going to grab both of them and haul them back to Aunt Birdie or maybe even throw them in jail.

Looking up at the sheriff, Lily said, "You scared us. We're trying to find out if our sister, Caitlin, might be around the train depot. Have you seen her? She looks a lot like me, except older and more of a lady."

"Nope, Ah haven't Lily. But ah'll keep my eyes open for her. When was the last time ya both saw her?"

"A few days ago now," Lily said.

Lily was nervous and was talking as fast as her mouth could move. "When we got up and went down for breakfast one morning, about three days ago, Aunt Birdie told us Caitlin had run off with a lover during the night and left us. But that's not true, Sheriff. Caitlin would never do that. And we haven't been able to find her, and she hasn't been able to come back to us. I know she is trying to get home, but someone must be holding her someplace. You have to help us find her, Sheriff. We have to find her before something bad happens to her." Lily's voice broke as she tried to tell the sheriff about Caitlin. "She would never, never leave us and we're getting pretty worried. How about it sheriff? Help us and I promise Granny Tomason will bake you biscuits every day if you want! What do you say?"

Benny broke in desperately, "Please Sheriff, if you help us, I will take care of your horse until you get old and die. I'm serious. I cross my heart and hope to die or I'll stick a needle in my eye." Benny made a cross over his chest and poked his finger onto his eyelid as he looked at the sheriff.

"Okay, okay. Ah'll help, but ya kids have to stay away from anyone who looks the least bit suspicious. Don't be going into any of the saloons and don't be out at night. And by the way, yor'ah Aunt Birdie is looking for ya and she told me she was worried about ya all." Andre bent down so he could stare directly into their eyes, "And by the way, wher'ah is yor'ah little sista Tessa? Birdie seems to think ya two ran off with her and she wants ya kids to go back home. What do ya have to say about that?"

Lily swallowed hard as she looked up at the sheriff and back to Benny.

"Well, we do try to stay away from Aunt Birdie, seeing that she is so mean and all — even when we are home. We get up early, do our chores and take off. Sometimes we go down to the river bottom to visit folks." Lily lied. She started twisting the ends of her curls that hung in her face and looked away from the Sheriff.

"We stopped at Granny Tomason's and Tessa stayed to help her out while me and Benny came into town to look for Caitlin." Lily figured she hadn't told but a little fib to the sheriff, so it might look real bad in God's book.

"Don't worry about Aunt Birdie, she's not worried about us none." Lily looked straight at the sheriff and kept her eyes staring directly into his eyes. Her face didn't show any emotion.

Andre could not tell if Lily was lying to him or not. He squinted his eyes and frowned as he looked down at Lily. "What a good lie'ah," Andre thought. "She could fool anyone if she put her mind to it. If ah hadn't heard those rascals in Granny's cupboard, ah would think for sure'ah she was telling me the truth."

Andre smiled at Lily and glanced over at Benny. Benny's face was red, but not as red as his ears were. Lily should get a new partner-in-crime. Benny's face was a sure give away. When Andre's eyes met Benny's, Benny looked down at his feet and started shuffling around.

"Okay kids," Andre said, "Ah'll be looking for yor'ah Caitlin startin', right now, but ya two go on back to yor'ah Aunt Birdie's house. Ah mean yor'ah house. Sorry."

"Thanks Sheriff!" Lily exclaimed. She gave Andre a surprisingly big hug and kissed him on his cheek. "I knew you'd help us. But we have to go to Granny Tomason's house and give her the money we're getting for her eggs. Granny said you were a nice guy, and now we know it for sure."

Andre hugged Lily back and ruffled Benny's hair. "Go on now, get on out of here'ah and don't let me catch ya two snooping around any place you shouldn't."

"Okay Sheriff," Benny replied. "We're going."

"Bye, Sheriff Beaumont. See ya later," Lily called as they walked away.

Andre watched them run off the platform and take off down the street, until their figures disappeared amongst the crowd of travelers and townspeople.

"Ah'm sure they aren't going to both'ah listening to anything ah just told them." Andre thought. He watched them as far as he could and then turned back to the train. As he looked at all the train cars, he wondered if Caitlin Quinn could have been put on one of them and taken out of Caruthersville, or maybe she was still in one of the private cars parked on the sidetracks. "Damnation" he thought, "Where should I start looking? She could be on a boat going down

CHAPTER SIX: THE DEPOT   75

the Mississippi or on a wagon train going out west, or she could be right here in Caruthersville inside someone's home."

As Andre leaned back against the wall of the train depot, he looked around at the people on the platform. What a display of human craziness. With the black smoke billowing out of the engine, the noise of the engine and all the yelling people, it was so loud a man could hardly think straight.

Except for a few, all the people on the platform looked familiar to him. A couple of dust covered, sweaty cowboys were trying to get their horses loaded. A few men were just watching, the same as Andre was doing. A woman dressed in an expensive, emerald green dress and hat stood beside a train window talking to a gentleman who was seated on the train. As Andre watched, the woman's face grew red with anger and he could tell she was raising her voice as she started speaking quickly to the man on the train. Andre couldn't hear above the noise as to what they were saying, but the woman was obviously upset. The man just kept staring out the window, glancing down at the woman and back up again as if he was looking for someone. It was obvious that someone else should have been there to catch the train. The gentleman didn't look pleased at all.

Slowly Andre walked to the other end of the passenger cars and then started moseying down to get close to the man and woman. As he walked past the train windows, he spoke to all the passengers he knew. Lucky for Andre, when he got one window away from the woman in the green dress, he spotted old Mr. Tillman.

"Hey Tillman," Andre said loudly. "How are ya? Goin' to see yor'ah daught'ah in New Orleans?"

"Well howdy, Andre. Yeah, I'm a'going on down ta visit Paulette and her young'uns. That gal o' mine has eight of them thar rascals now. All boys! I cain't stay down there too long 'cuz those young'uns of hers is wild as swamp critters. Them thar rascals are always a'climbin on me and a'pullin my hair. Sometimes I'm a'wonderin how I ever get home with any hair left on my head a'tall.

Why, last time I was a'visitin, one of them there young'uns came a'struttin out of the house and onto the front porch like an ol' banty rooster. He was jest a'struttin and a'grinnin' from ear to ear as he high-stepped it in a pair of my best trousers and my Sunday-go-to-meetin' shirt. He even had my Sunday hat on and hit was pulled down so low his ears were a'stickin straight out! I swear he had the devil's own mischief in his eyes. He stops right dab in front of me and says loudly 'Hi, Pappy' and then he takes off a'runnin' and a'whoopin' down the steps and out onto the road a'for I could blink an eye. I had to nab a couple of her other wild young'uns to run after that little rascal and fetch my duds back. All the rest of them thar rascals took off a'running after the one I sent to fetch my duds. Even the youngest one took off a'toddling after the rest of 'em. They caught that bugger and darn near tore my duds up a'getting them offa the little rascal. Then he comes a'struttin on back to the porch jest as naked as a jay bird and a'laughin' like that there was the funniest thing he ever done. He walks right up to me, naked as he was, and says in the deepest froggy voice of a young'un I ever did hear and with a big ol' smile says; 'Pappy, I sure do love them ther'ah duds o' yours.' So I go on ahead and give him my shirt. It ain't worth wearing by then anyway.

Mr. Tillman was smiling, with a twinkle in his eyes the whole time he was telling the story.

"But, I tell you, Andre, it was purt near worth the price of them there duds just to see the fun those rascals had wrestling each other. All eight of them thur young'uns is as pretty as new born pups, but, they sure are a handful for my Paulette. She just laughs and tells me they mean no harm, that they're just being boys. I'd a never thought my blonde haired, blue eyed pretty little Paulette would end up marrying up with that thur wild Cajun cousin of yours and having a passel of wild young'uns of her own and all of them a'looking just like their pappy with thur black hair and black eyes exceptin' that thar littlest one. He's a looking jest like my Paulette with his curly blond hair and blue eyes. I reckon hit must be that there Cajun blood of their pa's that make'em all so wild."

Tillman laughed as he looked out at Andre and winked.

"Ahreckon so." Andre laughed back.

"Well, my Paulette is expecting another young'un come harvest time. She really hopes hit's a little gal child. I told her maybe she should be a'hoping hit's another boy child; seeing that the rest of them thur rascals be so wild and all. If'en hit's a little gal it will probably be just as wild as the rest. Whatever hit is, hit's just fine with me. I got myself one child but the good Lord gave me nigh on nine grandchildren. Life is good; yep, life is good to me." Mr. Tillman flashed Andre another big smile.

Everyone knew Mr. Tillman was crazy about his Paulette and her wild young'uns. His wife had passed on when Paulette was little, so Paulette was all Mr. Tillman had of value – as Mr. Tillman always said. Paulette married Michel Beaumont, Andre's cousin, two weeks after they met and then she up and moved to New Orleans with him. Paulette and Michel had a good marriage. But their offspring were wild.

"How's your sheriffin' coming along? Catch any crooks lately?"

Just as Mr. Tillman said the word "sheriffin", Andre felt, more than saw, the woman standing at the next window stiffen. The woman spoke loudly to the man on the train and it was pretty obvious that she wanted Andre to hear what she had to say.

"She should have been here by now. What's keeping them? Oh dear, I am starting to worry about the dear girl. I surely am starting to worry. Maybe I should go and check on the dear child."

Out of the corner of his eye Andre could see her look over at him, but Andre kept his face turned toward Mr. Tillman as he continued to talk about Andre's catching crooks.

"Well, dear," the woman continued, "have a safe trip, and I'll see you when you get home. I will go out and check on our dear niece immediately and see what the problem is." She leaned up and the man leaned out of the window and she kissed him on the cheek. As they pulled away from each other, they whispered something and the woman turned quickly and walked away. Andre kept talking to Tillman as if he had heard nothing.

As the train began to pull away, Andre told Tillman goodbye and to be sure and say hello to Paulette and his cousin Michel for him when he got into New Orleans.

"As soon as I get there I'll do that Sheriff, and if I have any sense left by the time I get back, I'll let you know what he has to say." Tillman called out.

Andre laughed, waved and walked away from the moving train. As he glanced at the window where the gentleman sat behind Tillman, he could see the man had raised the window glass up and was staring at him. Andre smiled and nodded. The man did not return the nod.

"That sure'ah was strange," Andre muttered. "Both of those people appear'ah to be mighty nervous about something in particular. And I don't believe it was just a niece not showing up for'ah the train." Andre left the train platform and quickly walked out onto the street as he tried to see which way the woman had gone.

Looking down the main street, he did not see one buggy or a wagon with a woman dressed in green sitting in it, and he could not see the woman walking anywhere. "She must live fairly close," Andre thought to himself. But she was not in sight, and Andre, as hard as he tried, could not remember ever seeing her before.

80 *Lily and the Ghost of Michael Thorne*

CHAPTER SEVEN

The Saloon Escapade

ANDRE DECIDED TO TAKE A WALK along the back streets of town just to see if he could spot the woman in green. As he walked behind the Ruby Slipper, he kept his eyes and ears open. Nothing seemed to be going on except the usual — a couple of girls from the Ruby Slipper Saloon were standing outside the back door laughing and gabbing with one another.

"Hey Sheriff," one of them called out. "How are ya? Come on in for a drink. We haven't seen ya in a while."

"Hello ladies. Not today, mind you, but maybe anoth'ah time. Did ya ladies happen to see a woman in a green dress and hat pass by the alley, maybe going up to Church Street ther'ah? Just about two or three minutes ago?"

"No, Good Lookin', we haven't, but we haven't been watching for women either. Now...if it was a good-looking man you were looking for, we could probably tell ya right off if he had passed by." Both girls laughed at the same time.

Andre smiled, shook his head and turned around to walk up Broadway.

"Nice talking to ya, Sheriff" Pearl and Opal called out in unison. "Come on in and keep us company for a while."

"Ah don't think so, ladies." Andre smiled at them as he looked back over his shoulder.

"What a pair," Andre thought to himself. "Good looking, happy, friendly girls, but not a hope in the world of livin' a long life. Not unless they can get out of the business of serving drinks to drunks".

Andre walked along Broadway for a while but saw no one in a green dress and hat. As he turned back toward Waterfront Street, he heard yelling coming from one of the saloons.

"And don't let me see you two in here again. You hear me? Next time I'm going to call the sheriff and have both of you thrown in jail. I don't care if you are two skinny kids. Get out of my saloon and don't come back!" Someone bellowed.

"Damn! I bet it's those two Quinn kids again." Andre thought, as he started running toward the saloon. "What are they doin' in a dang saloon?"

"Hey! Hey! Come here'ah ya two." Andre yelled as he spotted Lily and Benny. "Ah thought ah told ya two to stay away from these here'ah saloons."

Lily and Benny came to a screeching halt. Their shoes actually made dust fly up around their ankles as they stopped running away from the saloon. "Aw, horse patoot!" Benny thought.

The sheriff had them. "We were just asking some questions, Sheriff," Lily said to Andre as they turned around to face him.

Benny pulled Lily behind him and hissed. "Shh. Let me do the talking."

"Sheriff," Benny said, "I was going into this particular saloon all by myself to see if old Mr. Tillman was in there. He goes to this saloon most days around this time to get a bite to eat, and I was going to ask him a few questions. You see, his daughter Paulette got married and moved on down to New Orleans, so Caitlin always takes him meat pies a couple times a week and I thought maybe he had heard her say something that would help us out in our hunt for her. Lily was supposed to stay outside and not go in.

But she went in anyway, and when she heard a man talking bad about all of us Irish living around here, she announced that she had heard just about enough slander about the Irish. Then, she just up and jumps on his back and started biting his right ear."

With that said, Benny started smiling.

"It would have gone okay if Lily would have just obeyed me and stayed outside where I told her to stay."

Lily glared at Benny. "OBEYED? How dare he say that to the sheriff!" she thought to herself as her face turned red with anger.

"OBEYED!!! I am going to kick his behind all the way across this river!" she thought madly. She could almost feel steam coming out of her ears.

Benny continued talking as if he had not even noticed Lily's anger.

"I've been in that saloon many times before and the barkeep doesn't really care. The only time he gets mad is when a bunch of us young guys go in and bother his regular customers.

Well, as soon as Lily jumped on the big guys back, he started in swinging his arms around trying to grab for her and then she bit a chunk right out of his ear. The piece was just hanging there by a little bit of skin, dangling like a pair of britches hanging on a clothesline and just a'flapping in the breeze. He was cursin' and swearin' and spinning around trying to get a hold on Lily's arm or leg. But then he swung around by the bar and she reached over and grabbed a bottle of whiskey and hit him on that bitten ear, real hard. BOOM! He hit the floor like a boulder dropping off a mountain top — with Lily still on his back. When he hit the floor, she jumps right up and starts kicking at him. Then every man in the bar started in laughing and the guy with the bitten ear started rolling around on the floor moaning and groaning. That was when all the men in the bar started in moaning and groaning, just like the fellow on the floor, and then, to make it worse, some of the fellers fall down on the floor beside him and started rolling around moaning. Well, the laughter got louder still and that was when the barkeep grabbed Lily and me and tossed us out.

Sheriff, I was so shocked at Lily I couldn't do anything. I couldn't even think as to how to get my legs moving and get us out of there. Thank goodness that barkeep shoved us out the door or I would still be standing there with my mouth hanging wide open staring at Lily and that bloody ear. I just couldn't believe it Sheriff. Lily was like a hungry dog with a bucket of garbage. It was the funniest gol'durn thing I have ever seen in my life. That big galoot is going to be hotter than a boil on the bottom of your bu… behind."

Andre took a tight hold on each of their shoulders and quickly started walking down the street toward the jail. "Ya two are going to stay right here'ah inside my office for a while, until ah say ya can leave. That man is going to be plenty mad when his head and ears stop ringing, and he's going to come looking for ya Lily."

"Sheriff," Benny said as he hop-walked along side the sheriff, trying to keep up, "I just couldn't believe it. Lily just jumped right up on his back and started biting."

Once again Benny went through the motions for the sheriff.

"You should have been there! What a sight to see! It was great! And she sure was a wild and woolly thing when she had her temper up. It was a great sight to see! Imagine that, Lily got the best of a grown-up man! She was like a mad-man!"

Benny was almost dancing a jig, grinning from ear to ear. One would have thought his sister had become a saint and saved the world from a terrible disaster.

"She sure is something, isn't she Sheriff? Yeah, it was a funny sight, alright. Those men in the saloon will be talking about this for a long time. How a small boy, which they thought Lily was, bested that galoot. It was exciting I tell ya, it was just plain exciting and you should've been there to see it. Those other men were having the biggest laugh ever. When Lily was on the back of that galoot I heard some of the other fella's taking bets on how long she would stay on his back. The whole crowd was cheering Lily on. Yelling things like, 'Hang on thar short stuff!' or, 'Grab his hair boy, grab his hair and don't let go!' If I'd had any money in my pocket I would have put in a bit myself. I knew Lily could hold on as long as he was standing up, but I didn't have any money and I was too stunned to even think straight."

"She's something all right. That big galoot, as ya call him, is going to be as mad as a hornet." Andre said forcefully. "She's going to get herself hurt real bad. Ya two have got to start behaving yourselves," Andre told them sternly. "Lily, ya need to start wearing a dress, ya hear'ah? Like right now today. If ya wear a dress, that galoot won't know you're the boy who jumped on his back ther'ah in the saloon. Now get in my office. We need to talk."

Andre pulled them both into the office and shut the door. He went to each window and pulled the shutters closed.

"Okay, let's have an honest-to-goodness talk. No more telling lies. If ya want me to help ya find Caitlin, yor'ah gonna have to be truthful with me. Lily, from the time ya discovered Caitlin was missing until this morning, what happened?"

"We already told you Sheriff Beaumont," Lily sputtered, wiping some of the galoot's blood off her coat sleeve. "We woke up in the morning and she was gone. Aunt Wad… Birdie told us she ran off with a lover and wouldn't be back."

"What happened during that night? Did either of ya hear'sh any strange sounds a'tall?" Andre asked

"Well, I woke up during the night and heard some mumbling and bumping around outside the house. I lay there thinking it was Elmer and one of his drunken buddies just coming home from the saloon. They always stumble and mumble around the yard when they're drunk and trying to find their way into the barn. I didn't get up and look out because I really didn't want them to see me looking out at them. They can be kind of scary sometimes, you know. Anyway, the next morning Aunt Birdie said Caitlin ran off. It's not true Sheriff. We know it's not true."

"Yeah," echoed Benny, "And Aunt Wa…Birdie slapped Lily when Lily told her she was a liar and that Caitlin would never leave us. But that's the truth sheriff, she really wouldn't. Caitlin would never leave us, and that's the gospel truth. That mean old Aunt Waddle is telling lies about her and I plan on doing something about it. Caitlin loves us too much to leave home and not tell us."

"Aunt Waddle?" Andre spoke up, "Who in the world is Aunt Waddle?"

"It's really Aunt Birdie," Lily sighed, "Benny we have to stop calling her 'Aunt Waddle', it isn't something Tessa should be hearing from us."

An instant picture of Birdie and her "sunshine" hole drawers popped into Andre's mind.

Sheriff Beaumont smirked but said nothing. "Dang!" he thought, "Ah can't start thinking about that again."

"Okay. You two have to try and help me out here'ah. Do you really think Elm'ah had anything to do with Caitlin's disappearance? When ah spoke to him and yor'ah aunt this morning, he didn't act like he had anything to do with it. It was kind of like he knew something about it, but hadn't done anything bad himself. What do ya two think?"

Lily and Benny looked at each other for a while and then looked at Andre, then back at each other. "You know Sheriff, Benny and I kind of liked Elmer at one time. When he and Aunt Birdie first came to our house, he seemed pretty much okay, sort of different and kind of dirty, but okay. He never said much to us, or Aunt Birdie, come to think of it; all he did was work and drink. Well, he and Benny did the work. Did he ever say much to you, Benny?"

"Not really," Benny spoke up, "But he really did help with all the work. Most mornings he was up and about before I could get out to the barn. He never said anything bad about anyone to me. In fact, he didn't say anything about anyone, good or bad. He just worked, ate, and went off to the saloons with his saloon friends. He would mumble a 'thanks' when he needed to. I know he always says 'thank you, ma'am' when Caitlin gives him something or does something for him. It seemed as if he just had more respect for Caitlin than he did for anyone else."

"Don't know why I felt that way, I just did. Benny said, "With everyone else it was just 'thanks'. That was about it, unless he got with his drinking friends, and then he would become pretty loud and rowdy. But then that's true with most of the drunks around town."

"Why do you ask, Sheriff?" Lily inquired.

"Well, ah have some thoughts about this whole thing. Ther'ah was some shady characters at the train depot this morning and ah'm just wondering about some things that went on ther'ah. Lily, do ya have a dress to change into at Granny Tomason's house?"

"Ah, why should I have anything there Sheriff?"

"Lily, ah know yor'ah stayin' ther'ah, and to tell the truth, ah think yor'ah bet'ah off ther'ah than at yor'ah own house until this whole thing is settled. Now, always tell me everything you know and don't hide anything and ah'll do the same — if ah can. Okay?"

"Okay." Lily replied softly. "Yes, I have a dress at Granny's house. I'll put it on as soon as we go out to her house. You just keep your word, Sheriff Beaumont, and help us find Caitlin."

"Ah'll do my best. Try not to worry and please," he paused, "stay out of trouble. Now, get on home to Granny's house and stay ther'ah. You've been in enough trouble for one today. Get on out of here'ah and don't let me see ya in town again today. Ya hear'ah?"

"Alright Sheriff, we have to run back and get Granny's basket of eggs Lily left under the train platform and drop them off at the bakery and then we'll go on back to Granny's house."

Lily and Benny walked out of the sheriff's office and turned back toward the train depot. Lily had completed forgotten about the basket of eggs under the platform.

"Come on Lily," Benny said, "Let's go. If we hurry maybe we will see something at the depot. Keep your eyes and ears open."

CHAPTER EIGHT

Pete Turnkey and Pearl

THE TWO OF THEM RAN as fast as they could back to the train depot. Lily knew Sheriff Beaumont would be mad if he found out they were still snooping around, but this was too important to ignore. If the sheriff had seen something, maybe they would too.

As they approached the depot, Lily and Benny slowed down. "Okay," Lily said, "Let me grab the egg basket first and then we can take a quick snoop around."

"All right," Benny replied, "but keep your eyes open for those men from the saloon and pull your hat down some more. You still have on the same clothes, and they'll know you right off. Here, give me your coat and you take mine. Maybe that will help."

As Lily and Benny switched coats as Lily looked up and saw the ticket master dozing at the window. "Come on," Lily said to Benny.

"Hey Pete," Lily called out, as they walked over to the ticket window. "How are you today? We were wondering if any strange things have been going on here at the depot. Like maybe you've seen our sister Caitlin in the last couple days?"

"Hello Lily, hello, Benny. How are you two doing?" Pete replied, as he leaned out his ticket window to get a better look at them. "Nope, sorry, I haven't seen Caitlin in a while now. Come on up here and we

89

can chew the fat a while. How is she? I sure do miss talking to her every day. She usually brings me a sweet roll or something tasty. Why would you be looking for her here at the depot?

"She disappeared a few days back and we're trying to find out if anyone has seen her or if anything suspicious going on."

"Disappeared? Well let me ponder that for a while. Let's see here, maybe it was yesterday — I'm not really sure now — but there was a couple of men standing over by the tracks having a long talk, and I did hear one of them say, let's see, what are the right words, oh yes, the words were: 'she's a looker, should get a whole bag full for that one. The problem is, we have to get her all the way down here to the train from way out Yoder's way.' At the time I thought they were talking about that new filly everyone has been talking about. But after they left, I said to myself: 'self, now that new filly is out at Jeff Goodwin's place? Wonder if Yoders has a new filly also? And then," he paused, "I said to myself: 'Self, old man Yoders moved on over to Memphis with his daughter, no one is living out there.' But right then the train got here and the whole thing just flew right out of my mind like a scared bird. But now that you mention it, now that I know Caitlin is missing, maybe they weren't talking about a horse filly. But just maybe they were talking about a young gal filly."

Pete's eyes looked off in the distance like he was in a trance. Or maybe he was just pondering on it some more.

Lily sucked in her breath with a gasp. "Oh my goodness, you think so, Pete? Were those the exact words they used?"

Pete darted his eyes back to Lily as he started thumping his finger on the window sill; he answered her in his get-your-tickets-here voice. "Yes sirree! As sure as I'm standing here, those are the eeexact words they used right there. Those are the exact words!" With every word, Pete thumped his finger on the windowsill.

Pete Turnkey reminded Lily of an owl. He was tall, even for a man, and his face was quite pale. His shoulders were hunched over as if he had lugged a heavy load during his lifetime. He had huge, thick, black glasses sitting on the bridge of his long, narrow nose and they were pushed up as far as they could go, making his long eyebrows stand up straight behind his glasses. His face matched his nose: long and narrow. His hair was blond and straight but it stuck out from his head like feathers. His clothes and body were always clean, and his hands looked as if they had never done a full day's work. The best characteristic of Pete Turnkey was that he could read any legal paper anyone asked him to read, and he could tell you exactly what it meant. If it pertained to the law, he could interpret it to its fullest extent. If a person didn't know how to read, he was the person to go see. He read for most of the non-readers in town and never told another soul anyone else's business. Pete could walk down the worst street in Caruthersville without being bothered – everyone knew that one day they may need him. He knew a lot about everyone's business, but all that information was safely hidden inside Pete's brain. No amount of threats or gifts could make him dishonor a promise he made to the people who trusted him.

Some say that at one time Pete had been a big-time lawyer in New York City but had gotten into business with some shady characters and had to flee for his life. But no one really knew his story, and he sure didn't tell.

Honest, clean, and an excellent reader. That's the description everyone gave of Pete Turnkey. Smart, honest and clean, but he seemed to sleep most of the day as he sat at the ticket window on the train platform he called his own.

Pete looked at Lily and Benny through his thick glasses. "Whoa doggies," Lily thought as she stared up at Pete. "He looks more like an owl today than he does most days; he must have washed his hair last night — it's sticking out all over his head."

Pete had a frown on his face as he said in a quiet voice. "Oooooh.... this is in-ter-est-ing! Have you two been to see Sheriff Beaumont? I'm sure he would find this very interesting. Go on over there real quick-like and tell him what I heard. Have him come on back here quick-like and I'll do some more pondering while you're gone. Maybe I can remember some more important facts. Hurry up now. Go, Go." Pete shooed them away with his hands. Benny grabbed Lily's arm and pulled her off the platform.

"Come on, let's go! Maybe he has something here. Maybe he can help. Put those eggs back under the platform and let's run."

"Okay, okay! Hold on a minute." Lily yelled to Benny as she put the eggs back under the platform and took off running after Benny. They ran as fast as they could back to the Sheriff's office.

Benny burst through the door and they both stumbled inside. Instantly they stopped in their tracks and stared. There was Pearl, from the Ruby Slipper Saloon, sitting on the sheriff's desk with her legs crossed, leaning toward him as if she was waiting to be kissed.

"Great gobs of goose grease," Benny thought as he smiled. "I do think she likes the Sheriff. Yep, I would say so."

Sheriff Andre jumped up from his seat at his desk so quickly he knocked Pearl onto the hard floor in the process. Pearl landed hard on her backside and instantly fell back and banged her head on the floor. Her legs whooshed up over her head and all you could see were bloomers and legs. She let out a loud "oof" as the air in her lungs rushed out.

A few seconds of silence, and then: "Dang, Sheriff, you didn't have to push me, I'm quite capable of getting down from your desk by myself, and in a more ladylike fashion, I have you know. Damn! Sheriff Andre that hurt my backside! Ya big oaf! What's the matter with you? I couldn't breathe there for a minute, you gone loco or something?" Pearl gasped.

"Pearl," Sheriff Beaumont stammered, "Watch your language around these kids"

Benny's mouth was wide open in an enormous smile as he stared at Pearl. His smile was the biggest smile Lily had ever seen on his stupid face.

"Good Lord, what's a pretty girl like this doing sitting on the sheriff's desk all leaned over waiting for a kiss? She must work over at the Slipper." Benny was thinking. "Wow, she sure is a pretty thing!"

"Goldurn, Sheriff!" Benny croaked, all the while still bug-eyed at Pearl, "What-cha doing with this gal in your office sitting on your desk? Don't you know this is no place for that kind of thing? I'm just young and I know that. What's the matter with you? Everybody can walk right into your office, it's a public place and I really don't think a good sheriff should be having ladies sitting on their desks like that, do you? What's the matter with you?" He asked again. "You gone loco, like she said?"

Lily couldn't stop looking at Pearl. Pearl's skirts were still up above her knees and she was just sitting there with her black stockings and high-heeled shoes showing as if she were still too stunned to move. Maybe the sheriff isn't the one for Caitlin, if he carries on with women like this. Caitlin didn't need him and he isn't good enough for her. This dog-eared sheriff is a womanizer. That's what he is, a womanizer and a scoundrel! What a flop-eared, egg-sucking hound!"

Lily turned around and stomped out of the sheriff's office. "Come on Benny, let's go. Dad-blame him, he's a womanizing rascal of a mule's hind end! We are not asking him to help us find Caitlin! We can do it ourselves. Come on," Lily said angrily, "We can do this with Pete Turnkey's help. We don't need the help of an old, womanizing, scally-wagging, flop-eared dog."

When Benny didn't answer her Lily turned around to tell him again and discovered that Benny wasn't behind her. He was still in the sheriff's office. Lily stomped right back into the office and stopped with her hands on her hips. Benny was leaning down to help Pearl up off the floor. He had a tight hold on one of her arms.

"Well that's a fine howdy-do," Lily stammered, "now my stupid pea-brained brother thinks he has to help this woman up."

She was so mad. If she had a stick, she would hit both Benny and the Sheriff upside the head and maybe she could smack some sense into their empty brains.

"Let her get up by herself; she just said she was capable." Lily stated loudly.

"Here ma'am, let me help you up." Benny said, ignoring Lily as she stood in the door tapping her foot and watching. "Sheriff, take hold of her other arm and we can lift her up onto this chair."

Sheriff Beaumont was still standing there staring down at Pearl with his mouth open until Benny spoke up. Quickly he stepped around and grabbed one of Pearl's arms and both of them lifted her onto the chair.

"Well I never," thought Lily, "I don't remember Benny ever helping me up, even after he pushed me down. Even if I stumble and fall down, he hasn't bothered to rush over and lift me up real gentle-like. Heaven help these empty-headed donkeys! They don't have the brains God gave a goose, and geese brains are about as big as a pea."

"You dumb ox, you're just as bad as Sheriff Beaumont." Lily wanted to say the words out loud, but didn't want to hurt Pearl's feelings. After Pearl was seated in the chair, Benny told the sheriff that we needed to talk to him in private. "Alright," Sheriff Beaumont said softly. "Pearl, do ya think ya can walk on back to the Slipp'ah by yourself?"

Pearl glared up at Sheriff Andres with fire in her eyes. "I walked over here by myself didn't I? I'm not a child, you stupid horse's patoot. I've been takin' care of myself since I was eight years old. I don't need some dumb-cluck of a man to help me find my way back down the street to Ruby's. That wasn't a very nice thing to do, Sheriff. I've never seen you be so rude to a lady."

"Lady my hind-end," Lily thought.

"Pearl, ah am so sorry, Ah really didn't mean to knock ya off the desk. It's just that these here'ah kids surprised me and it was just a reaction. Please excuse my rudeness, Pearl" the sheriff drawled gently.

"I think I am going to lose my breakfast all over this floor." Lily thought.

"Well, don't ev'ah do it again, Sheriff," Pearl shouted, mocking Sheriff Andre's accent. "Or you will nev'ah be seeing me again, ev'ah!" Pearl replied.

As Pearl stomped to the office door where she stopped, looked at Lily and said loudly, "Young lady, men are stupid. Never ever marry-up with one of these creatures. If you do, you will forever be sorry and depressed about it!"

With that, she walked out and slammed the door shut. At that moment, Lily decided she liked Pearl.

"Well," the sheriff drawled with a grin on his face. "I just don't understand women no matt'ah how I try. Even when ya say sorry, they are nev'ah happy."

"Sorry," Sheriff Beaumont said as he turned to them. "Benny and Lily, that was kind of embarrassin' for me. Yor'ah right Benny, ah shouldn't allow Pearl to sit on my desk when she comes to visit. Ah guess it isn't very official like."

"I don't reckin it is, sheriff." Benny said, "Even though she is a might pretty lady and all, it probably isn't very official like."

"Okay, let's hear'ah what ya two have to tell me. It bett'ah be good, because ah told ya two to get on ov'ah to Granny's house."

"Well," Lily spoke up, "before we start in talking, both of you better use your shirt tails and wipe that drool off your chins before it runs down onto your necks!"

Sheriff Beaumont and Benny turned and looked at Lily with puzzlement. "What in the world are you talking about, Lily?" Benny asked.

"Wipe your chins off, you clabber-heads, you're still drooling."

"Sheriff," Lily said stiffly, "When we went back to get Granny's eggs from under the train platform, Pete, the ticket master, was just sitting there as usual, with his eyes half closed doing nothing. So we started asking him some questions about seeing any suspicious-looking people hanging around the depot as he sits there during the day. And low and behold, he did hear something kind of suspicious about two days ago. He said he heard some men talking about a new filly out at Yoders' place and wondered why they said 'Yoders' place'. He wondered, because the new filly is out at Jeff Goodwin's, not Yoders. He now thinks they might have been talking about Caitlin, and not a horse. He wants you to hurry on over to the depot, because he is going to ponder on it some more to see if he can't remember other things that might have been said on the platform in the last couple of days.

But if you're more interested in those girls at the Ruby Slipper, we don't need your help in finding Caitlin. We wouldn't want to upset your life of pleasure. Caitlin doesn't need a scally-wag making cow eyes at her. So if you'd rather go on over to the Ruby Slipper, that's fine. Benny and I can do this by ourselves."

"Lily, just calm down," Andre said staring sternly into Lily's eyes. "Ah'm not going over to the Slipp'ah and ah'm not a womanizing scally-wag. Pearl had a legitimate reason for being in here and ah'm not in a mood to listen to any wet-behind-the-ears kid lecture me. Now, ah'm going to the train depot and yor'ah both going home to Granny's. Now, get — right now!"

"We can't, Sheriff," Lily said forcefully. "We left Granny's eggs under the platform again. We're going with you." Andre rolled his eyes skyward and mumbled a prayer.

"You know, since this whole thing started yesterday, ah have started mumbling to myself and praying more than ah ev'ah have in my entire life. Come on then, let's get ov'ah to the depot so you can get those eggs."

Andre, Lily and Benny stepped out of the sheriff's office and hurried down the wooden sidewalk toward the train depot with Lily almost running to keep up with Sheriff Beaumont and Benny.

When they got to the depot, Pete was pacing in front of the ticket window. "It's about time you got back here," Pete stated. "I remember some things that might come in handy with your case, Sheriff."

"Like what?" Lily and Benny spoke together.

"Well," Pete replied, looking at Lily and Benny, "like seeing your Aunt Birdie out on the platform talking to some fellers that came in on the late train yesterday. They all stepped over to the side of the platform and talked for about fifteen minutes and then the whistle blew and the two fellers got back on the train and Miss Birdie left. Kind of strange, don't you think Sheriff? What would Birdie Quinn be doing talking to some fancy-pants city fellers? They were all slicked up in their city clothes and their boots — looked like they just walked off the shelf of the Paris Bootery. They weren't relatives or friends, or she would have taken them on home for a visit. If they were salesmen, they would have spoken to more people in town than Birdie Quinn. And if they were church folk, they would have gone on down to the Reverend's house. It all seems kind of strange to me. How about you, Sheriff Andre? What do you think? Kind of strange isn't it?"

"You're right Pete. That ther'ah does sound a mite strange."

"And," Pete continued, "Some strange fellows have been hanging out around the depot, like they're waiting for something, or someone. What do ya think Andre? Ya think something's going on here? What-cha thinking, Sheriff? Maybe those bums have Miss Caitlin and are just waiting for an 'all clear' signal from someone so they can put her on one of the trains going down to New Orleans. What-cha think? Whatever you think I should do Sheriff, I'll do it."

Pete was so wound up he was pacing up and down the platform talking as fast as a magpie. "Yes sir'ee, yes sir'ee, I'll do whatever it takes to help find Miss Caitlin. Why, she's a real lady. I knew Michael too, he was her beau, ya know. He sure was in love with Miss Caitlin. She was mighty broken-hearted when he didn't come home from that war." Pete shook his head as he continued pacing.

"She sure was broken-hearted," Pete said again, his voice getting soft. "Yep, she was mighty broken hearted. Sometimes when she was in town she would come by for a chat and we would talk about her

Michael. She had a hard time getting over him. Yes sir'ee, she surely did."

"You see," Pete continued, "Michael was a good man. He and I became good friends the day I arrived here in Missouri. I met Michael when I stepped off the train. You see, I was having trouble with my carpet bags and Michael happened to be on the platform; when he saw how I was struggling, trying to get my bags off the train and all, he came right over and lent me a hand."

Pete seemed to be talking more to himself than to anyone else. "Well, he took me right on over to the saloon and bought me a fine glass of whiskey. He asked me all about life back east and I asked him all about life here in Missouri. Well, after I heard him tell of life here in Carutherville — in particular — I decided right then and there to stay right here in Carthursville, Missouri for the rest of my life."

Pete blinked his eyes, his mind coming back to the present time. "She would have done well by marrying up with him."

Pete stopped suddenly and glared at Sheriff Beaumont. "And he would have done well by marrying up with her! Sheriff Beaumont, Miss Caitlin did not run off with a lover and don't you let anything happen to her. In memory of Michael, I guess maybe I should have been watching out for her."

Sheriff Beaumont scratched his chin and thought for a few minutes. Then he started pacing up and down the platform, just like Pete.

"Cri-min-y Christmas!" Lily finally said, "Will you two stop walking and start talking? Sheriff, what are we going to do?"

Andre stopped and looked at Lily as if he just noticed she was standing there.

"We? Ther'ah is no 'we'. 'We' aren't going to do anything. Pete and ah are going to do something and ya two kids are going on back to Granny's and staying ther'ah until ah tell ya it's okay to leave that house." Andre bent down, looked Lily right in the face and said very firmly, "Now, do ya understand me?" She could have punched him right in the nose, but she knew he would get mighty mad and maybe

98 *Lily and the Ghost of Michael Thorne*

throw her and Benny in jail and throw away the key.

"Ah don't want two mor'ah missin' kids to be looking for. One is enough," he said sharply.

"Sheriff," Lily said indignantly, "Caitlin is not a kid; she is a grown woman and a very pretty one at that! And I'll mind you to treat her like a lady when you find her, and not get all womanizing around her! If you do, you'll be sorry for the rest of your miserable life!"

"Is that so? Well ah'll make sur'ah and treat her like the lady she is and not let her set on my desk when she talks to me. Is that alright?"

"You best behave yourself. You're the sheriff around here and should have more manners than those rascally sailors walking the streets!" Lily almost shouted at him. Andre ruffled Lily's hair as she ducked away; he laughed with a deep chested chuckle.

"Okay Lily-girl, ah'll behave myself. Now ya two get out of here'ah right now," he drawled.

"Sitting on your desk? What's that all about, Sheriff?" Pete asked.

"Nothing a'tall Pete, nothing a'tall," Sheriff Beaumont answered.

"Come on Lily, let's go." Benny pulled on Lily's sleeve and said, "Let's get Granny's eggs and get over to the bake shop."

100 *Lily and the Ghost of Michael Thorne*

CHAPTER NINE

Mr. Johnston and Aunt Birdie

LILY AND BENNY HURRIED down the steps to the street and Lily grabbed the egg basket. Slowly they shuffled down the street, all the while watching the hustle and bustle of the town. The day was warm and everyone seemed to be doing outside work and running errands so they could enjoy the warm sunshine.

"I think spring is on its way out the back door and summer is running in the front door, isn't it?" Lily said to Benny after they walked a while.

"Yeah," Benny said. "You know, Pete sure seemed concerned about Caitlin. If I had known he was such good friends with Michael, I would have gone to him the first day Caitlin went missing. Did you know they were friends?"

"Nope," Lily replied, shaking her head.

As they entered the bakery, Lily walked up and put the eggs on the counter. She called out "hello" to Mr. Johnston, the baker, and started looking through the glass at all the sweets lined up in perfect rows. If reminded her of all the tasty sweets her mama used to make.

"Hey Benny, I'm sure hungry for something sweet. What do you think?" Lily spoke up, "Shall we get some of those cherry tarts? Look at them, don't they look wonderful?"

"Lily," Benny said, "Stop looking at them. These eggs are Granny's and she didn't say we could buy tarts or anything else."

"I know, I know, I'm just dreaming," Lily replied.

"Howdy children," Mr. Johnston said as he walked in from the back of the bakery. He had been in the back with the oven. "Ye got some eggs for me? I was hoping Granny Tomason would come along today. At this very moment I am right out of eggs. How about a cherry tart for the two of ye? Doesn't that sound good? Fresh out of the oven they are. And they're pretty tasty if I have to say so myself. Don't want to toot my own horn, but well, they are the best you'll find in this county. I cannot say they aren't!"

Mr. Johnston's accent sounded a little like their Pa's.

Mr. Johnston and his wife Nora had been the bakers in town way before Lily and Benny came along. Their Mama and Pa had told them that the Johnston's were already in Caruthersville when they had arrived years ago. Mr. Johnston and Nora had settled in Caruthersville a good long while before their own children come along.

"Me lovely Nora," Mr. Johnston would say when he spoke of his wife, who had not lived past the first year of their youngest son's birth. Much to the dismay of the town widows, Mr. Johnston never remarried. He raised his sons alone, teaching them the skills of baking and books. Both sons turned out to be hard workers, and highly educated as well. His eldest son was named Mo, after the state he was born in, and his youngest was Noraman, named after his mother.

Mr. Johnston was one of the proudest parents in town. His boys went off to the war, met two Yankee sisters and decided to stay back east to marry the sisters and raise their families. Having opened several bake shops in and around Boston, both of Mr. Johnston's sons were doing quite well in life. Mr. Johnston wasn't too happy about their decisions to stay in the east, but there was nothing he could do about it. So every year he sent them all Christmas presents and asked them to come to Missouri and live close to him. Every year they would refuse, but they promised to come and visit for the holidays — which they did. Every other Christmas, his sons, daughter-in-laws and grandchildren would fill his house and bakery. On the off years, Mr. Johnston would travel back to Boston and stay with his sons for the whole month of December and well into January. When he returned from seeing his grandchildren he was the happiest man in Missouri. He would always contemplate moving back to Boston, but once he got back into the running of his own bake shop, he just couldn't leave Missouri.

"One day," he would say with a laugh and a smile on his face, "I will leave this wilderness and live among the civilized people of society once again. But for now, I still like it here among the happy, rowdy, uncivilized folk of Missouri."

He was a tall, stout man with white-blond hair and sparkling bright blue eyes. His eyebrows and eyelashes were the same color as his hair, which made his eyes seem to jump right out of his face. When a person was speaking to Mr. Johnston, they always looked him straight in the eyes – they were mesmerizing to look at. His eyes had the look of the clear blue waters off the Caribbean islands; at least that was what the sailors all said. If Mr. Johnston had warts and toads living on his face, no one would notice. All a person remembered about him was how blue his eyes were. He was a very nice jolly man, always ready with a laugh.

At the moment, he was covered from head to toe with flour, especially his hair. He must have tried to wipe the flour off his face when he heard Lily and Benny come in, because small parts of his face were the only areas not powdered with flour. Flour was still attached to his mustache and eyebrows. He looked quite comical as flour continued to slowly sift down from his eyebrows.

"Thanks Mr. Johnston, but these eggs are Granny Tomason's, not ours, so we really can't buy anything today. But, they sure do look good, and smell even better." Lily said.

"Well here, take these four that didn't really bake the way I like them to. They won't sell for me and I'll end up throwing them out to the hogs. Take one to your little sister and one for Granny Tomason. I hear ye children are staying out at Granny's house for a while. What's going on with that? Nothing is wrong at ye own house now, I hope."

Lily and Benny looked at each other. "My goodness," Lily thought. "Nothing is a secret in this town."

"We just decided to visit Granny for a while," Benny said quickly.

"Well, here are some nice hot tarts for all of ye. Take a dozen of them. They make a wonderful, tasty treat with your milk in the morning. Just don't mention it to that aunt of yours; I'm not giving anything to that woman! Pardon my saying so, but she needs to stop eating all those bitter greens. Maybe she would be a little sweeter."

Mr. Johnston winked and chuckled at his own joke as he handed Lily and Benny a bag full of tarts. When he laughed, flour once again floated down from his hair like a soft shower of powdery snow.

"She would scare the devil himself if he ever noticed that scowl on her face. Here ye go, here's the money for Granny's eggs. Tell her I said thank you and that she is a woman sent straight from heaven for letting me buy her eggs at such a low price. And be sure and bring me all the eggs ye can get."

Flour now covered the counter; Lily was sure the floor was also covered with it.

"Well, children, I be running off at the mouth again, I am sure Miss Bidy — sorry, Birdie — might just be a right nice person if one got to know her."

"I doubt that," Benny mumbled.

"It's okay. Thanks Mr. Johnston," Lily and Benny said together. "We'll make sure and give Tessa and Granny some tarts."

Lily and Benny walked out of the bakery and started up the road to Granny's house. As they walked past the door to the Ruby Slipper Saloon, Lily caught Benny trying to look in the door.

"What a pea-brain," she thought to herself. "Just like a grown man, even at his age they have no brains."

"Itty-bitty brains must come with all baby boys," Lily thought. "No wonder God decided to create a woman. He sure messed up on that man he started with. All they can see is the way a woman looks. They seem to forget that God really did give women brains. If all the men in this town put their brains together in a bucket, it still wouldn't be as smart as a woman's brain.

"Stop acting like a simpleton, Benny Quinn," Lily hissed as she jerked on Benny's sleeve and pulled him away from the Slipper's door. "You don't have the brains the good Lord in heaven gave a goose."

Just as they turned the corner behind the Ruby Slipper, both of them started running until — SMACK! They slammed right into the backside of Aunt Birdie's derrière.

"OH CHICKEN POOP!" Lily gasped.

"WHOA!" Benny sucked in air.

They both spoke at the same time as they came to a screeching halt. Spinning around like tops they took off running back around the corner as Aunt Birdie flung herself around and started moving as fast as she could to try and catch them.

"You two stop this instant!" she yelled out. "Get back here right now! Someone help me! Those two br... children are mine! Help me! S-stop them! Bring them b-back!"

Birdie was huffing and puffing as she tried to catch up with Lily and Benny. Her legs were pumping up and down and she was breathing so deeply she could hardly yell. Her face turned bright red and sweat started running down her neck. It ran down her back and soaked into her dress.

"Oh Lord," she whizzed. "I have to stop. Those wild heathens are like animals! I am going beat them when I finally get my hands on those creatures. Where is that little Tessa? She'll be easier to handle. Those two are just too wild and that's what comes from being the spawn of that no-good, backwoods mother of theirs!"

Birdie kept mumbling to herself as she stopped in front of the bakery and sat down on the bench in front of the window. She had a difficult time catching her breath and her heart was pumping so fast she could see her bosoms moving up and down.

"I'm going to get rid of those woods-colts if I have to do away with them myself," she muttered.

Birdie didn't feel bad at all about getting rid of the Daniel and Molly's children. All she could think about was that she could finally get back at that Molly woman for marrying Daniel and taking him away from her. Daniel had left her for that wild woman with the awful red hair flying around her head. Wild as a savage she was. Always laughing and touching Daniel's arm or hands in front of God and everyone else. What a floozy she had been. Well, he had fallen for her wily-ways and look what that had gotten him. Dead! That's what it had gotten him. That wicked woman had been the reason Daniel died. The woman he thought was such a beautiful lady had killed him.

"Ugh," Birdie thought, "Lady? Not in the least. Molly Donaldson was nothing but trash and a conniving tramp that tricked Daniel into marrying-up with her."

Birdie kept right on muttering to herself as she sat in front of the Johnston Bakery. She was oblivious to all the other pedestrians walking by and staring at her.

"Molly Donaldson was worse than a saloon girl." she muttered loudly, "She pretended to be a high-society lady and all the time acting like a floozy. From the wrong side of the tracks was what she was. She may have lived in a big, beautiful house with all the servants she wanted, but that didn't make her a lady," Birdie continued on as if she was by herself in her own house. "From the wrong side of the tracks, is where she was from! She didn't even have a mother to teach her how to be a proper lady. All she had was a stupid old man for a father who was more interested in teaching his daughter to ride astride and shoot a gun than to be a lady. What had Daniel seen in that woman? Molly had thrown herself at Daniel, and being a man, he just couldn't resist her witching ways. That had to be the reason."

"Well, that woman will be clawing in her grave when I finish with those wild savages of hers," Birdie said. "She thought she was so smart taking my Daniel away. Well, I'll show her. I'll have her house and everything in it and her wild, heathenish excuses for children will be gone to join her. Ha! I'll show her! Daniel should have stayed on the farm and helped me!" Birdie kept right on muttering to herself.

She was so deep in her ranting about Molly Quinn the rest of the world was blocked out of her thoughts. All she could think about was Molly Donaldson and how much she hated her.

She sat there for a good while trying to catch her breath and talking to herself. It was becoming harder and harder to breathe after doing anything the less bit taxing.

"Those insolent street-rags," she said again, as she started breathing easier, "I'll get them yet and sell them to the highest bidder. And forget that paper money. I want GOLD!"

Lily and Benny ran as fast and as far as they could to get away from Aunt Birdie. They ended up on the opposite end of town from Granny's house. Now, they would have to walk all the way back through town to get home — or walk through the woods.

"Wait a minute Benny," Lily gasped. "let me take a minute and catch my breath. That was a close call. Too close for me! I was so surprised to see her I almost wet myself."

"I could feel her breathing right down the neck of my shirt!" Benny gasped. "She scared the be-jee-bees out of me! We were so close I could smell her onion breath. Cri-min-y Lily, that was close! I thought my skin was gonna jump off my bones and take off running." "Come on," Lily pulled on Benny's sleeve, "let's go on back to Granny Tomason's house and see what's on the stove to eat."

"Let's take the path through the woods," Benny stated.

They were both breathing heavily as they started walking back to Granny's house. They decided to go through the woods instead of going down the main street of town and taking the chance of seeing Aunt Birdie again.

CHAPTER NINE: MR. JOHNSTON AND AUNT BIRDIE

The narrow path was uneven, and most of it was overgrown with grass and weeds. The sun was still shining but the afternoon was quickly coming to a close.

CHAPTER TEN

Mr. Bushman

ON THE WAY BACK TO THE FARM, Lily and Benny didn't have much to say to each other as both of them were once again trying to figure out a faster way to find Caitlin while staying away from Aunt Birdie or Elmer.

Lily put her hand in her pocket and slipped it around Caitlin's hair comb.

"I wonder where this came from?" she thought to herself. "It just seems strange that Tessa found it outside the shanty."

The further they walked from town, the thicker the forest became. Saplings, flowering bushes and shrubs filled in most of the open spaces throughout the larger older trees. Here and there, they would come upon a path leading out into the forest. Magnolia and dogwood trees were starting to bloom, and wildflowers had their eyes open in the warm soothing spring sunshine.

Lily could sense the winds changing direction, blowing in from the south and bringing with it the sultry hot weather of summer.

"Well, slap my arse and call me Spanky," came a booming voice from the thick forest. Lily and Benny came to a startled stop as they whirled around and stared into the woods. "If'n it ain't them thar' Quinn critters! How ya'll been? Mighty fine to see ya critters again, yes sir'ree, mi'tee fine. Wait up fer an old feller, would ya? Yer a'walkin way too fast. Hold up thar'."

"Well!" Benny called out with a big grin on his face, "How-do, Mr. Bushman. Where you been hiding yourself? We haven't seen you in a month of Sundays. You been up there in the Ozarks, living with the bears and the hill folk? Or maybe hibernating with the bears? Come on along with us, we're on our way to Granny Tomason's house."

"Ouch. I don't think I can do that thar'," Mr. Bushman bellowed laughingly.

"Granny Tom-a-son doesn't rightly fancy up to me. I'm not clean enough she says. She would be a'puttin me in a worsh tub quicker'n a lightin' bug's flash and be a'scrubbin my hide right off my bones." He let out another booming laugh.

"Well! Miss Lily, yer a'looking as pretty as a picture. You sure enough look like yer Aunt Maggie Mae. That Maggie Mae is a mighty fine lookin' lady, I tell ya. She be the darling of me life, the moonlight on a cloudy night and the sunshine on a rainy day. That she is, that she surely is. She stole me heart clean out of me chest, she did. There be an empty spot where me heart used to be." He put his hands over his heart and looked toward the sky. Sometimes Mr. Bushman spoke with a horrifyingly fake Irish accent.

He stood poised as if reciting Shakespeare.

"Well, never mind that," he bellowed still grinning from ear to ear as he waved his hands above his head; as if to scatter his thoughts.

Rumor had it that it was love at first sight for Mr. Bushman when he met Aunt Maggie Mae. He was so in love, it was said, that he pretty much made a fool of himself. He kidnapped her away from Boston, but Aunt Maggie Mae insisted she had to honor her marriage vows and return. Supposedly, Maggie Mae promised Mr. Bushy that if anything ever happened to her husband, he would be the first to know and she would consider marrying him. Reluctantly, Mr. Bushman took her back to Boston to the man he called a coward.

The coward had never found out about the abduction and was no more the wiser as a broken-hearted Mr. Bushy returned to Missouri and his mountain.

"So how ya two critters doin'?" Mr. Bushy asked.

Lily could not keep from staring at Mr. Bushman. He was exactly what everyone called him: a bushy man! Lily didn't know whether that was his real name or if folks just called him that because of the way he looked. He stood almost six and a half feet tall and was as broad as the side of a barn. His hair and beard reached almost to his waist, and both were red and curly. He had a big, toothy smile and bushy eyebrows. His eyebrows were so bushy a person could barely see his eyes.

When the days were sunny, he wore his eyeball covers – that's what he called them. He had made them from thin pieces of wood cut to fit each eye. He then cut openings across the middle of each eye. The openings were nothing more than oblong holes cut into the thin pieces of wood and covered with very thin pieces of black sheer fabric. They were held to his head with a long strip of very thin leather woven into the side of each eyepiece and across the middle of his nose. He said they kept the sun out of his eyes and made it possible for him to see things, in the glare of the sun, other men could not see. He refused to leave his cabin without them.

Sometimes, like today, he wore them pushed back onto the top of his head, making the hair around his face stand on end in a big feathery poof that stood straight up in front of his floppy hat — sort of like a bonnet brim.

Pa once told them that Mr. Bushman was as strong as a team of oxen and Pa was forever asking him if he would pull the plow as Pa led the mules to plow up the soil in the spring. Since Mama always fed Mr. Bushy when he was at their house, Pa said he figured it was an even trade. Mama would shush Pa and Mr. Bushy would laugh and tell Pa that on the day Pa talked Maggie Mae into leaving her coward, he would "plow the whole dang field fur free".

CHAPTER TEN: MR. BUSHMAN

With the exception of Granny Tomason, all the Quinn family dearly loved Mr. Bushman. But Lily was quite sure Granny just liked to pester Mr. Bushman. Lily always thought Granny really did like him quite a bit.

Mr. Bushy had arrived in Missouri a long time before Molly and Daniel H. Quinn. Supposedly, he met the Quinn's while he was on one of his travels that ended up in Boston and immediately took a grand liking to Daniel and his pretty wife Molly. It was during that time that he talked Daniel and Molly Quinn into moving to the Missouri wilderness where they could own their own land and live in peace with clean air, beautiful mountains and crystal clear streams.

He also met and fell in love with Mama's sister, Maggie Mae. There were many secrets about Mr. Bushman and Aunt Maggie Mae that Lily couldn't get out of anyone. Maybe someday Lily would find out from Granny or Caitlin and her curiosity would be satisfied.

Molly and Daniel had indeed fallen in love with the land and people of Missouri. They built their home and raised their children in the "wonderful wilderness", as Pa called it, of Missouri. Missouri was very unlike the crowded farm on which Pa had been raised.

When anyone asked Mr. Bushman where he hailed from, he would simply say "way down yonder, deep in the Oh-zarks". No one knew exactly where "way down yonder" happened to be. He called himself an inventor, trapper, and traveling mountain man. He was a sight to behold that was for sure.

Lily walked over to Mr. Bushman and gave him a big hug. He smelled of tobacco, horses, and sweat. It wasn't a bad smell; it was just the smell of a mountain man.

"Howdy, Mr. Bushy," she said with a smile. "We sure are glad to see you. You see, our Caitlin went missing and we've been trying to find her. She disappeared a few days back and the Sheriff and Pete Turnkey, the ticket master, are helping us find her. Do you think you can help?"

"What's that you say? Caitlin's missing?" Mr. Bushy said in a whisper, leaning in close to Lily and Benny.

"Yeah," Benny replied as he told Mr. Bushman the details of Caitlin's disappearance.

"Well, you don't say. I'll be a sawed off donkey's ear. This here is a strange thing for sure. Yep, mighty strange." Mr. Bushman looked around the woods as if checking for other people, then he once again leaned down closer to their faces as he whispered.

"Let's go have a sit-down over yonder on that thar' fallen tree for a few minutes and take a load off while I tell you two critters something I need to be a'telling ya."

They all walked over and had a sit-down on the fallen tree and Mr. Bushman looked at both of them for a second or two.

"Ya see here, critters, what I'm a'goin to be a'tellin ya sounds right loco. But it is the honest to goodness goldurn truth! It all started about a week ago when I was down in my mountain a'sittin outside my cabin jest a'gettin' ready to bed down fur the night and all, ya see. Now, I usually sleep outside my cabin unless it's too cold fur a human bean to last through the night. The fresh air of a mountain night is a right fine thin' for the human body and soul.

Well, after my horse, Digger, was all set for the night, I et' my supper and got my night fire a'burnin low. I lit my ol' pipe and just sat thar smokin' and a'listenin' to them thar crickets and bull frogs a'singin them thar love songs to each other. The breeze was a'blowin real soft like so I just sat thur watchin' as the sweet smellin' smoke from my ol' pipe drifted up and disappeared amongst the tree. Ever so often I'd join in and whistle a tune or two right along with them forest critters. Well, hit was a'gettin' on to be close to the witchin' hour and all, I believe hit was."

.Mr. Bushy paused a bit and then said, "Now, you critters know how those mountains have a soul of their own and all, and there's times when you can almost hear and feel it a'breathin right beneath ya? Well, that night, my mountain seemed to be a'whisperin' in my ears, like a bumble bee a'buzzin around a daisy. It was as if it was just a'tryin to wrap me up in its warmth and start a'tellin me secrets. Well, I start in being real quiet like, thinkin' maybe I could hear what she was a'whisperin, but I couldn't hear nary a thing. Now, I love my mountain and when she talks to me that way I listen and I feel all warm and safe from anything that might be a'lurkin around. So I go on ahead and clean up my grub dish and pulled out a blanket, in case the night chill got heavy.

Well, I weren't really sound asleep none, just kinda like a'startin off being pert near asleep, kinda fuzzy in the brain, ya know, when all of a sudden-like, I feel something's a'bumpin on my shoulder real steady like. Bump, bump, bump. Well, I slapped at what I thought was ol' Digger there," Mr. Bushy pointed to his horse. "And my hand hit nothing but jest plain ole air. I thought to myself, 'Well, the dad-blame old horse moved pretty durn fast getting' away from my slap.' I didn't even bother opening my eyes none since I was plum tuckered out and all and had just a'startin' off to dreamin'. So I just tucked my hand back up under my blanket and went on back to sleep. Well, about five minutes later, I reckon it was, the bumping starts in again. Only this time it pert near pushed me over onto my belly."

"Now, this belly here," Bushy said, patting his stomach with a big grin, "Ain't no little bitty thin' like you critters have, you see, so that was some pretty dad-blame hard pushing on my shoulder. Well now, I whirls around as fast as I could," Bushy whirled around on the fallen tree, demonstrating, "and I yells out 'Digger, get on out of here ya bag o' fleas, ya hear? Leave me be!'. Well, it weren't Digger a'tall." Mr. Bushy whispers, as he leaned in about two inches from Lily and Benny's faces. "What was a'squattin' right close to me, was a sure 'nuf confederate soldier. A'squattin' right there beside me. He was a'lookin right at me and he had on the whole kit and caboodle soldiering uniform. Hat, pants, boots, jacket and everthin' else. His hair was long and his face was real thin-like, but I knowed right off who he was."

With his hands on his knees, Bushy leaned back a bit, and said haltingly, "It was Michael Thorne! Yes sir'ree, it sure 'nuf was Michael Thorne. God as my witness, it was him.

Well… I jumped right to my feet and put out my hand, a'wantin to shake his hand, and I start in a'talkin. I said 'Michael my boy, what a fine sight you are. I am right happy to see ya, where ya been boy? Come on over here son, let's have us a sit-down. But first let me give ya such a hug your belly button pops right on out.' Well, I reached out to give the boy a belly-button-popper hug, but he steps back and shakes his head, with a smile. Then I knowed right off, this weren't no actual meeting with a long lost soldier-boy. Something weren't right and I knowed just what was a'happenin'. I stopped and squeezed my eyes a bit to peer at him real close-like, and low and behold I could almost see right through him. Not really, but… kindly like. He was all shadowy; kindly like a thick cloud, but it sure 'nuf was Michael. He smiled and spoke to me with his usual slow raspy Tennessee voice and says, 'lo, Bushy. How are ya? Sorry, no more belly-button poppin' for me. I'm just here to ask a favor and then I'll be on my way. I need to ask ya to help find my Cait'. Well, I just stood there with my mouth a'hangin down to my own belly-button. He spoke again in that soft, low drawl, and says, 'They need your help in finding her, Bushy. I know I can depend on ya. When ya find her and she's safe, tell her that she's in my heart for all eternity.' Then he reaches up, pulls his soldierin' hat a little further down on his head, gives me one of them there soldier hat salutes, a smile and a nod as he says, 'had a mighty fine time knowing ya Bushy, you're a good man.' He then just up and walks away. Kindly like a'meltin' in with the trees and bushes and there I stood, just me and ole' Digger there, a'lookin' like scared jack-rabbits. My heart had jumped right up in my throat and was a'dancin' a jig on my tonsils to get out through my mouth. It was a'poundin on my ears like an Indian war drum, and I was a'sweatin like a buff'lo in a stampede! Digger had backed up and was just a'lookin off into the forest where Michael had melted away."

As Bushy told his story, he acted out each and every action for Lily and Benny.

"It was one of the strangest durn things I have ever seen in all my born days. Now, those thar hill folk say they see spirits and spooks and all." Bushy leaned close again and whispered. "Even say the dead can talk to the livin' and tell them things. Now, I always was a'thinkin it was just the jibber-jabber of them thar' women folk a'talkin and a'squackin' about ever'thin and them thar tales was just a whole lot of passin' the wind. Pardon me Miss Lily, but now I'm a'thinkin they may be some grit to them thar tales."

Mr. Bushman was looking off into the woods as if he was talking to himself. "Ya jest never do know, ya never do know fer sure." He blinked his eyes and came back.

"Well, after all that thar happened, I decided not to sleep out under the stars and all, so I marched right back up onto my porch, turned around and sat right thar against the house with my rifle handy and watched until the daylight lightened the sky just a wee bit, and then me and ol' Digger here took off lickety-split to check up on you Quinn critters. We spent some scary nights in them thar mountain's while I was a'walkin and a'riding down here. I was kind of jumpy-like, so I had to keep a far going all night, but nothing happened and there weren't not even a whisper of a haint. Next thing I know'd is, I see you Quinn critters and you tell me Caitlin really does need help."

Bushy looked at Lily and Benny with a look of awe on his face. Now, don't ya be a'lookin' at me like I be gone loco. Both you critters know I ain't no more loco than your ma and pa was. Why I can't hardly believe the whole thin' myself. But hit's the honest to goodness truth. I will stand before the good Lord in Heaven himself on judgment day and testify that it's all the truth. I wouldn't have been more surprised if I'd ah seen the Mother Mary herself a'standin' thar!"

"Oh no, Mr. Bushy," Lily whispered. Her throat was tight and her skin was clammy. "I most certainly do believe you. Something quite like that happened to me. The person didn't carry on a conversation with me but he did call out my name and seemed to want me to go to him. But now I think it must have been Michael and maybe he wanted to talk to me about Caitlin. I was scared out of my skin."

Lily told Mr. Bushman what had happened on the way to Granny's house on the night she had dragged Benny and Tessa out from under the dock.

"Well, I'll be a flap-eared hound-dog," Mr. Bushy said, looking at Lily with relief. "I thought you critters would think I'd gone loco. Now," he paused, "are ya sure it was a soldier-boy and not just one of them thar river rats, a'hangin around the town in the fog?"

"Nope," Lily replied swiftly. "It was a soldier. I could see that plain enough. I couldn't tell who it was, but it definitely was a soldier, and a confederate one at that."

"Well, critters," Bushy said. "I guess I'm a'gonna have to go on in to Granny Tomason's house with ya after all. I can't have ya running around here by yourself a'looking for Caitlin and maybe runnin' into more spooks. Because if'en that was Michael's spook, I'm a'knowing he wouldn't hurt anyone of ya, but if Michael's spook is out there, maybe someone else's spook is out there too, and they may not be a good'un. Let's go get this torture from Granny Tomason over with." He let out a big sigh and got up from the fallen tree.

"Good Lord on high, please give Granny a kind heart today for this poor wanderer," he muttered.

As Lily, Benny and Mr. Bushy neared the back of the house from the path going through the woods, Benny called out, "hello the house"; as was customary to do when one approached anyone's house from the back area (or even the front, if you were a stranger to the house). If a person did not "hello the house", most farmers would think the person was a thief or someone up to no good, and may take a shot at whoever it was. It was an unwritten law that everyone must "hello the house" to announce themselves. If a person was shot by a farmer because he had not called "hello the house", the law was on the farmer's side.

CHAPTER TEN: MR. BUSHMAN   117

So Benny called out, just from habit, as they approached Granny's house. Pie Eater came bounding out to meet them, jumping up and trying to lick their faces. "Hello, Pie Eater!" Benny said as he rubbed the dog's head.

"Let's get in the house," Lily said. "I'm hungry and we can have these cherry tarts after supper. The two of them took off running toward the house, jumped up onto the back porch and knocked on the door.

"Granny," Lily called out. "It's us, Lily and Benny. We have another guest with us; he came to help us find Caitlin."

Tessa threw open the door to great them. "Well, fellers!" she said with a wide grin. "Me and Granny sure are glad to see you. We thought maybe you had gotten eaten up by river monsters or something. We made sweet biscuits and fried apple pie."

"Fellers?" Lily thought, "When did she start saying 'fellers'?"

"Mr. Bushy!" Tessa yelped as she spied Mr. Bushman. Off the porch she jumped and raced into his open arms. "I am sooo glad you came to see me. I sure need your help. My Caitlin is gone and I need you to find her for me."

Tessa considered Caitlin, as well as Mr. Bushy, to be her personal property. She figured Caitlin was just on loan to Lily and Benny once in a while. Tessa leaned into Mr. Bushman's shoulder and kissed him on his hairy face.

"Ah, me lovely darlin' Tessa. If we ain't careful, someone will steal you away as fast as they did your Caitlin. You be a'lookin more like yer pretty mama each time I see ya. Yer pa was a mighty lucky man if ya be askin' me. But then, he was like a leprechaun with a pot-o-gold tucked under his arm when he was with yer mama. " Mr. Bushy always spoke with his very bad Irish brogue when he was having a conversation Tessa.

"How ya been, ya little red haired whipper-snapper? Ya been a'actin like a young lassie should or a wild honey-bee, a'buzzing around everbody's head?" Bushy grinned at Tessa.

Granny once told them that Mr. Bushy had taken a powerful liking to Tessa the day she was born. He had lost his wife and his own little red-haired, green-eyed daughter in a fire when the baby was but a couple years old. Both of them had been gone a few years when Tessa was born, and Granny guessed that Tessa's red hair and mossy green eyes was the reason Mr. Bushy had a special place in his heart for Tessa.

"Oh Mr. Bushy," Tessa giggled, "It's no fun being a proper lassie. It's more fun being a honey bee and buzzing around." She giggled and gave Bushy another big hug.

"Well, Tessa, me darlin', let's go in and buzz around Granny for a while and see if she gives me the boot and sends me packing out to the barn," Bushy said with a deep laugh. Tessa jumped down, grabbed Mr. Bushy's hand and pulled him toward the house.

As they all walked into the house, Granny turned from her big stove and gave them all a big hello.

"Granny, Granny!" Tessa said excitedly. "Look what I found! It's Mr. Bushy! Isn't he wonderful? He'll find Caitlin for us, won't you Mr. Bushy?"

"Well, Alexander," Granny grinned. She always called Mr. Bushman by his given name. "Have you taken a bath since last fall? I didn't smell you coming in the door, so you must be fairly clean."

"Aw, Granny, you wound me heart to me very soul. You be a wonderful sight to behold. Is that ham I smell cooking? And fresh hot biscuits too? Oh — coffee to go with hot biscuits maybe? You are a woman dear to me heart. You are full of kindness for me poor stomach. Me belly is a'bowing down to my knees, giving ya praises. Your wonderful cooking and memories of Maggie Mae are me only pleasures in this wild and wooly world. Other than these here Quinn critters, that is. I already give thanks to the good Lord above for just the smell of yur vittles." With that he let out one of his booming laughs and sat down at Granny's table.

"Get on with you, Alexander. You are full of malarkey. All of you have a sit-down and the girls and I will spoon up the food. Benny, did you take care of Alexander's horse?"

"Yes ma'am, Granny. Digger is in the barn as happy as a coon with a fish pie."

CHAPTER ELEVEN

The Tales

AFTER FILLING THEIR STOMACHS with Granny's wonderful food and doing all the evening work that needed to be done, they sat down in the parlor and talked the rest of the day away. Mr. Bushy entertained them with tales of his adventures and travels amongst the mountain folk, Indians and wild animals of the Ozarks. He told them about the time he was way over on the west side of the Ozarks and a mama bear chased him up a tree. The mama bear stayed at the bottom of the tree with her three cubs until the wee hours of the morning. Mr. Bushy said he fell asleep in the oak tree's branches, thankful that the tree was huge and the fork in the branches was "better than sleeping in a bedroll." When the sun came up the next morning and just as he was about to drop from the lowest branch of the tree, a family of skunks came strolling by and stopped right beneath him as they searched for grubs. As his feet hit the ground, he landed on the tail of the mama skunk and a wild frenzy of yelling and hopping began, along with the continuous streams of skunk spray. He was instantly covered with the sweet perfume of skunk. The skunk family took off and Mr. Bushy lost what little food he had in his stomach. He threw up on his own clothes, on his shoes and all over his beard. His hair was covered with spray and his eyes felt as if they were on fire. Thankfully, he had turned his head in the nick of time so his eyes had not caught the full force of the spray. Since Digger had vanished the night before when the mama bear surprised them, Bushy had to walk miles back to his cabin, stopping every so often to throw up. By the time he got back to the cabin, he was thirsty and his stomach was chewing on his backbone in hunger. And there was Digger, inside his lean-to, peeking out as he watched Mr. Bushy walk in. As Bushy got close to the cabin, Digger started pawing at the ground and shaking his head. He took a few steps outside the lean-to and snorted, all the while looking at Bushy. The horse took off down the path at a full run trying to get away from the smell and he didn't come back for two days. In the meantime, Bushy had to shave his hair, mustache and beard off. He had to throw his clothes into the fire and burn them. He scrubbed and scrubbed in the creek until he thought his skin would come off. Nothing worked. He just had to live with it until the smell left on its own. He walked around without shoes for a full week until he could find a peddler and trade some of his furs for boots. The peddler gave him a good bargain on the boots and then made a quick getaway after the smelly deal was completed. Mr. Bushy told of how the mountain folks and the Indians pointed and laughed at him and wanted him to take off his hat so they could rub his bald head.

Granny, Benny and the girls all laughed at Mr. Bushy until their sides hurt. Around dusk, Mr. Bushy started in telling them about the strange things that would happen down deep in the valley of the mountain where his cabin sat. He told us about the evil apparitions which appeared to ride in on the wings of the hot winds in the middle of the night, when the sounds of the forest muffled their voices as if to keep their whereabouts hidden. The sweltering heat of the afternoon lingered long after it should have left, and the stars and moon were covered with dark clouds, keeping the night air as hot as the mid-day heat. He told how sometimes he would wake up and feel something watching him. The presence of the being would be so intense, he could barely force himself to get up and light a lantern. He could feel — not see — someone next to his bed. But once he managed to light his lanterns he could almost see the presence melt away through the cracks in the walls.

He told of other nights when the heat was thick and the only things he could hear were the crickets and bull frogs singing their songs; it was so dark he couldn't see his hand in front of his face. It was as if all the worlds' darkness had crept into his house for a visit, and decided to stay the night. Suddenly the crickets and frogs would stop their singing, and that in itself would wake him up from a sound sleep. It was at that point when he heard it — the soft rustle of leaves from afar off getting louder as it came closer. Every time this happened, he would jump out of his bed or, if he was sleeping outside, would rush into his house to shut and lock all the windows and doors. He lit all the lanterns he had and sat them all over his small cabin, "lighting it up like a house afire" he said. Then he would sit in his chair by the door. Sometimes the winds would whip so hard it seemed as if it was trying to disregard his locks and open the door and push the shutters in.

Mr. Bushy spoke in a whisper, leaning close to his audience so they could all hear him. Granny sat in her rocker with her knitting needles clicking faster and faster, nodding her head as if in agreement with him.

He then went on to tell of still other times when the wind, which felt evil and dark, managed to creep into his house through the cracks, like the fingers of darkness were trying to crawl right into him and grab his soul. He was sure ol' Lucifer himself would, at any moment, start banging on his door with vengeance. Maybe Lucifer was low on fuel for his fire-lake and wanted to drag him off and throw him into the flames. Mr. Bushy said there had been a few times when he was so "scare't" he started singing Amazing Grace at the top of his deep voice.

"I've done more than my share of wrong in this here lifetime, but I ain't ready to walk into those fary flames with that ol' boy just yet. Nope, I'm not a'goin' jest yet. I still have me some livin' to do on this here earth and I plan on doing it. That old boy can just wait awhile. Maybe the good Lord on high will see fit to take me in with him. Maybe I can do some good thin's down here a'fore I take a dive in the dirt," Mr. Bushy said with a chuckle and a smile.

"Maybe I can find your Cait," he said with a big smile. "And then the next time that ol' boy comes a'callin' I can tell him, 'here's my boot, don't come back.'"

"But now listen here ya critters. Let me tell ya some more about my mountains. My mountains aren't usually like that. Only once't in a while does an evil wind come a'blowin' and a'sneakin' through my forest. My mountains are like a wall guarding everthing and everbody who lives there.

Why, I've seen angels a'walking amongst my trees. I've felt the spirits of my good friends and ancestors, and I've felt the breeze a'whisperin' in my ears warning me of dangers. That mountain breeze has saved my life more than once't, I tell ya, and I sure do 'preciate it."

Suddenly a huge grin spread across Mr. Bushy's face and laughter swelled up from his chest. "Well, critters," he said, "let me tell ya a story that is the dad-blame truth." Granny's knitting needles stopped as she looked real sternly at Mr. Bushy, waiting for him to stop cussing and start in on one of his tales.

"One time I was over yonder a'visitin' them there Oh-zark hill folk, and they was a'havin' a big 'ol shin-dig cuz one of their kin was a'marryin-up. I just happened to be there and they all insisted I stay around. Said it was gonna be the best shin-dig they ever had put on since this here was a marrying-up between two old people who had never gotten married-up a'fore.

Well, I obliged and started in a'havin' me a grand ol' time. I was a'dancin and a'talkin and havin' me a good time when low and behold I suddenly realized I was as drunk as ol' cooter Brown. So I just decided maybe I should stumble on out into the woods a ways and sleep it off a while. Well, I no more than had my first dream a'goin' when I felt someone just a smoochin' away on my face. 'Well this ain't so bad' I'm a'thinkin' to myself. I'd been a'dreamin' of your pretty little Aunt Maggie Mae, and what do ya know — here she is in my dreams, just a'smoochin on me! So in my half asleep stupor, I just start in a'smilin' and puckerin' up my lips as she's a'smoochin' away. I lean over and wrap my arms around her neck jest a'tryin' to give her the biggest ol' kiss right on her sweet lips. I had a lip-lock on those beautiful lips of hers and I was a'thinkin' hit was pure heaven. Well all of a sudden-like, I hear this here loud squealing right in my ear! It was so loud, my eyeballs start a'bouncin' around inside my head and it takes me a second or two to get them back into my eyeball holes. Well, when I finally manage to get my eyeballs popped open all I see is a hog — a big ol' mama hog just a'starin' and a'squealin' at me real close like with them there beady little eyes and the biggest snoot I ever did see, right up against my lips. And that there ol' sow's snoot was completely covered with molasses.

Well I jumped right up from that there tree, reached up to wipe my mouth off, and there was molasses all over my face. Then I hear'd this here loud laughin' and looked up to see four of them there skinny little mountain fellers, couldn't be more than twelve years old, a'taking off into the woods. Just a'whoopin and a'laughin' their dang heads off and luggin' that big ol' jug of molasses with them. I start in a'yellin' at them and that there dang mama sow runs right into me, knocking me down onto the ground as she tried to get out of there. Well, I'm half way to getting up when that there mama hog gets her foot hooked in my 'spenders and there I go again, right down on top of her. She takes off a'runnin' like lightening and there I am, a'hangin' on for dear life. She's still a'squealin' and I start in a'yellin'. She takes off lickety-split for home with me on her back. My 'spenders won't come off her leg, so all's I can do is hang on and ride it out. That there hog was pert near as long as I am tall, so it was a wild ride. I got my arms hooked around her neck and my legs around her middle and she's a'runnin' straight out. Well after a minute or two, I start in a'laughin' and cain't stop cause she was a'swayin' back and forth and a'gruntin with each step she took and I was a'slidin' from the left to the right, back to the left and back to the right again. It was the most fun I've had in my whole dang life!" At this point Mr. Bushy was standing up and acting out his hog ride.

'Well, lo' and behold," he continued, "After about five minutes, that ol' sow just dropped to the ground. She was dead! Just as dead as old Abe himself. I thank the good Lord on high that I was on her left side when she went down on her right side. But dead she was! There she lay, just as dead as if I'd a bonked her on the head with a hammer. Well, I managed to get my 'spenders off her front leg and stood there just a'lookin' at her. I got down on my knees and puts my ear to her heart area, and sure 'nuf — no heart beat! I knew right off that who-ever owned her was gonna be purty dang hopping mad-as-a-hornet when they found out that sow was a goner, so I just scurried right on back to that thar' house, where the shin-dig was still a'goin on, grabs Digger and high-tailed it right on out of thar'. I still had molasses all over my face and my 'spenders weren't doin' a very good job of holdin' up my britches, since that thar' hog had pulled them apart. But I jumped on 'ol Digger, held my britches with one hand and the reins with the other and away we went.

Haven't been back to visit them thar particular hill folk since, and I don't plan on a'goin' back any time soon."

Mr. Bushy sat there laughing so hard his belly was jumping up and down, and the rest of us, including Granny, were laughing so hard our eyes were watering.

"Now," he said, "one more story of my adventures and I believe you critters better hit the hay."

"You're absolutely right, Alexander," Granny spoke up, "One more tall tale and that's it for tonight."

"Well, Mrs. Granny Tomason, these here ain't no tall tales! As the good Lord is my witness, all these tales be the honest gospel truth!" Mr. Bushy sounded quite offended by Granny's remark.

"Ok Alexander, start in with the telling," Granny replied.

Granny still had her knitting on her lap, but she was just as enthralled with Mr. Bushy's stories as we were. She didn't pick her needles up; she sat waiting for him to start telling.

"Well, this here story happened a while back. I was off on the other side of the Oh-zarks doing some trappin' and such. It was only me, Digger and an ol' pack mule we took along to help carry our load of furs, — and that mule was a stubborn old cuss! We just came away from that there big Oh-zark Lake and was a'headin' down the side of the mountain, when that ol' mule stopped and wouldn't go another step. I tried and tried to get that ol' cuss to move but everthing I did jest didn't work. Finally I says to Digger, 'well, Dig my boy, let's just camp here for the night. It's way too early, but if this here ole' mule won't go, he just won't go.'

So I set up camp, unloaded that mule, took all my gear off Digger and turned them both out to find their own food. The day was pretty on that mountain, jest as it usually is, so I took my time a'fixin' my grub and a'cleanin it up after I was done. Since the day was still young, I decided to take me a walk around for a look-see.

Well, I start in a'walkin' toward the west and go about a mile or two when I come upon an old Injun burial ground. There was still a lot of them thar poles with some tattered feathers still a'hangin' on them, and the big body-burnin contraption was still a'standin. You know, the thing where they burn their dead a'fore they put 'em in the ground. Well, I guess that's what they do. I ain't never been to one of them thar buryin ceremonies, so I don't rightly know for sure jest what they do.

Anyway, I stopped before I got onto the grounds — out of respect for their dead and all — and started in a'thinkin about how far around I should walk to stay respectful but not take forever and a day to do it. And I sure hoped none of them thar warriors was still out there a'keeping watch. Well, I start in a'walkin around the place, trying to be respectful and all. I get to the other side in no time a'tall and lo' and behold, there sat an ol' Injun, just a'watchin! Well, I make the peace sign of the Osage and the Kickapoo, hoping he's one of them. Sure enough, he signs back, so I know'd right off that he was Kickapoo. They're a friendly folk and all, so I sit down beside him and we just sat there for an hour or so. Not saying nary a single word or looking at one another. That's the polite thing to do among the Kickapoo. If you don't mind someone a'sitting by ya, ya just stay, but if ya don't like it, ya get right up in a hurry and walk away. Well, I took it that he didn't mind me a'sittin there, since he stayed right beside me fur so long.

Then, real sudden like, he gets up, nods at me and walks straight through the burial grounds and disappears. I just stay right there. The view was nice and the tree I was leaning against was feeling mighty fine. I leaned my head back and decided to take me a little snooze, ya see. Well, I start in a'dreamin about that there burial ground. I dream that all them there Injuns that died came right up out of their graves and came over to sit all around me and the tree I was a'leanin against. There was warriors, squaws, babies, and all other ages of people. They were all Kickapoo except one. Sittin' right in the front, right close to me, was this here little white gal. She had on a beautiful Injun dress and moccasins with all sorts of beads and feathers on both her dress and mocs. And her hair was as white as the clouds on a sunny day and long 'nuf to almost touch the ground. And her eyes were as blue as a robin's egg. I remember, as clear as day, seeing her hair a'blowin kindly soft-like in the breeze and she had a big smile on her little freckled face. She was as cute as the little pup she was a'holdin' onto. She looked to be about nine or ten years along. She sat with her legs crossed, like most Injuns do, and I could see the markings on her ankle. The ankle markings said she was of the Kickapoo tribe.

Well she just sat there for a while a'smilin at me, and then she said in a soft little gal whisper, "Would you tell my mama I can't go home, 'cause me and Bluebonnet fell into the river. The nice Indians found me and pulled me out. They tried and tried to get me to breathe again, but me and Bluebonnet were already someplace else and couldn't breathe anymore. Please tell my mama and papa that they buried me here with my Bluebonnet and that I'm sorry I fell in the water. Bluebonnet fell in first and I just wanted to try and get him out. But it's all okay now. The Kickapoo gave me the name Sooleawa, which means Silver — they didn't know my real name and they said my hair looked like silver. They gave me a pretty new dress and shoes and drew a pretty picture of a little girl like me, and wrote the name Sooleawa on my ankle. Tell Mama, Papa, Granny and the boys that I love them. Would you do that for me, mister?"

Well, in my dream, I told her that yes I would certainly do that, but I didn't know who her mama was or where her family lived. She told me her name was Hannah Barnes and her mama and papa's names are Anna and Jonathan Barnes and they live in Eden Bend along with her granny and her brothers. She told how she had gone on over there and tried to talk to them after she drowned, but no one could hear her. She didn't know why, but she was able to talk to me but not to anyone else.

Well, in my dream, I tell this little Hannah gal that I sure will do that, as soon as I can get over to Eden Bend. She gives me another big smile, tells me 'thank you kindly, Mister,' and then her and all them there Kickapoo just up and vanish.

Well I woke up with a start, and sweat was jest a'pourin' down my back. I look around that there burial ground. Nothing had changed. It must have just been a dream, I tell myself.

Well, I take off back around that there burial ground to my campsite and ol' Digger and that mule were still a'choppin on the grass, so I start makin' up my sleeping blankets for the night. Well I'm a little uneasy, cause of the dream and all, but I'm a'telling myself, 'it's just a dream, ol' boy, it's just a dream.'

Well along about midnight I finally fall asleep, and I don't dream a single thing! And seeing that I always start in a'dreamin' as soon as I fall asleep, that's mighty strange. I get up the next morning and I have the vigor of a fifteen year old boy!"

"Well," Mr. Bushy continued, "To shorten up this here adventure of mine, I high-tailed it down that there mountain as fast as that mule would go, stashed my furs and started in a'huntin for Eden Bend, since I ain't never in my life heard of such a place. I asked everbody I met up with but nary a one of them had ever heard of such a place. Finally I give up and start on back to collect my furs and go on into St. Louie to do some tradin'. I surely felt mighty bad about not being able to keep my promise to that little gal, I sure did feel bad about that.

Well, I get a day or two closer to St. Louie and along the way I run into a feller coming down from St. Louie a'goin towards New Orleans area to do some trappin' and tradin'. One of his pack mules had lost a shoe, so I stop to help the feller unload the mule and fix it right up with a new shoe. Well, we strike up a talkin' and he seems like a pretty likeable feller, so we decide to set up camp together for the night. And what do ya know but lo' and behold, he had some homemade shine with him. So we started in a'sharin' it and we get to talkin' and a'drinkin', and a'gettin' purr-ty dang gabby when we decide to swap our stories about spooks and haints and such.

Well, after he told me a fist-full of his strange happenin's, I start in. I start out by a'tellin my tale about that there little white gal. Well, he sits there a'starin' at me with his mouth and eyeballs wide open, and when I'm all done with the tellin', he sort of swallers and says in a low whisper, 'we looked for little Hannah for weeks. We never did find hide nor hair of what happened to her. We all ended up thinking some mountain man snatched her right up or maybe a bear or panther got ahold of her. Her ma and pa grieve for her still. That was nigh on a year ago now. I'm her Uncle Benjamin.'

Then all of a sudden like, he stops talking, jumps up and whips out that there long skinning knife he had and says, 'Bushman, if you took our little Hannah and are just making this up, I'm gonna skin you alive!"

Well I just shook my head, held out the palms of my hands towards him and tells him, 'No, Benjamin, I didn't take your little Hannah. I lost my own little gal some years back and I'd never do that to any ma and pa's young'un.'

Well, he just stares at me for a good long while then sits right back down and starts in a'weepin. I didn't rightly know what to say to help him out, so I just sat there and let him weep for a while. I didn't want to embarrass him, seeing that he was a pretty big feller and all."

By this time, Granny was silently crying, as were we girls. Even Benny was blinking his eyes.

"After a while," Mr. Bushy continued, emotionally, "he stops a'weepin' and shakes my hand and tells me he would let Hannah's ma and pa know what happened to her. I tell him 'no, I had to do it myself since I had made a promise to that thar little gal.'

Well, along about daybreak, the next morning, we start on out for Eden Bend. Eden Bend is jest a few homesteaders out on one of the points in the Mississippi. Not too far from St. Louie. When we finally get to the Barnes cabin, Benjamin walks right in and pulls me along with him. The whole family is a'sittin around the table eatin'. There was food piled high enough for the whole northern army. The two women get right up and gives Benjamin a hug and he introduced me all around. There was the little gals ma Anna, her pa Jonathan, her little brothers Seth and Jacob, and her granny, Pansy. Well, her pa invites us to have a sit-down, and so we do and we all start in a'eatin'. Good food and plenty of it. I hadn't had good food like that in a coon's age. My belly was a grinning from my belly button to my backbone."

"Come on Mr. Bushy," Tessa says, "tell us what happened when you told her ma and pa about little Hannah."

"Okay, Okay. Well after we all 'et, Benjamin asked if the two of us could speak to Hannah's pa in the barn, so the three of us went on out.

Benjamin gave me a nod and I started in with my tellin'. At first Jonathan looked angry. As if maybe he wanted to pick up his gun and shoot me, but Benjamin told him how he had run into me on his way down to New Orleans and that I had never heard of Eden Bend in my life and that he himself believed me.

Finally Jonathan started in a'askin me all kinds of questions about that little gal. I answered them the best I could. He wanted to know how she looked and if she looked happy. I told him about her little pup she had in her arms and he shook his head yes, he had just found her a pup and sure enough she had named it Bluebonnet.

I don't think he knew what to do, but he knew he had to tell Hannah's ma about it, so we all went on back to the house and he tells his boys to go on outside and do the evening chores. We all sat back down at the table and he starts in a'tellin Anna and Pansy about the dream I had.

Well, Anna just stares at me and all of a sudden-like tears just start in a'pouring down her face like water coming out of a bucket. Granny Pansy just sat there at that table the whole time a'noddin her head as if she already knew what was being said was true.

Granny Pansy leans over and puts her arm around Anna's shoulders and says, 'Anna girl, I knowed she was happy. I knowed all along she was gone from us, but she is fine now. She's at home with our maker. He always knows what's best, Anna my daughter. He knows what's best.'

Let me tell you critters, it was all I could do to keep my tears from a'pourin out of my own eyeballs as I was a'watchin Anna weep over her little lost gal and my heart was a'breakin' for her. Now, that is a true story, and the good Lord in heaven knows it is. I will never, in my life, forget that thar little gal and her family. Not everbody would believe it, but it's the truth."

We all just sat there staring at Mr. Bushy, Granny included. "Well, Alexander," Granny finally spoke up, "That was truly a wonderful thing you did and you did a wonderful thing by going to her ma and pa. I surely do have more respect for you now. You are welcome to this home, whether you are clean or dirty, anytime you want."

"Mr. Bushy," Tessa said, as she climbed up onto his lap, "You are an angel come down from heaven aren't you?"

"Now Tessa me-girl, don't be a'goin that far. I only did what any good man would do. That's what the good book be tellin' us to do, so that's just what I did."

After a moment's pause, Mr. Bushy said, "Okay critters, off to bed with ya. I'm a'goin out to the barn and havin me a good-nights sleep for once." Mr. Bushy announced.

"No, you are not," Granny spoke up, "Alexander, you sleep in my fourth bedroom down the hall. No one is sleeping in there, and I insist. Just take yourself right on down there and crawl into that bed, or you won't be getting any breakfast in the morning."

"Well, Granny," Mr. Bushy said with a grin on his face, "if you put it that there way, I guess I'll have to oblige ya. Thank ye ma'am."

134 *Lily and the Ghost of Michael Thorne*

CHAPTER TWELVE

Yoder's Farm

"Oh Lord, what happened to my head?" Caitlin moaned and groaned as she tried to turn over onto her side.

"Nope, that's worse than on my back," she mumbled.

Caitlin lay there for a few minutes keeping her eyes closed. She felt sick, as if someone had beaten the side of her head with a board and then taken all the food out of her stomach. Her stomach was growling and she was as hungry as a grizzly bear in the spring.

"What happened to me?" She tried to remember where she was and what could have caused her misery. After a while, it all came back to her.

The last thing she remembered was opening her bedroom window for Benny, or so she thought. She had wondered why he was knocking on her bedroom window instead of coming in through the back door. She remembered thinking maybe Aunt Birdie had locked the door on him again, and since his bedroom was on the second floor, he was trying to come in through her room. She had opened her window and leaned out to give Benny a hand as he climbed in her window. That was all she could remember.

She opened her eyes and looked around the room. This was not her room — that was for sure. It was very small and smelled of old musty wood. There was dirt around the edges of the floor, as if someone had made an attempt to sweep and then decided just to leave the dirt there. No one seemed to be in the room with her, so she moved her head to get a better look around. "Where in the world am I?" she thought.

Slowly Caitlin sat up, trying to keep her stomach from coming up into her throat. She eased herself out of the bed and stood there for a few minutes trying to steady her spinning head. Once she got her bearings, she tiptoed over to the window. The dirty rags, thrown up to the windows as curtains, were drawn shut, but the sun was shining in through the rips and holes torn in the rags. Slowly she moved the edge of the rag a bit and looked out. The sun was straight up, so it must be around noontime, she thought to herself.

Great jumping Jehoshaphat! There was nothing but trees in every direction she looked. She was looking out a back window from a room on the second floor of a house. There were outbuildings and a faded grey barn behind the house. The outbuildings had fallen to the ground and were now overgrown and weedy and the barn itself looked as if it was ready to join them. The barn leaned to one side with boards braced to hold it up off of the ground. It reminded Caitlin of an old man leaning on a cane. The barn was missing so many boards, she could see right through it. There was a horse corral at the back of the barn; Caitlin could see two horses inside the corral. The dense forest started at the back side of the horse corral and continued on as far as her eyes could see. The trees were thick and dense with undergrowth covering most of the trees trunks.

She walked over to the second window in the room and looked out. She could see what looked to be a wrap-around porch coming from the front side of the house. There was an old dirt road, partially covered with grass, leading from the barn and going out into a thick pine forest facing, what she figured, was east. The forest in front of the house was full of the tallest pines she had ever seen. Their branches started twenty feet off the ground, but the pines were thick and close together, so it was quite dark under the branches.

"That must be the road back to town," Caitlin thought to herself. "I'm in the middle of nowhere!"

With nothing on her feet but her night stockings it made it easy for Caitlin to walk quietly across the room and put her ear to the door. She could hear a faint sound of voices and the clatter of dishes downstairs.

Dishes! She could smell food cooking.

"I'm starving," Caitlin whispered to herself. The voices grew loud and angry.

Slowly she opened the door. With one eye, she looked out the tiny crack of a doorway. Slowly, slowly, she opened the door a little more. Her heart was pounding in her ears as she held her breath. She eased her head out the door and looked down the hall. She was in the last room at the end of a long hall. The walls in the hall were faded and the old wallpaper was peeling off in large coils. The sun was shining brightly outside, but the hall was dark. In addition to the room she was in, five other doors were in the hall. The house had the smell of musty dirt, and the feeling of neglect hung thick in the air, as if the soul of the house had left with the people who once called it home. In the hallway and in Caitlin's room, the floor was covered in dust along the edges. Thankfully, the darkness in the hall would cover her footprints when she decided to leave.

"This must be the Yoder's place," Caitlin thought. "I don't know of any other abandoned farms around here unless I have been taken further away than I hope."

Caitlin opened the door ever so slightly, in hopes of making it easier for her to hear the angry voices coming from the downstairs rooms.

"You say I stupid because I ask you how close you get to New Orlean in two hour? It because I Chinese? You think all Chinese stupid?" A man yelled at the top of his voice. "You the stupid cow-pie!" the same voice yelled again.

CHAPTER TWELVE: YODER'S FARM

A second man's voice yelled back, "No, ya id-jet, what I'm a'sayin is, ya Chinese think ya have all the brains. I'm a'sayin that I cain't figger out how fur I can get to New Orleans in two hours, and that doesn't mean I'm stupid! It means you cain't figger it out either, so ya must be jest as stupid as I am!"

Trying to get a better look at the two men, Caitlin tiptoed down the hall, her hear beating quickly, toward the top of the staircase. She stayed far enough back so that if one of them looked up, they would not see her.

At the top of the staircase someone had knocked holes in the walls. Some holes were large and some were small. Squatting down and peeking through a small narrow hole, she could see three men sitting at a large kitchen table.

One of the men was sitting with his mouth hanging open looking at the other two men as they yelled at each other.

"No! You ask stupid question because you think I stupid. I know what you mean!" yelled the Chinaman. The second idiot stood up from the table and leaned across to get closer to the Chinaman and shook his fork in the Chinaman's face, all the while flinging food all over the table.

"No! I'm a'calling ya a stupid donkey-behind because you think only Chinamen have the high-faluttin'privilege of havin' more brains then everbody else in this here country, and your always a'takin' advantage of everthin in this here country just whenever ya be a'wantin to!" At this point, his voice had gotten high and squeaky, like a woman's, and he put his hands on his hips and swished his hips around. Evidently he was trying to act like a high-society woman.

"I hate Chinamen!" he continued loudly, "You always be a'thinkin yer better then everbody else and a'hoggin all the brains, and, as a matter of fact," his voice going back to normal, "yer always a'hoggin all the coffee up! Ever mornin', no matter if we're a'campin' or in some ol' house, I'm always a'havin' ta snatch up my coffee just as soon as

I'm a'thinkin the coffee's done, or, by golly, next thin I know hit's all gone down yer gullet."

As he was yelling at the Chinaman, food was flying out of his mouth and landing in the bowls of food which were sitting on the table. He was leaning so far over the table his dirty shirt was hanging in the gravy bowl. His pants were up under his armpits and his suspenders looked as if they had, at one time, belonged to a five-year old boy. They drew his oversized pants up in peaks at the front and back of his body. From where Caitlin squatted, she could see that his pant legs were rolled up to the middle of the calves of his legs. In previous years his pants must have belonged to a much heavier, taller man.

"I going to kick you all way to China, you STUPID cowboy donkey! You too STUPID to get coffee when ready, then no coffee for you!" the Chinaman yelled back, waving his arms around as he yelled.

The Chinaman was very short, thin and wiry, with a long black thin braid hanging down his back. His hat was so big it was resting on the top of his ears, making them stick straight out from his head. He took his hat off and threw it on the floor as if getting ready for a fight.

"Well jest a'come on over here, ya sawed off little woodpecker, and give 'er a try if'fen yer a'thinkin' ya can finish the job! I'll whoop ya so hard you'll be a eatin' with yur belly-button!"

The third man, who had been in a trance watching the two idiots argue, shot to his feet, picked up the full plates of food and slammed them onto the tops of their heads without missing a beat. He dropped the plates back onto the table, whipped out two pistols, pointing them at the arguing men and started in yelling.

"SIT DOWN! SHUT UP AND SIT DOWN! You two are dumb as dirt, and I'm getting tired of hearing your yammering. I've met smarter buckets of mud. Where in the world did you find these two, woman? I'm thinking they left their brains a'flapping in the breeze on some woman's clothesline. Between the two of you, you don't have enough brains to fill a thimble! So do as I say or, by God, I swear I'm gonna shoot ya both right between the eyes!"

"What woman?" Caitlin mumbled.

The two men stood there looking at the plate-slamming man with their mouths open and food sliding down their heads. The Chinaman had a fried egg slipping down his forehead, almost covering his right eye, and his other two eggs were sitting on top of the bacon, which was sitting on top of his head like a little brown greasy hat. Gravy already covered both sides of his face, hair and shoulders and his biscuits were on the floor. The cowboy had one egg on his head and one egg on his right shoulder. His bacon was stuck on his ear and the gravy was slipping down the front of his shirt. They both looked like two mud-ugly women with greasy gravy hair.

The idiots looked at each other, looked back at the plate slammer and apparently decided he was serious. The Chinaman took the egg from his eye and put it back onto his plate, then leaned over to let the other two eggs and the bacon slide onto his plate.

The other man snatched the eggs and bacon off his head and chest and slammed them back onto his own plate. They both wiped some of the gravy off their faces with their shirt sleeves, not bothering to clean their hair or hands. Then they sat back down at the table, picked their forks up off the floor and started eating again without a word.

As the cowboy bent over to pick his biscuits up off the floor, he let out the loudest fart Caitlin had ever heard in her life. The explosion seemed to go on for a good half minute. The sound was like the long rumble of thunder before a storm. He stayed bent over until the loud blast ended. He then acted as if nothing unusual had happened, sat back down in his chair, released a huge sigh and said "Ah that felt good." He shoved a biscuit in his mouth, turned his head toward the floor to spat out a chunk of something which had evidently been on the floor and stuck to his biscuit.

Caitlin squatted there on the hall floor in amazement as she watched the plate slammer sit back down. He sat looking at the idiots for a few seconds, then muttered "filthy pigs", picked up his fork and once again started shoveling food into his mouth.

The Chinaman sat staring at the cowboy. "Stupid stinking cowboy," he said and went back to his eating.

A fourth person moved into Caitlin's line of sight, and she could see the person's shoes. It was a woman all right.

"Come on, come out and let me see you," Caitlin thought to herself.

With an "Ugh", the woman stomped out of the kitchen and into another room.

The plate slammer set his fork down, looked up at the two idiots and calmly said, "If you two make her mad and she stops cooking for us, you are both going to become pig slop. And by the time I get done with you, no one will ever know what happened to you or where your bones are buried."

Once again he picked up his fork and returned to eating. The other two looked up from their plates with eyes wide and mouths open. "Sorry, boss, hit won't happen again," stuttered the cowboy.

"No, boss," the Chinaman said. "Not ever again."

Slowly and quietly, Caitlin stood up and quickly tiptoed back down the hall to the room she had woken up in. It was cold in the room and her feet were freezing, but at least she still had a winter nightgown and wrap on, so her body was okay. She started looking around the room for something to keep her feet warmer — maybe some regular socks or shoes. Under the bed she found an old pair of boots. They looked way too big, but they were better than nothing at all. Caitlin picked them up and sat them on the bed.

"If I manage to get out of this place, these will do fine," she said to herself.

"Okay, what am I going to do next? And how long have I been here? My stomach says months, but probably not that long since I can still walk and think. And why am I here?"

Caitlin squeezed her eyes shut and tried to remember what had happened after the hit on her head. Nothing. Nothing at all came to mind. She felt around on her head and – ouch! There it was; a bump on the side of her head above her right ear.

"Well, they must have known just where to hit me," she thought. "It's as big as a goose egg. No wonder I was out so long."

"Those dirty stinking polecats!" she whispered softly. "They knew just what they were doing. I'm probably not the first person to experience their handiwork. I wonder who else they've done this to."

Caitlin walked back over to the door and listened. No sounds were coming from outside the door. As slowly and carefully as she could, she turned the knob and opened the door a tiny crack.

No one came running up the stairs, so they must not have heard her during the fracas.

"Well, cri-min-y," Caitlin whispered to herself. "Somehow I'll just have to find a way out of this mess and get back home. I sure hope they haven't taken Benny, Lily or Tessa."

Caitlin stepped out of her room quietly and, as softly as possible started tip-toeing down the hall when one of the floor boards squeaked.

Instantly Caitlin froze. Holding her breath with her heart pumping so fast she could feel it in her chest, she waited a few seconds. Other than the stairs leading down to the kitchen, there was not another way out that she could see. Maybe one of the doors led to another staircase, but she couldn't risk making any more sounds. The doors were all too old to open quietly. She would have to wait until it was dark to try again.

Suddenly she heard an outside door open and slam shut and the men started talking again. A different male voice floated up the stairs.

"I'm as hungry as a horse and dog-tired. Give me some grub, woman, or I'm gonna start chewing on old Fernando here."

"Yeah, well you just give it a try Mac, and I'll shoot your knees off. I've put up with these two stupid jackals all morning and I'm in no mood to put up with your mouth," the plate-slammer said.

"Whoa doggies, what got into you, Ferd? Had a bit of a fight maybe? Give me some food, woman!"

"Get your own food," a woman mumbled. "I'm not one of your servants. I'll cook the food but I'm not waiting on you." All the men laughed loudly. Once again Caitlin heard the woman stomp out of the room and slam a door.

Afraid to take another step forward, she turned around and went back toward the room she had been in.

"I cannot do this right now," she told herself. Quietly she returned to the bedroom. She put the boots back under the bed and laid back down. She tried to remember which way she had been when she woke up. Not being able to remember, Caitlin decided to lie on her side facing the wall.

"I'll wait until dark and then try again," Caitlin told herself. "Maybe after they all go to bed and are sound asleep, I can sneak out of here."

Slowly the hours ticked by.

"Oh chicken-poo, if I don't use the privy soon," she thought, "I'm going to have a big problem. There's going to be water dripping downstairs any minute". Quickly she got back up and looked under the bed for a chamber pot.

Nothing.

"Oh shucks on a corncob," she whispered. "What am I going to do now?"

"I guess there's just one thing to do. I'll have to use one of those old boots as a chamber pot," she thought. "Wait, wait, wait; maybe there is something else around here." Caitlin looked around the room.

There was an opening that looked as if it had once been a clothes closet.

"Ah-ha! Here's something!" In the corner of the closet was a glass canning jar with something brown in the bottom. Caitlin picked it up, unscrewed the top and looked in. Only mold. "This will work just fine," she thought. She smiled with a sigh of relief.

"I'll leave it in the kitchen when I ever get out of here and maybe one of those polecats will be drunk and think it's a jar of whiskey."

After using the jar, Caitlin screwed the top back on and placed it on the floor under the bed. She couldn't help but quietly laugh about her idea.

"I sure wish I could see their faces when they pick up that jar and take a big swig," she thought. She sat down on the bed and tried to arrange the blanket the way it had been before she woke up.

Next thing she heard was the sound of someone coming up the stairs. Her heart started thumping in her chest.

"Oh Lord," she thought, "They're coming up here to get me." Quickly she forced herself to lie down on the bed. Her body wanted to open the window and jump out.

One of the doors down the hall opened and slammed shut. Next she heard the same door open and the fourth man's voice yell out.

"One of you better check on that gal. I'm not gonna do it. I've been up all last night and this morning a'watchin for the dang sheriff. Who, by the way, never did show up and I'm dog-tired."

Slowly Caitlin got out of the bed and walked to the door, hoping she could hear a reply from downstairs, she put her ear against the wood.

"Okay," one of the men yelled up from the kitchen, "we'll do it. Just shut up and go to sleep or you're gonna wake her up and then there'll be hell to pay as we fight her into that carriage."

"You stupid donkey's hind-end!" came a woman's voice. "That girl will be out for another day or two. Did you see the size of that bump on her head? She may never wake up – and then she'll be worthless. Did you two idiots think you were handling a grown man?"

"Just shut-up Bird," one of the men spoke loudly. "Next time maybe you can do the dirty work and handle it better. Let's see you lug a limp body from Caruthersville all the way out here and not make anyone suspicious. That was the hard part. Thank the devil himself for the dark clouds and all the city folks being either at home or at the saloons. We better get a lot for this one, or I'm about done with this work."

The man from the second floor yelled down, "We've been here too long and that sheriff is gonna start sniffing around. Mark my word. We never should have taken that gal. Those two younger kids are slicker than snot. They seem to be everywhere, asking questions, looking into every shack along the river. Why yesterday I saw those two under the train depot platform. What in the tarnation were they doing under there? What's the matter with you, Bird? Can't you keep a handle on those two? And where's that little sister of theirs, huh? She run off too?"

Caitlin eyes opened wide as she put a hand over her mouth trying to stifle the gasp as she whispered, "Bird? Did that man really say 'Bird'? And did that woman say 'Donkey's hind-end'? That's what Aunt Birdie calls Elmer whenever she gets upset with him. That's Aunt Birdie down there! What is going on here?"

Caitlin knew her Aunt Birdie was not a very nice person, but to kidnap her own niece, her brother's daughter and have her brought out to this place! Aunt Birdie was Pa's sister! She wouldn't do anything harmful to her own brother's children, would she? She knew Aunt Birdie didn't really like them, but to physically hurt them was hard for Caitlin to understand.

'Maybe she would for money." Caitlin thought to herself.

Caitlin thought back to when Mama and Pa were alive, she and the other children had never seen Aunt Birdie — or remembered seeing her. Pa had said it was because Aunt Birdie felt she had to stay on the farm to prove she could run it properly. Every Christmas, Aunt Birdie sent all of them beautiful gifts; as well as on their birthdays. But not once did Caitlin remember meeting her. Mama and Pa saw her once in a while when they went downriver to New Orleans. Caitlin could remember Mama and Pa going to New Orleans about twice a year and coming back to say that they had gone out to the farm and visited with Aunt Birdie. There were no pictures of Aunt Birdie, and no one had ever commented on what Aunt Birdie looked like. All Pa mainly spoke about was how well she was handling the farm. Mama always talked of how she missed Aunt Birdie and would love to have Birdie close so they could visit like old times. But it seemed like Aunt Birdie was always way too busy with her farm, and Mama and Pa were too busy with their farm to make any arrangements.

Late at night, when Mama and Pa thought all the kids were asleep, they would sit in the kitchen and talk in quiet whispers. Caitlin remembered once, as she got up to use the privy, she heard Mama say, "I hope Birdie is doing better, I worry about her so." Then Pa replied, "Don't worry about her, me Molly, she's a grown woman. There's nothing we can do to change her at this time in her life." Pa always called Mama 'me Molly' when he had his arms around her or was trying to make her feel better about something.

"Maude is there with her, and she will let us know if Birdie gets worse. Maude is a good keeper," he had whispered to Mama.

Now Caitlin wondered what had happened to Maude. Had she ran off and left Aunt Birdie? Maybe Aunt Birdie was not the nice sister Pa remembered.

Tears came to Caitlin's eyes as she thought about Mama and Pa, and how terribly she missed them. Why did they have to die? Why couldn't it have been Aunt Birdie?

Life was not fair. Lily, Benny and Tessa were way too young to be left without parents. All these questions and concerns ran through Caitlin's mind as she stood by the bedroom door listening. She wondered if anything had happened to Benny, Lily and Tessa. Had Aunt Birdie sent them off on a ship? Had she and Elmer hurt them?

"No, I don't think Elmer would hurt the little ones," Caitlin thought. "He may get drunk most nights, but I don't think he would hurt children. Hopefully he won't. I sure hope they are safe. Maybe they went to Granny Tomason's house when they discovered I was gone."

"Okay," Caitlin whispered to herself. "What am I going to do now? I have to try and leave as soon as it gets dark. That's the only chance I have."

Quietly Caitlin walked back to the bed and sat down on its edge. "If anyone comes up here I'll act as if I'm still asleep and then I'll try and get away from this place as soon as it's dark enough. This place has to be west of Caruthersville. It must be the Yoder's farm. Either that or some other abandoned farm. If I can get a horse, I can make it back to town."

Caitlin crawled back under the blanket and faced the wall. "Maybe they won't come up and check on me until tomorrow," she thought to herself.

No such luck!

Caitlin heard stomping feet coming up the stairs, then in the hallway coming towards her. Whoever it was stopped outside the door as if listening. Caitlin shut her eyes and tried to breathe normally.

"How does one breathe when they're asleep?" she thought wildly.

She heard the door open and someone walking softly into the room. The person seemed to stand there at the door for a few seconds, and then slowly walked over to the bed. Caitlin felt as if she was going to throw up. She willed herself to calm down and stop shaking.

"Well girlie," Caitlin heard Aunt Birdie whisper, "when are you going to wake up so we can get rid of you?"

"Caitlin! Wake up girl!" Birdie almost shouted. "Wake up!" She shook Caitlin' shoulder sharply, but Caitlin went limp and let herself flop around.

"Thank God you're still breathing," Birdie said loudly. "Don't become a worthless poke of trouble and die on us, girlie. At least stay alive until we can get you on that train tomorrow."

Birdie shook Caitlin's shoulder once again. Caitlin's arm flopped over the side of the bed but Caitlin didn't attempt to move it back onto the bed. "Play dead," Caitlin encouraged herself.

"You complete waste of a girl," Birdie said loudly. "I should leave you here to die. Well, if you don't wake up by tomorrow, that's just what I'm going to do, leave you here. I'm sick to death of dealing with these four butt-ugly men. Let them take care of getting rid of you and all the rest of this mess for all I care. I'm going home in the morning."

Caitlin heard Birdie stomp out of the room muttering the whole way. After Caitlin heard the door slam and Birdie stomp back down the hall, she let out her breath with a deep "whoosh".

"Well chicken pooh! What a mean old witch she turned out to be! Well I'll show you, Aunt Birdie, I'm getting out of here tonight before you try getting me on that train tomorrow, or I'll die trying!"

Caitlin stayed in the bed a little longer, then got up and walked around the room trying to stretch her legs.

The hours seemed to drag by, she heard the three men leave the house and not return until late afternoon. Aunt Birdie came back up once in the late afternoon and just stood at the end of the bed muttering.

Once again Aunt Birdie tried to arouse Caitlin before she went back down to the kitchen. Then she heard the sound of pots and pans clinking. Aunt Birdie must have started cooking again — Caitlin could smell the wonderful fragrance of ham frying.

Caitlin stayed away from the window and quietly walked around the room until it started getting dark.

Then she heard the man called Mac leave his room and stomp down to the kitchen. It sounded as if all the men were back in the kitchen eating. Aunt Birdie was yelling at one of them to stop eating out of the pan and sit down at the table like a civilized human.

Caitlin opened the door a crack and tried to hear their voices a little better. Aunt Birdie and the men were not talking loud enough for her to make out what they were saying. She would have to walk down the hall again and maybe find out the plans they had for her.

When she got to the top of the stair, she once again peeked through one of the narrow holes in the wall.

She heard Aunt Birdie say: "Mac, you go on into town and ask around in the saloons and see if you can figure out what that Sheriff is doing about finding Caitlin."

"That's a right fine idea." Mac replied, "I can wet my whistle while I'm at it."

Quickly the man called Mac got up from the table and walked out the door. The rest of the men sat there a while and grumbled because they weren't the ones going into town.

"We're taking her into that train tomorrow." Aunt Birdie spoke up, "and if she still isn't awake, we're leaving her here to die. I'm tired of dealing with her and those smaller children are much easier to handle. You men get ready to leave first thing in the morning."

"Good idea" all three of the men said at the same time.

Caitlin crept back to the bedroom and eased the door shut. She walked to the window and peeked out through the crack in the curtain and watched Mac as he rode away. So the road to town was exactly the way she had figured.

She stood looking out the window until the sky turned shades of pink and purple, and the clinking of dishes, along with the sound of voices, stopped drifting up to her.

She sat on the bed waiting as long as she could; her stomach was growling loudly and even though the night was chilly, sweat was running down her body. She was nervous, hungry and thirsty.

She went back to the window to make sure it was completely dark. She listened for a door to shut downstairs. Surely Aunt Birdie slept downstairs.

She opened the bedroom door just enough to see the light in the kitchen. After a while, she finally saw the light move away from the stairs and heard a door shut. Aunt Birdie must have carried the lamp into her bedroom. Quietly she closed the bedroom door and one by one she heard the men climb the stairs and enter a bedroom.

At long last all the shuffling and bed squeaking stopped.

Quickly the night became quiet until the snoring started. After a few minutes she was able to determine the three different snores. So, she then knew all three men were sound asleep.

Still, she stayed in the bed until she was quite sure they were all asleep, including Aunt Birdie, and they wouldn't be easily aroused.

She lay there on the bed for what seemed like unknown hours, wide awake and waiting until she felt it was safe to try and leave.

CHAPTER TWELVE: YODER'S FARM

"Okay, here we go," she finally said to herself.

She tiptoed to the window. The moon was full and bright. There were small splotches of moonlight scattered among the trees. Everything on the farm was clearly outlined in shadows.

"Okay," She thought to herself. "Let's do it. Get yourself out of this fine kettle-of-fish and away from this horrible nightmare."

She collected the boots and canning jar from under the bed and crossed to the bedroom door. She opened the door a crack to listen. No sounds, except for the snoring, came from the downstairs room. Caitlin grinned as she thought of those scallywags opening the canning jar. She felt a nervous giggle coming up in her throat and had to swallow it back down.

"Serves them right!" she thought.

Slowly she pulled the door knob and eased it open a bit. It creaked; she stopped instantly. Holding her breath, she listened for movement from the other bedrooms.

Nothing.

For some reason, the darkness of night amplified sound. She would have to be extremely careful getting out of the house. She opened the door a little more and finally had enough room to squeeze through. Grimacing, she pulled the door shut. If they didn't discover her absence until morning it would give her more time to make it into town. Caitlin stood outside the door until she worked up enough courage to start walking down the hall. As she looked around the hall, she decided to walk along the edge of the hall floor again – maybe the floorboards wouldn't squeak.

"Okay, me-girl. Let's go," she said to herself.

She was so hungry and scared her legs were shaking, but she tiptoed down the hall. Past two doors, then past another two doors. At the top of the stairs she stopped, cocked her head and listened. Nothing moved. The snoring continued, somewhat louder than before. She also heard the loudest snoring coming from Aunt Birdie's room.

Thankfully the kitchen was brightly lit up by the light of the moon.

She took the first step down and waited. No squeaks and nothing moved within the bedrooms. Stepping extremely slow, she continued down the stairs. When she got to the bottom of the steps, she was in the kitchen. The first thing she did was walk to the water pail and took a huge drink of water.

"Ah; that's the best water I have ever tasted," she thought. "No telling what was in it, but it sure felt good going down."

Next, she looked around to see if there were any biscuits on the stove. Not only did she find biscuits, but also some slices of ham.

"Oh yes, I'll just take most of these with me," she thought. She popped five biscuits and three big slices of ham into her night-wraps pocket. Looking around the kitchen she saw dirty dishes stacked everywhere. Dried food was stuck on the table and the floor. Some of the breakfast food from the day before was still on the floor — bacon and smeared gravy. It looked as if someone had slipped on the gravy and landed on their backside. This certainly wasn't the clean sparkling kitchen Aunt Birdie kept at their house — that was for sure.

She sat the canning jar down next to the pitcher of water and smiled. Then she turned and tiptoed to the back door. There was not a bar on the door, so it should open quite easily Caitlin thought as she gently eased the door open a little at a time. It squeaked a bit, so each time she moved it and it squeaked she stopped and waited a few seconds; she eventually got it open enough to slip out as quietly as she could. Instead of closing the door, she let it stay where it stopped on its own. As she stood on the back steps, she looked around the farm buildings. About fifty feet in front of her was the barn. It looked as if the horses were still in the corral behind the barn.

"Now for the get-away," she mumbled.

152   *Lily and the Ghost of Michael Thorne*

CHAPTER THIRTEEN

The Getaway

CAITLIN RAN TO THE BARN and slipped in through the missing boards. The barn smelled of rotted hay and horse manure. Moonlight flooded in through the holes in the roof and walls, making everything in the barn visible –that was a good thing she thought to herself. The light streaming through the roof created a cathedral effect as the beams of light reached down to touch the barn floor. The wooden supports in the barn were sagging, and most of the loft had fallen into the main part of the barn. When she looked up at the roof, Caitlin could see two huge owls sitting in the opening. Their eyes were gleaming in the dark as they stared at her.

In what remained of the loft, Caitlin could hear rustling and meowing.

"It must be a mama cat and her kittens," Caitlin thought as she bent down and pulled on the old boots. When she straightened, the mama cat and her babies were sitting there staring at her. She reached down to pet the cats, but they all jumped back a couple feet but they crept right back up to her after they realized she just wanted to pet them.

"If Aunt Birdie thinks she is going to get all of us kids out of her way, she's in for a big surprise," she told the kittens as they wound around her ankles.

All of a sudden, she heard one of the house windows being forced open. Her whole body froze in fear. Whoever was opening that window had to bang it open.

"Chicken-pooh," she thought.

She peeked around the edge of an opening in the boards. If she did not stay completely hidden, she knew whomever was looking out the window would be able to see her in this bright moonlit night.

The man was peeing out his bedroom window! And he did not bother to close the window when he had finished. "Oh, yuck!" Caitlin thought.

She walked over to an upturned barrel and sat down. She would have to wait until the man was once again sound asleep before she could make her move.

As she sat there holding the mother cat, her mind started racing with thoughts of how she was going to get out of this place. Maybe she should just start walking. She could stay in the woods and maybe they wouldn't be able to find her. Nope, that wouldn't do; she had no idea where she was, and the men had horses and Aunt Birdie had a carriage. They would quickly find her.

Maybe she should take one of the horses. That's what she would do! But the men would probably catch up with her since she didn't know where she was going. "Well, I'll just take all the horses!" she told the mama cat.

After a while, she grew tired of waiting so she sat the cat down and walked toward the back of the barn to pick up a bridle and some lead ropes. She could ride bareback and hopefully these horses were gentle enough; hopefully they wouldn't start a ruckus when she tried putting lead ropes on them. Out through a section of the missing boards she slipped and stepped into the horse corral.

All five horses turned their heads to look at her. "Well," she spoke in a whisper, "Which one of you will let me ride you?" As she looked at the horses, one of them trotted up to her.

"Tabby!"

Aunt Birdie must have hitched Caitlin's own horse, Tabby, to the carriage when she rode out here.

"Well, Tabby girl," Caitlin whispered, as she rubbed the horse's nose. "Aunt Birdie did me a favor and she doesn't even know it." Tabby nickered back at Caitlin and bumped her shoulder.

"Shh, Tabby-girl, we don't want to wake up Aunt Birdie and her trolls." Caitlin slipped the bridle on Tabby and led her to the fence. Quickly she stepped on one of the rails and slid onto Tabby's back. She trotted Tabby over to the other four horses and put lead ropes on the first two. The third horse didn't want anything to do with the rope and neither did the fourth — they both started snorting and prancing away.

"Okay boys," she spoke softly to the two big black horses. "Calm down. I won't use a lead rope on you. We'll just let you out of the corral and hopefully you will follow the rest of us."

"Come on Tabby, let's go." She held the two lead ropes and the two mares started walking along beside Tabby. Caitlin trotted Tabby over to the corral gate, leaned down and opened it. The gate squeaked loudly and at the same time she heard the back door of the house bang open. Caitlin looked up toward the house and her heart skipped a beat.

There stood the blurry eyed, dirty "cowboy", his hair looking like a scarecrow lived in it. The gravy the plate-slammer had dumped onto his head was still there and it must have dried because part of his hair was standing on end in thick clumps and the rest of it was slicked back. His eyes were squinted and he had a deep frown on his extremely dirty face.

"HEY! Get back here, girl!" he yelled.

"Get down off'en that horse and come back in here!" he shouted as he jumped down off the porch and started running toward the corral.

"HEE-YAA!" Caitlin yelled to the horses.

She gave Tabby a sharp kick with her heels and the horse took off like a shot.

CHAPTER THIRTEEN: THE GETAWAY

She didn't look back as she bent low over Tabby's back, holding onto her mane with one hand and the lead ropes with the other. She knew if she looked back she may lose her grip or her balance, and that would be the end of her. Caitlin heard the slimy toad yelling as he ran after her.

"I'm a'gonna beat ya to death as soon as I get a'holt on ya gal!"

One of the other men must have heard the yelling and ran down the stairs and out the door, because a different voice started yelling at her also.

"You be sorry you ever was borned!" yelled the Chinamen.

"Get back here ya stupid gal, Bird is gonna kill ya unless ya get back here, now!" yelled the first bum.

She had gone a short distance when she heard another horse coming up beside her. Her heart started hammering faster and faster.

"Oh no!" she thought. "That ugly buzzard has caught one of the other horses and is catching up to me." She kneed Tabby trying to make her move faster.

Caitlin turned her head to the left, and out of the corner of her eye, she could see a big black horse's head coming up beside Tabby. All of a sudden, the black horse shot past them; close behind him was the smaller black horse. Both horses were riderless as they passed Caitlin and Tabby as if they were standing still.

What a magnificent horse!

The bigger black horse probably stood about seventeen hands high, and his coat was as black as midnight and as shiny as satin. His mane and tail were almost horizontal to the ground as he ran in full stride. His mane and tail hair was not straight; it was wavy – even when he wasn't in a full run. The long, feather hair growing around the tops of his hooves made it look as if he was floating.

What a beauty! That horse must have been stolen. Such a magnificent horse could not possibly belong to any of the riff-raff back at that farm.

"I'll make sure he gets back to the sheriff as soon as I can get myself to safety," she thought.

Again, she nudged Tabby to get her going a little faster. Caitlin and the three mares galloped for a long time. There were no forks in the road and no paths leading off into the woods. The road just kept on going straight as an arrow.

"I sure hope this is the right way to town," she whispered to no one.

Caitlin heard the sound of labored breathing as the two mares behind her started tiring, so she pulled back on Tabby and slowed them down a bit. The last thing she wanted was to have one of these horses collapse and die on her.

"Okay Tabby-girl," Caitlin said loudly as she pulled on the reins a little more, "let's give these ladies a rest." She let the three mares walk for a good long while as she watched the changing of the night into day.

The sun was slowly creeping over the horizon. It wasn't complete daylight yet, but the sky was starting to illuminate itself in the east and rays of early morning sunlight were slipping into the forest.

As Caitlin and the mares walked further along the road, the abundance of tall pine trees started to thin and was replaced by huge oak trees. About a half mile ahead it looked as if the oak trees were leaning across the road, blocking out the glow of the early morning light. The giant trees were bending inward over the narrow road as if they were trying to pull the road into the forest.

Caitlin, by this time, was trotting all three horses. The big black horse and his buddy were long gone. Not even an echo of their distant hoof beats could be heard. For some reason Caitlin felt more alone without the two bigger horses. She would have felt safer had they stayed with her and the mares.

"Where is that feeling coming from?" she said out loud. "I think I'm losing my mind. They're just horses, the same as these three."

But for whatever reason, she kept her eyes on the road ahead looking for them. The deeper she went into the forest of oaks, the colder she felt. Goosebumps popped out on her arms and the back of her neck tingled. She felt as if someone was watching her. A feeling of unease started to build in her stomach like a hand squeezing her body and working its way up into her throat.

She was slowly entering an emerald green tunnel formed by oak trees. Up ahead, she could make out a turn in the road which blocked the open end of the tunnel from her sight.

The two mares trotted up beside Tabby and started pulling on the lead ropes as if they wanted to run.

The anxiety in her stomach made her want to stop — maybe she should wait?

"Wait for what?" she asked herself in a sharp whisper. "Wait for Aunt Birdie and the river rats to catch up with me? Not a good idea." she said loudly. "Let's go girls. We're going to make it through these woods and into town."

Just as she started to give Tabby a nudge, she realized the early morning sounds of the forest were gone. It was as quiet as a tomb.

No birds were chirping as they called out to the world to wake up and see the sunrise; no small animals were scurrying around trying to find an early morning breakfast.

Absolutely no sounds could be heard. The soft echo of horse hooves trotting along the narrowing road was the only sound in the forest. Slowly, Caitlin urged the mares further into the forest tunnel. Fear and unease hung thick in the air as the tunnel surrounded them in its chilly embrace.

She knew the trees were not that close, but in her mind it felt as if the forest was closing in on them. The end of the tunnel was not yet visible, and the oaks were growing larger and it was getting darker as the trees blocked out the early dawn. When she turned her head to look back, the entrance into the emerald tunnel was hidden, the green canopy made an arc over the narrow road which in turn formed the tunnel of emerald leaves. She could not see the beginning or the end of the passageway. They were totally enclosed within the long tunnel of trees.

Then she heard the sound the horses and other forest creatures had already sensed. From the hills around them came the scream of a black panther. Black panthers were abundant along the Mississippi river bottom. They were black as midnight and their screams were like the screams of a woman.

Everyone knew the stories of men going out during the dusky late hours of the day trying to find the woman they heard screaming, only to be attacked by a black panther.

It was unusual to hear them this early in the morning, so this one must be hurt or still hunting. Whatever the reason, Caitlin wasn't about to stick around to find out which one it was. Seldom did the panthers come close to civilization; but then again, this area was not civilization.

The scream came again, louder this time, as if it was on the run and coming closer to her and the mares.

All three horses had become skittish and anxious to run faster. When the screams echoed off the hills, Tabby and the other two horses needed no urging to run. Tabby took off like a bullet, and the two mares were right behind her. All Caitlin could do was to hang on tightly to Tabby's mane. She knew if she fell off she was a dead woman — either from the fall itself or from being panther breakfast. She held onto Tabby's mane with one hand and hugged the horse's neck with the hand that held the lead ropes.

All of a sudden, her hand holding the ropes was jerked back; she either had to let the ropes drop or be pulled off her horse. Instantly she dropped the leads and grabbed Tabby's neck with both hands. As she hugged the horse's body she turned to glance back. One of the mares had stumbled.

"Come on girl, get up! Get up!" she yelled loudly to the mare. "You can do it, get up!"

The second mare was keeping up with Tabby; in fact she was less than a necks length behind them. When Caitlin glanced back again, she could see the fallen mare getting to her feet and, amazingly, start to run.

"That's it girl, come on now, catch up."

When the panther screamed again, the fallen mare needed no encouragement. Her head came up and immediately she was in a full stride. "Good girl, come on up, come on!"

As Caitlin turned her head back around to see where Tabby was taking them, she saw the big black horse up ahead. He and the smaller black had returned for some reason.

He was prancing around in circles and looking back as if to make sure they were coming. The smaller black horse was standing further down the road waiting for him. When Caitlin got closer, both of them once again took off running at a full gallop. Caitlin felt both surprise and relief when she saw them.

"Okay, come on girls, let's get up there with our boys," she said to Tabby. The horse seemed to realize what was being said because she increased her speed.

As they came around the bend in the road, Caitlin saw the end of the tunnel. Relief flooded her body when she caught sight of the early morning sun with its golden fingers slipping over the top of the hills and softly tumbling in to caress the fields. The dense forest had thinned into a meadow with only a scattering of oak tree clusters among the tall field grasses.

They ran another mile or so when the horses started slowing down. All three horses were lathered with foam and breathing heavily. The two black horses were not in sight.

Gently she pulled back on Tabby to slow all of them down. Caitlin knew, unless she had missed a horse, that Aunt Birdie and the river rats had no way to get away from the farm unless they started walking. And if any of them had started walking, they would not be close behind her.

The horses needed to stop and rest for a bit and it would also give Caitlin time to wipe the horses down and find a stream of clear water for them to drink. Caitlin started looking around for a tree stump she could use to remount Tabby once she slid off of her back.

A short distance down the road, she spotted a large cluster of oak and aspen trees which started at the edge of the road and went back more than fifty feet.

Slowly she walked the horses through the line of oaks and discovered a small clearing within the circle of trees and it was well hidden from anyone passing along on the road. The trees around the clearing grew in a large circle. There were probably more than one hundred trees surrounding the clearing and it was covered with spring grasses and fallen trees. It was a perfect place to rest and hide from prying eyes.

Caitlin stopped Tabby in the center of the clearing next to a fallen tree and slipped off her back. She picked up the lead ropes and tied them to a branch on the fallen tree, just in case the horses decided to stray. She surely didn't want that panther to have them for breakfast and the good Lord was the only one who knew, other than the panther himself, where that black devil was. She probably shouldn't linger in these trees too long.

Caitlin bent over and pulled a hand full of tall grass and started rubbing Tabby down. When she was finished with Tabby, she pulled some more of the tall grass and slowly approached one of the other mares.

"Okay girl," she whispered softly, "let me rub you down. I'm sure you will feel better."

The mare stood there looking at her with big brown solemn eyes. She waited calmly as Caitlin rubbed the foam from her body.

"Well girl," Caitlin spoke to the horse softly, rubbing her nose and head. "You haven't had very good care now, have you? You probably belong to one of the filthy rats out there with Aunt Birdie. What a shame. Well, if I have anything to do with it, you aren't going back to any of those rascals. They don't deserve to own a pig, much less a wonderful horse like you."

As Caitlin pulled more grass for the third mare, she started softly singing an Irish lullaby her Pa had sung to his "wee lad and lassies" many years ago. She stood up and looked off into the forest. "It all seems so long ago," she thought to herself. "Sometimes I forget how Mama and Pa looked when we were all together around the table and Pa was making us all laugh. Sometimes it seems like a fairy tale."

Once in a while when Caitlin went to her parents' graves to sit and visit, it seemed as if she could hear her mama speak to her in a gentle voice telling her, "go on home now Caitlin. Live your life to the fullest and don't worry about your pa and me. We are together and happy, so go along my sweet girl, and don't cry over us. Your sisters and Benny need you."

Softly she started singing to the mares, hoping it would help calm the third mare so she could wipe the foam off her body.

> *My Mother sang a song to me*
> *In tones so sweet and low.*
> *Just a simple little ditty,*
> *In her good old Irish way,*
> *And I'd give the world if she could sing*
> *That song to me this day.*
> *"Too-ra-loo-ra-loo-ral, Too-ra-loo-ra-li,*
> *Too-ra-loo-ra-loo-ral, hush now, don't you cry!*

She took her time as she rubbed the third mare down. By then the horses all seemed to have calmed and were not as jumpy as they had been when she first led them into the clearing. All three were munching on the lush grass growing in the meadow.

Picking up the lead ropes to the two mares, she tugged on Tabby's halter and led them over to the tree stump where she slid onto Tabby's back. "Okay, Tabby girl, let's get going again. We don't want to be panther food if we can avoid it."

As she started walking the horses toward the road, she heard the sound of a horse approaching from the direction of the farmhouse. Caitlin immediately stopped Tabby and slid off her back. As quickly and quietly as possible, Caitlin looped the lead ropes over a branch and ran to the edge of the road. Squatting down behind an oak tree surrounded by thick brush, she watched for the unknown horse's approach.

Lily and the Ghost of Michael Thorne

CHAPTER FOURTEEN

The Road Home

CAITLIN HEARD THE VOICES before she saw the riders.

"Slow down would ya, I'm a'fallin off'en his hind-end. Pull up and slow down a mite, would ya?" One of the riders yelled.

It was an old mule with two riders on his back.

One man was on his stomach with his arms wrapped around the lead rider's waist and his feet were flapping out behind the mule's hind quarters. He was hanging on for dear life.

It was the cowboy and the plate-slammer. The old mule was running as fast as he could go, and with each stride of his legs, the cowboy would flop up and slam back down onto the backbone of the poor old mule. The cowboy's hat had evidently fallen off, and now all of his hair was slicks down on his head. His pant legs, which were rolled up to begin with, were almost to his knees due to flopping up and down on the mule's back; his filthy socks were so big they had fallen down and were completely covering his shoes. His legs looked like sticks flapping in the wind. It was one of the funniest sights Caitlin had ever watched. The skinny cowboy was flopping like a dead chicken tied to the back of a running dog.

The plate-slammer wasn't paying any attention to the cowboy; he just kept right on kicking his boots into the sides of the poor old mule. The mule, the plate-slammer and the cowboy went right on past the spot where Caitlin was hiding.

"Good Lord on high," Caitlin laughed. "Where did that mule come from? I sure didn't see a mule around the barn." Caitlin said in amazement.

"Well," she thought to herself, "that ends our journey for a bit. We'll have to stay here until they go back to the farm. I sure don't want to meet up with them on our way to town." She turned the horses around and led them back into the clearing; hoping the black panther had decided to stop roaming the hills around them. She ground tied the horses with their lead ropes and sat on one of the fallen oaks.

"Okay Tabby-girl, we'll have to wait a bit. But if they don't return soon, we'll have to keep going. Only now we'll have to go through the woods."

After a while, the forest once again came alive with the sounds of life. The sky was crystal clear and as blue as Michael's eyes. Bees were buzzing around the early spring flowers and a woodpecker, high in one of the trees, starting its rhythmic knocking. The rustling of small scurrying animals and singing birds once again flooded the forest. A soft breeze moved gently through the aspen, bringing with it the sweet summer smell of wild honeysuckle and generating the familiar rustle of aspen leaves. The rustle would grow as loud as a waterfall and then, when the breeze softened, it become as quiet as the whisper of a bubbling stream.

Caitlin lay down on a smooth part of the large fallen oak and watched two eagles as they flew around the tree tops. They were catching the wind as it brushed the tops of the tallest trees and carried them away. After they were carried a good distance they would flap their wings and soar back to catch another current.

The giant oaks stood tall and majestic, guarding the smaller aspen and flowering bushes that littered the clearing. Flowering bushes filled in the gaps between the giant oaks surrounding the clearing. The clearing was a perfect place to hide.

The cooing of doves and the chatter of squirrels lulled her into a state of contentment. She closed her eyes as she felt the sunshine caress her skin and soothed her nerves.

"This is so nice," she thought as she curled into a ball on the fallen oak tree. "There is absolutely nothing in this world better than a nap in the warm morning sun."

As she closed her eyes and drifted into a state of remembering. Her mind drifted back to the short time she had spent with Michael. She smiled as she remembered his smell when he came to visit and the warmth of his arms around her when he hugged her before he went to war. She could visualize that day so vividly; he had stood so proud and anxious to defend his beliefs and his love for his country.

Oh to have Michael back again; along with Mama and Papa. That would be wonderful. She lay there for a while daydreaming about the people she loved who were now just a memory, as well as the people she loved who were still with her.

The sun was now completely up and warming the tree trunk; the heat intensified the intoxicating smells of spring time. Her night-wrap was almost too warm. She could not keep her eyes open any longer –slowly she slipped into a slumber.

Caitlin awoke with Tabby pushing at her shoulder with her muzzle. The two mares were standing on the other side of her with their faces not even a foot away from Caitlin's. The sun had passed the high noon mark and was on its way down. It was probably three o'clock, or there about. The birds were still singing, but the eagles had moved on. The clearing seemed so peaceful; Caitlin did not want to move. But they had to start out for town again. She sure didn't want to be out here during the night with no protection.

She stretched and sat up. Tabby and the mares moved back as if they knew they needed to be moving on. In the distance she could hear the sound of approaching hoof beats. This time the sounds were coming from the opposite direction.

"It must be the plate-slammer and the cowboy again," she thought to herself.

CHAPTER FOURTEEN: THE ROAD HOME

Scrambling off the fallen tree, she picked up the lead ropes for all three horses and quickly wrapped them around a branch. Quietly she hurried out to the same large oak tree she had previously hidden behind. Squatting down, she peered around the tree.

And there they came. Sure enough, it was the poor old mule, the plate-slammer and the cowboy. The cowboy was still holding onto the plate-slammer and the plate-slammer was still kicking the old mule in the sides to make him run faster.

"Where is that stupid girl?" the plate-slammer yelled back to the cowboy.

"I cain't hardly hold on, Mac, much less think 'bout whur that thar gal is," yelled the cowboy.

The cowboy had managed to get his legs up and around the belly of the poor old mule. His long arms were stretched out around the plate-slammer's waist and his behind was sticking way out over the mule's behind. His skinny legs were clamped around the mule's belly so tightly Caitlin could see the depression in the mule's side. Thankfully, the cowboy had his face turned away from Caitlin or he would have looked right at her hiding spot as they passed.

She walked back to the horses and led Tabby to the fallen tree so she could slip onto her back without falling off. Slowly she walked the three mares back to the road.

"Well, that was another sight to behold and this road must lead into a town. Let's get going and see how far we can get before it turns dark. Hopefully this is the right way to Caruthersville," Caitlin said to Tabby.

So off they went. The two mares were following close behind Tabby and Caitlin as if they knew there could be danger awaiting them. Caitlin started the horses off in a slow trot so as to not alert the cowboy and the plate slammer to her whereabouts. She sure didn't want them to turn around and start chasing her. After a while, the road turned and ran along beside a stream. Caitlin stopped the horses and let them drink from the cool water while she herself ate some of the food she had stashed in her pockets.

When she and the horses drank their full from the stream, they started out again. This time Caitlin urged them into a faster gallop. The afternoon was getting away from them and it would soon be dark. The last thing Caitlin wanted to do was to stay in the forest all night. After encountering the screams of the black panther in the early morning hours, she sure didn't want to encounter the actual creature tonight. She tried pushing the horses a little faster.

Within minutes, the giant oaks clusters totally disappeared and the land became full of tall prairie grass with only a few trees scattered along the sides of the road. They came to a fork in the road and Caitlin stopped the horses.

"Tabby-girl, which way do you think we should go?"

Not getting an answer from the horse, Caitlin laughed at herself and leaned to one side of Tabby trying to get a better look at the dirt as she walked Tabby a short distance in each direction. She soon discovered that the road leading to the south seemed to have more hoof prints than the one leading north.

"Okay girls, this is the way we are going to go." She said to the horses, but they just looked at her, not knowing that she had just made a huge decision for all of them.

Not wanting anyone ahead or behind them to see the dust they were creating, Caitlin kept the horses going in a fast trot.

They must have gone five miles when Caitlin spotted a wagon coming toward them.

Quickly she stopped all three horses and strained her eyes to see if she could make out who was driving the wagon. It looked as if it was a man and a woman.

As the wagon drew closer, Caitlin could see that it was indeed a man and a woman on the front bench, and in the back of the wagon there were four little blond heads peeking over the sides rails staring at Caitlin in the same manner in which she was staring at them.

Caitlin pulled her horses into the tall grass at the side of the road and waited for the wagon to approach and pass.

CHAPTER FOURTEEN: THE ROAD HOME

The man pulled his wagon to a stop beside her and the mares.

"Howdy ma'am," he spoke with a thick southern accent. "Are ya okay way out here by ya'self? We sure will help ya; if need be. Ya know yur a long ways from town. Hit's about ten more miles into Caruthersville and hit's a'gonna be dark here just in a bit. I'm David John and this here is my lovely wife Katie Nicole. We be the Levi's and hail from way over Georgia-way. These here young'uns be: Mary Queen of Scotts, Henry the Fifth, we'd a'named him Henry the Eighth, but ol' Henry the Eighth weren't a very nice feller my Katie Nicole tells me. And a'sittin' next to Henry there is Jethro John the Baptist and Arthur Coydon is the one a'laying down a'sleeping, we'd a named him King Arthur, but Katie Nicole liked Arthur Coydon, and this'n right here be little Josephine Pansy. She be named after ol' Napoleon's sweetheart. Now, I know'd Napoleon weren't no fine feller and all, but we figured Josephine might have been just a right nice lady. Katie Nicole here loves the name Josephine so we just went right on ahead and named our little gal Josephine. We be expectin' another in just a few months." David John grinned as if he had accomplished a grand deed, and just went right on talking, "and if'fen hit's a boy-child, he'll be named after his great-grandpappy and be called King David, being that his great grand-pappy came over here from the old country and all. But if'fen hit's a girl-child she'll be called Catherine the Great, since Catherine the Great was such a great woman and all. I know'd they all have grand fancy names but hits because Katie Nicole here is a fine educated lady from Baltimore, Maryland. But we don't never call them by their given names; unless Mama here is upset wth 'em all. We just call them Queenie, Henny, JJ, Bugpappy and Josie. Now if yur a'wondin why we call Artur Coydon, Bugpappy. Well, hits because he truly loves ever ol' kind of bug there is. Ever kind you can think of, he likes 'em. Why once't on a Sunday morning, he took his jug o bugs into the house of God, without us a'knowin', mind you. Well, that thar preacher-man starts in a'shoutin' about how we'll all be free and a'flyin' around with wings when we get to that great promise land and our lil' Bugpappy here start in a'cryin and opens his jug-o'-bugs and yells out at the top of his voice, 'You're free, bugs! Go on now and fly into the promise land whur there be lot's o skitters fur ya to eat.'

Why there was more yellin' and shoutin' and a'jumpin up and down, and a'tryin' to get away from them thar bugs on that thar particular Sunday morning gatherin' than there ever was in all them tent revivals put together. And even though he be just a little'un, the church folk wouldn't let him back in the doors. Right then and there I decided to take my family and find a good place to farm where everbody loves the gifts God gives us in our young'uns. Ain't no man on this here green earth gonna be mean to my young'uns. So we be headed on up to Eden Bend, closer to St. Louie. We plan on startin' up a farm and living there for many years iff'en the good Lord sees fit and we don't get flooded out."

David John had to stop and take a deep breath when he finished telling his story. His wife, Katie Nicole, smiled at Caitlin and nodded her head in agreement.

Caitlin could see why Katie Nicole had fallen for David John. He was a very handsome man and he sure loved his children.

Four little faces were still peeking over the wagon rails at her. They were all as blond as could be and as cute as buttons with grins spread across their faces.

All of a sudden another little head popped up from the wagon floor.

"That must be Bugpappy," Caitlin thought to herself.

This little guy was cuter than the others; if that was possible. He had huge, dark gray eyes outlined with long beautiful black eyelashes. His hair and eyebrows were as white as cotton and it was sticking straight out all over his head, Plus he had a splash of freckles across his nose and cheeks. He looked to be around six years old, and was grinning from ear to ear as he looked at Caitlin.

"Howdy ma'am, it's a right fine day today isn't it?" he called out in a high, squeaky, little boy's voice. "I'm Bugpappy and I'm almost a grown up man. I have some nice brothers and sisters here if you want to meet them. And I even have my jug-o-bugs with me. What ya doing out here by yourself? You getting' ready for bed this early? It's not even dark yet. I like your horse. She's a beaut' and I'm going to get me a horse when I'm a full man. Yes, I'm going to get me a dandy fine horse! What's your name ma'am? Do you have a grand name like we do? You probably do since you're so pretty and all. You want to hold my jug-o-bugs? I have some beauties in here! Here's the biggest old bug you ever did see right here," Bugpappy said as he pointed to his jar and held it out for Caitlin to see, "and you would really like them I'm sure. We are moving to a big farm and we are going to help Pa build it up! I'm going catch every bug on our farm. In fact I'm going to have a bug farm. I just now thought of that. That's a right fine idea isn't it ma'am? What cha doing with three horses? You can only ride one at a time. If you see any good bugs, just send them our way." Bugpappy scratched his head and grinned wider yet as he informed her: "Yes ma'am, there will be lots and lots of bugs on our farm!"

"Katie Nicole is doing a wonderful job with her children's grammar if all of them speak as well as Bugpappy," Caitlin thought to herself before she answered his question.

"My name is Caitlin Violet Quinn. And it is very nice to meet you, Bugpappy."

"It's mighty nice meeting you also, ma'am," Bugpappy announced loudly as he stretched out to shake Caitlin's hand. "My real name is Arthur, but I like Bugpappy," he said with a big smile. Caitlin took the small outstretched hand and was surprised at the strength in the little guy's handshake.

"Bugpappy," his mother turned and spoke to him softly, "Mind your manners, now. Pa was talking. Don't interrupt. Maybe you can talk to this nice lady when we finish our visit. Don't release your bugs, and please hold onto your sister so she doesn't fall over the side."

As little Bugpappy did as his mother instructed, she spoke to him again softly and with a smile. "Thank you, Bugpappy, that's very kind of you."

Katie Nicole turned back and smiled at Caitlin. "I do apologize, Miss Caitlin, he means no disrespect. He just loves to talk and gets a little carried away sometimes."

"Katie Nicole is well-educated," Caitlin thought. "No offense taken at all Mrs. Levi. I have a brother and two little sisters myself. I truly understand. Your children are beautiful, and I'm sure you will all have a wonderful farm since all the land up north, closer to St. Louis, is very fertile and the farmers always have good crops during harvest." Caitlin smiled at the little faces peering over the sides of the wagon grinning at her.

"Well, ya be careful now, young lady," David John stated. "Iff'en ya get caught out here in the dark, afore ya can get to Caruthersville, there be an old abandoned shack 'bout five miles back on down the road. We spent the night there last night. We didn't get an early start out this morning; ol' Blue here lost one of his shoes and hit took me forever to fix it. These young'uns ain't big enough to help much yet, but they'll get thar in a few more years. We plan on spendin' this here night just makin camp out in the forest. Ya don't know of any empty farmhouses out this way, do ya?"

"Well, no. But I do know of a large grove of giant oaks a ways up the road that may give you some shelter. There's plenty of grass for the horses and a good clear stream for drinking just before you reach it." Caitlin replied. "As a matter of fact, I would like to give you these two mares of mine. I really don't need them and I was just going to give them to anyone who could use them once I get into Caruthersville. They often get away from me and I'm just tired of chasing them all over the county. If you would take them off my hands I would really appreciate it and it would save me the trouble of leading them along the next ten miles and maybe having to chase them down again. That way Tabby and I can go a little faster. How about it? Could you use two extra mares on your farm? You're more than welcome to them if you like. I have no use for them."

"Well, Miss Caitlin," David John slowly replied, eyeing the horses. "Hit don't feel right: me just takin' them from ya. Let me pay ya in some way. We can make a trade here. What would ya like? We have plenty of food and all kinds of kitchen things ya might like. Take yur pick. Hit's yur pick."

"Well, I could use some food for the night. Whatever you have, just a little bit will do for me. My horse can live off the grass and the stream water."

"Katie Nicole, love, get this here gal some food stuffs, and maybe a jug o' that there milk from the mulch cow."

With the help of her husband, Katie Nicole climbed over the bench and into the back of the wagon. David John jumped down from the wagon, took the lead ropes from Caitlin and tied the two mares to the back of the wagon next to their cow.

Katie Nicole had a burlap flour bag and was stuffing it full of food and other items.

Caitlin didn't say anything, because she didn't want them to feel as if they had cheated her.

David John handed the bag up to Caitlin and smiled broadly as he said, "Miss, ya have helped us out mighty fine and we sure do thank ye. Ya be a blessin to us."

Katie Nicole gave Caitlin a beautiful smile and nodded her head. "You are very welcome," Caitlin replied. "I should also let you know about a couple of things to watch for. Today in the early hours of the morning, I heard a black panther scream a few times as if maybe it was hurt. And the second thing is, when you come to the first fork in the road, don't go west, stay on the road to the north. Down the west road a ways is an old abandoned farm, but it's full of some very bad folks. They won't hesitate to take everything you have and may even steal your children and sell them down the river. They will also take your wife if they get a chance. They may be trying to walk or ride an old mule back to town, so keep a sharp eye out for anyone walking or riding a mule. I know they have one old mule, a carriage and maybe some more horses by now, so if they stop you and try to talk you into helping them out or giving them the horses I gave to you, don't do it. Get your gun out and have it ready as soon as you see them coming and have your children hide. If I were you, I would also give your wife a gun. Even if she doesn't know how to use it, it will be a backup for you. I know for a fact that there are at least four men and one woman, and there could be more. They are all in cahoots with the slavers along the river.

If the sky is clear tonight I am going to try and get into town. If I were you all I wouldn't chance running into those evil people.

When you get to Eden Bend, please sent me a letter and let me know you arrived safely and everything is okay. Just send it to Caitlin Quinn in care of Pete Turnkey at the train depot in Caruthersville and he will see that I get it."

Katie Nicole's face turned a little white and David John seemed to, all of a sudden, be in a hurry. "Miss Caitlin, we thank ye much and wish ya luck in getting back to town but we better be movin' along now. We sure won't take the west road and maybe we will just keep on a'movin along until we can't go no further. We sure nuf' will send ya notice when we get to Eden Bend, won't ya Katie Nicole? And you be very careful ya'self, young lady. Thank ya much, Miss Caitlin, thank ya very much."

With that, the wagon moved out at a faster pace than a wagon should move. "Thank you Ms. Caitlin, be safe!" they all called out. "You are very welcome!" Caitlin called back.

Little Bugpappy was holding up his jug-o-bugs as he yelled out to her, "I know for certain you will love these here bugs once you get to meet them! They are right friendly most of the time. Come on in to Eden Bend and visit us and I'll let you meet them." Caitlin laughed and gave them all another wave. The five little ones and Katie Nicole all turned and waved at her until they reached the next bend in the road and were out of sight.

"Well Tabby, it's just you and me," Caitlin said to her horse. "I know I told a lie, but they seemed to be good people and they will take good care of those mares. I did the right thing and I sure hope they don't run into any of those men or Aunt Birdie. Let's get moving girl and see how far we can get before it gets too dark." Off they went again.

Even though it was only Caitlin and Tabby and they were moving fast, Caitlin could see the lengthening shadows of dusk as darkness began its rapid decent upon the forest around her. The clouds were rolling across the sky, chasing away any hope Caitlin had of being able to continue riding in the dark of night. Once the moon was completely covered, Missouri turned black as midnight, making it impossible to ride a horse and stay on the road.

She pushed Tabby into a run; a few miles down the road, she started looking for the old shack. The clouds were getting thicker and darkness was quickly closing in on them. Soon it would be too dark to spot the old shack.

Colder air was moving in and the forest sounds were changing from singing birds to hoot owls, crickets and bullfrogs. With dusk upon them, there also came the sounds of branches and bushes rustling – probably the larger night animals starting their nightly hunt for food.

Tabby must have sensed the urgency in Caitlin's movements; because she started moving faster than Caitlin wanted to chance. In the growing darkness, Caitlin needed to watch for holes in the road — or anything else Tabby may stumble over.

There it was! Off to the right about fifty feet from the road was the abandoned old cabin. There was no path leading up to the door. The slight bend in the tall grass, left from the Levi's wagon, was the only sign of anyone having been there. The structure of the old cabin looked as if it might, very shortly, be on its way back to mother earth. But at least it had four walls and a roof. The door was still attached and the windows had boards across them. There were wide cracks between the window boards, but at least the boards would keep the wild animals out.

"Come on girl. We'll both stay inside so that panther won't have us for dinner."

Carefully she walked Tabby across the field and up to the cabin. She slid off Tabby's back and landed on the rickety porch. Slowly she opened the door and looked in. It was better than she had expected. Evidently the Levi's has somewhat cleaned it up. She could barely see, but she could make out an old rusty lantern with a small amount of oil still in it and what looked like a box of matches sitting alongside the lamp. Stepping inside the room, she quickly lit the lantern and sat it on a tiny table leaning against the wall. The lantern lit up the whole place. The only furniture in the room appeared to be one chair and an old feather tick mattress lying on the floor. What had once been a cot was now in pieces in a corner. There was a pot-bellied stove in the middle of the room and a few short logs beside it. Caitlin walked to the back of the cabin and opened the back door. It led into a small lean-to which looked to be in decent shape.

"This will be fine for Tabby," she said to herself. Caitlin went back outside and picked up the sack Katie Nicole had filled for her. She led Tabby inside the cabin and through the back door to the lean-to. There were walls at both ends of the lean-to; so it must have been added on as an additional room.

"Well, tonight it's going to be a room for a horse!" she laughed. After closing the door to the lean-to, she walked over and opened the bag from the Levi's. Inside she found a blanket, a small knife and an old dress. Caitlin started laughing at herself because she had completely forgotten about being in her night wrap and the oversized shoes. Katie Nicole must have thought Caitlin was a run-away and needed some clothes. And the knife — Katie knew Caitlin might need some type of protection. Bless her for that. A woman alone in the woods at night could always use a little protection.

The bag was stuffed with more food than Caitlin would be able to eat. A small jug of milk was included. The food consisted of sweet potato pancakes, bacon, fried chicken and some kind of sweet bread. It was a feast!

She shut the outside door and blocked it with the table, pulled the rickety chair over to the table and sat down to feast. The chicken was the best tasting chicken she had ever eaten, and the sweet potato pancakes melted in her mouth. The milk tasted like honey going down her throat and at that moment the food tasted like food fit for a king.

After finishing her feast, she blew out the lantern and wrapped herself in the blanket. She wasn't just concerned with staying warm; she was also concerned about the bugs which may be hiding in the old feather tic. She curled up on the old mattress and immediately fell sound asleep.

CHAPTER FIFTEEN

A Night in the Wilderness

ALONG ABOUT MIDNIGHT (or so she guessed), Caitlin was awakened by the sound of clapping, laughing and music. She lay there for a few minutes trying to get her bearings.

Slowly, she sat up. "Where is that racket coming from?" she whispered to herself. She got up and peeked out the window.

About fifty feet further down the meadow, in a large clump of tall pines, she could see a camp fire. The tall pine branches started about twenty feet above the ground, so she could see everything fairly well.

The clouds had vanished, and the moon lit up the entire meadow. She could see men moving around the campfire. It looked as if they were dancing with each other!

Knowing that sounds are easily carried in the night, she quietly pulled the table away from the door, wrapped the dark colored blanket around herself to hide her light colored clothing, and slipped out the door. She didn't tug the door shut, knowing the noise would carry across the clearing. Instead, she stood on the porch watching for a minute just to make sure no one had heard her. Then she ran swiftly to the edge of the tree line and moved back into the thick brush which grew among the trees. Carefully and slowly, as to not alert any of them, she walked closer to the campfire.

When she was about thirty feet from the campfire, she stopped and squatted down behind a clump of pine trees and bushes. There were approximately fifteen to twenty men in a circle standing around the campfire. The fire was large and they were noisy. They were all up clapping and singing Camp Town Races at the top of their voices.

One of the men had on a bonnet. The bonnet looked new and was decked out with a lot of ribbons and bows. It was pink with blue ruffles all around the brim and neck. Actually, it was quite pretty – had a woman been wearing it!

One of the men, a little man dressed in a dandy suit and top hat, was standing on a large rock, and as the man with the bonnet danced with non-bonnet men, he would call out the dance steps and then yell out "Switch partners" and away the bonnet man would go with the next man in the circle. They appeared to be having the time of their life.

After each man had a go-around with the bonnet man, the short little man yelled out, "Switch the bonnet!" and the man wearing the bonnet whipped it off and plunked it onto the head of the man he was presently dancing with, and off they all went again. All of them were clapping, singing and dancing. One very tall, very skinny man with a huge nose and no teeth would, every time he switched partners, repeat an interesting routine. He would bow, break wind, snatch up his partner's hand, wrap his arm around his partner's waist and take off around the fire so quickly his bonnet ribbons were trailing out behind him. Before he changed to the next partner he would bow, break wind again and yell out "Thank'ye ma'am!"

This went on for a while until the little man doing the calling suddenly yelled out, "Okay boys, that's the whole lesson for tonight. I can't yell anymore and I have a powerful thirst coming on. Let's all have a drink. Break out the whiskey, John. Let's celebrate our dancing."

The dandy little man continued on with his speech. "The next town dance we come upon, you men will be the envy of every man in attendance. Ever last one of you is ready to impress every boney-fide and non-boney-fide lady we meet up with. I do have to say one thing though — I have done an excellent job of teaching you how to dance, and all of you have done an excellent job of learning. Welcome to the civilized world, boys! Yes indeed, welcome to the world of dancing with boney-fide ladies and sipping tea in a parlor. Tomorrow we will practice sipping tea one more time before we move on, and I am right proud of all of you and I do suspect many of you will soon be marrying up with the finest ladies in Missouri. By this time next year, we should be seeing some fathers among us — myself included, I do hope and pray."

" Now this here calls for some celebrating, if you ask me! Wrap up that bonnet for the next time and we can start our celebration. I salute you!" yelled out the little man as he held up a jug of whiskey and saluted the men.

There was a lot of whooping and hollering as they all sat down around the fire and John started passing the jugs of whiskey. As the jugs went around the group, they all started in teasing each other. Calls like, "Yur one fine lookin' boney-fide lady," were being loudly and exuberantly thrown around.

"I know'd I am, ya handsome city feller," one of the men said in a mocking high squeaky voice, "but I just cain't marry up with ya, Slim. Ever time ya changed partners ya broke an awful smellin' wind, and I just cain't put up with that there." They all laughed and kept on passing the jugs and harassing each other.

"Well, Jasper, you are a sweet charmin' lady," Slim replied. "But I don't think I could marry up with ya either. You be one fine dancin' boney-fide woman, but yur boo-soms seem to have dropped down and turned into a belly."

That comment brought another chaotic round of laughter from the other men, and more crude remarks were yelled out as they all pushed and shoved at each other. "I'd jest as soon meet up with one of them thar non-boney-fide ladies." A young cowboy yelled out, "I do think it would be a lot more fun. I ain't a'lookin' to get hitched up jest yet,"

"Go right on ahead, Job," an older man yelled back. "I'm a'lookin' fur me a wife. I'm 'tard of riding and sleeping on the ground. Hit's a'wearin' on my bones."

"Me too, I'm a'getting too old fur this," Slim yelled out.

"Same here!" called out the dandy little man with the hat.

All of a sudden, Caitlin heard yelling and someone came crashing through the edge of the woods not ten feet away from where Caitlin was hiding. She hunkered further down into the brush. When she looked up again, she saw two men running toward the campfire yelling at the top of their voices and waving their hands.

"We see'd haints! We see'd haints! Get out yur guns! We see'd some haints."

All the men jumped up, whipped out their guns and stood staring at the men as they continued to yell.

"What ya talkin about, Bones?" one of the other men asked. "Stop yer yammering and yellin and tell us what ya see'd," another man yelled.

All the men had their guns drawn and were staring, bug-eyed, out into the forest. Both men stopped yammering, put their hands on their knees with their heads hanging down, and tried to get air into their lungs.

"Well," one of them finally managed to get out, "Me and Jonesey here, we be over yonder by that thar old shack just a'nosin' around, and all of a sudden like, there be a man and a little white haired gal a'standin' right dab in front of us. He was one of them there soldier fellers. And that there little gal was all decked out in Injun' clothes and her hair was a'blowin straight out behind her head and there weren't no wind a'tall a'blowin around us. That there soldier boy was a'glarin right at us with red eyes. Hit looked like there was far a'comin' right on out of his eyeballs and hit was a'shootin right at us. Well, me and Jonesy stopped dead in our tracks. I was mighty scare't and my legs started in a'shaking and they froze right up on me at the same time and wouldn't let me move nary one bit. Now, me and Jonesy," He stopped and took a deep breath. "We ain't no cowards or nothing like that a'tall, but that there sure 'nuf was two haints we see'd. Hit was kindly like --we could see right through 'em. They was there alright, but we could see the shack right on through their bodies, and their eyes was on far! Well, the soldier haint calls out and says fur us to git on out of there and stay out, or we'll be on our way to the Pearly gates ta face ol' Saint Pete as quick as a flash. Ain't that true, Jonesy?" "Yep, boss, that there is just the way hit happened." Jonesy was stammering, and spit was flying out of his mouth the whole time he was talking. "Cept hit was worst 'en that fur me. I see'd that there soldier boy stretch out his hand and started in a'comin' right towards me. He was a'pointin' a finger at me and the end of his finger was on far and there was lightin a'coming out of hit. Bones here had done turned around and took off a'runnin, but I was still frozen solid right whur I stood. Well, as soon as I see'd that there far a'comin out of his finger, I just whipped my legs on around and took off a'runnin after Bones. We never looked back to see if they was a'follerin' us, but I didn't get any of them there lightin bolts in my back, so I'm a'guessin we out-runned them."

"Hit were the first time I ever see'd a haint up close, and I'm a'hopin hits the last," Bones said with a stammer and a sigh.

"Me too, boss, me too. No more haints for me. I'm a'stayin right by this here campfar ever night from here on out. I ain't even gonna go let water durin' the night," Jonesey said matter-of-factly.

Jonesey walked over to the fire, sat down with his gun drawn staring out into the woods as he watched for the haints.

The camp grew as quiet as a tomb as all the men slowly turned their backs to the fire so they could watch the forest. Even the little man with the dandy suit, who must have been the boss, looked uneasy. He sat next to one of the biggest men and had his own gun drawn just like the others.

CHAPTER FIFTEEN: A NIGHT IN THE WILDERNESS

Caitlin sat there with her blanket wrapped around her for what seemed like an eternity. Caitlin wasn't so calm herself — if there was something strange going on at the shack, maybe she shouldn't sleep over there. Maybe it would be safer staying right here close to the cowboys and their campfire. They didn't appear to be such a bad bunch.

But she had to go back. Tabby was there and she didn't want anyone to take her. She would have to go back before daybreak.

So, very slowly, she gathered the blanket around herself and leaned against the trunk of the tree. The thick brush would hide her body. Her eyes started to close and her head began to nod when she felt a warm hand on her shoulder and heard a soft voice whisper in her ear.

"Caitlin love, wake up. It's me, Michael." The voice said, "I'm here to help you. Run on back to the shack as fast as you can and lock yourself in when you hear the men yelling and shooting."

With a start, her eyes popped open and she was staring into Michael's face.

"Michael," she whispered. "You're home! Oh my goodness! I thought I would never see you again. Where have you been?" Tears had already started running down her face. She was quietly sobbing.

Michael squatted down beside her and wrapped his arms around her, holding her close.

"No, love," he whispered softly to her. "I'm not home to stay. I'm just here to help you get home safely."

Caitlin looked up at him, puzzled by what he had said. "What do you mean, Michael? Where are you going? You can't stay here with me? Michael, we need you. Mama and Pa are gone and Aunt Birdie may have the little ones. We need you Michael; I need you to stay home with us."

"I can't, love." He looked at her with sadness in his eyes. "I would love to stay here with you and take care of you, but it's too late for me. I'll be leaving shortly and I won't be back. You will find someone special to help keep the little ones safe. But it can't be me, love." He sighed deeply. "It can't be me."

He stood and pulled her up with him as he wrapped her in his arms. She felt the warmth of his body and the love in his heart pour into hers.

"I will always love you, my Caitlin. You will always be with me. But I want you to find another who will love you as much as I do. You will know him when it is time. Be happy and have a good life, my Cait."

With that said, he kissed her tenderly and backed away, as he once again told her to run for the shack when the men started yelling and shooting.

"Wait Michael, don't go. Please — don't go!" She whispered frantically to him. But Michael had already turned his back and was walking away. She watched him as he walked toward the campfire.

Suddenly she noticed he had not made a sound as he went through the brush. And there appeared to be a small child with him. They both appeared to be floating instead of walking. The child was a little girl with the longest, whitest hair Caitlin had ever seen. Her hair was flowing out behind her, fluttering in the slight breeze. She was dressed as an Indian child and had a small puppy under her arm. She held Michael's hand as she looked up at him and laughed about something.

The little girl's voice floated back to Caitlin as she spoke to Michael.

"Let's give them a real big scare for thinking of bothering your Caitlin, okay Mr. Michael?"

Michael looked down at the child, laughed and replied, "Okay, Hannah, let's do that. You startle them up and we will both give them a taste of what they get for even thinking of bothering Caitlin."

Caitlin stood transfixed as she watched them. Michael and Hannah approached the campfire and little Hannah floated up to one of the men who by this time had sat back down and relaxed; most of them probably thinking Bones and Jonesy had imagined the haints.

CHAPTER FIFTEEN: A NIGHT IN THE WILDERNESS

"Youuuu whooooo," Hannah called out loudly, not more than two inches from the man's right ear. "Get up, mountain man. It's the haints and we come to take all of you to your maker to get your just rewards for all the 'good' things you have done in your lives."

Pandemonium broke out. Men were scrambling up, pointing their guns and shooting at Michael and Hannah.

Michael and Hannah were facing Caitlin as they floated almost three feet above the ground, and all the men had their backs to her. Michael and Hannah were waving their hands above their heads and Hannah's hair was now floating straight up from her head. The men were in a panic.

Most of them started running around the campfire shooting into the night air towards Michael and Hannah. Caitlin noticed that two of the men had obviously wet the front of their britches, but they didn't stop. They just kept right on shooting into nothingness.

When some of them used up all their bullets, instead of reloading they just kept on shooting their empty guns. Michael looked over at Caitlin with a twinkle in his eyes; he blew her a kiss and gave her a big smile and a wink, telling her to run.

She stood there for a few more seconds, still mesmerized with the whole scene, and then she took off running as fast as her feet could carry her. She didn't look back until she got to the door of the old shack. Just before she opened the door to slip through, she looked back and saw the men scattering into the forest. The ones that were left were backing further away from the campfire.

Michael and Hannah had moved around the campfire and were now going back and forth between the forest and the men. When any of the men tried to leave in the direction of the shack, Michael would swoop in front of them, scaring them back in the opposite direction. Michael and Hannah were still flapping their arms in the air, and Hannah began dancing an Irish jig. Her feet were still three feet off the ground, and her little legs were going as fast as she could move them. Her hair was now flying around her head in a circle and she had her puppy wrapped around her neck like a winter muff. The puppy was howling at the top of his voice. Michael stopped waving his arms above his head and started playing an invisible banjo. Caitlin was sure the sound of the banjo could be heard throughout the forest. Michael was stomping out a tune and little Hannah's laugh could be heard clearly. They were making sure none of the men ran towards the shack and seemed to be having a great bit of fun doing so.

Caitlin slipped into the shack, barred the door and moved over to the window. In the few seconds it took her to cross from the door to the window, the men had mounted up their horses and were gone. Michael and Hannah were also gone. The only evidence left behind was the smoldering embers of the campfire, and even that was quickly dissipating.

Caitlin stood peering out the window for a while. Nothing was moving. Once again, the forest came alive with the sounds of the night. The frogs and crickets began their love songs and the barn owls were calling to their mates. The symphony of the forest was once again in full stride.

Caitlin moved across the room to check on Tabby. As she opened the lean-to door Tabby raised her head and looked at her as if to say, "Go away and leave me alone."

Caitlin walked back to the window and took another look-see. Nothing moved. Everything and everyone had vanished; as if it had never been there. She knew Michael and Hannah would not return, and she was quite sure the cowboys were into the next county by now. The stars sparkled in the sky and the moon lit up the forest. The campfire was completely out. The glow of the embers had now vanished and the lingering smoke had drifted up and out of the forest.

Sleep came on quickly as she once again snuggled into her blanket and closed her eyes.

CHAPTER FIFTEEN: A NIGHT IN THE WILDERNESS

Lily and the Ghost of Michael Thorne

CHAPTER SIXTEEN

Elmer's Confession

"**WELL, PETE,**" Andre said. "Ah think maybe Ah should deputize ya and then you and ah should take a look-see on some of those there'ah boats. What do ya think about that? That way you can point out any of the men ya saw on the train platform."

"Well, Sheriff," Pete replied with a grin on his face, "If need be, I think it's my duty to perform. If you need me to do it, that is. I would be honored to serve my state and Caruthersville as your Deputy Sheriff."

"Let's get it done then," Sheriff Beaumont replied. "Come on ov'ah to the office and we'll get it all set up." Andre and Pete went into the office and Andre got out a Deputy badge and his book about swearing in deputies. When he finished, Andre smiled, shook Pete's hand and told him, "Congratulations Deputy Turnkey, I am confident you will make an excellent deputy."

With a big smile on his face, Pete thanked Andre and promised to do his level best to uphold the law and help him keep the peace in Caruthersville. So Sheriff Andre Beaumont and Deputy Pete Turnkey walked along the dock, checking out each riverboat. The riverboat captains were all congenial and congratulated Pete when Andre introduced him as the new deputy of Caruthersville; most of them had no problem letting the sheriff and his new deputy search their boats.

Others who were carrying contraband gave them a harder time. But when Andre assured them that all they were looking for was a runaway young girl, they willingly let them on board. He really didn't think it was necessary to tell them that the young girl was in her twenties. Andre and Pete closed their eyes to any contraband they happened to see. But Andre did try to remember which riverboat captains were running illegal goods. Just for use in the future — if need be.

Andre and Pete thanked each captain and moved on to the next boat. After the boats had been searched, they walked back up the levee to the sheriff's office. Waterfront Street was busy with farm wagons and grist-mill wagons lined up one right behind the other all the way from the boats and up to Waterfront Street. The wagons were waiting their turn to unload their goods and reload the incoming goods. Most of the riverboats were shabby goods-haulers. They spent each day going up and down the Mississippi picking up farm goods and other supplies which people living along the way needed or wanted. Some of the livestock and machinery came up the river from the ports in New Orleans, and cotton, grain and cattle went down the river to Natchez and New Orleans.

Many of the triple-deck paddle steam-wheelers were for passengers. They carried very few goods, so the only stops they made along the river was to let passengers off and take passenger on. When they did happen to take on goods, it was because the price was extremely profitable and the passenger business was slow.

"Well Deputy Pete," Andre said as they walked along the levee, "nothing a'tall there'ah. What do ya think? Any idea's come to yor'ah mind about where to look next?"

"Let me do some pondering, Sheriff. I might come up with an idea or two."

Andre and Pete walked the short distance to the sheriff's office in silence and pushed the door open. Andre used his boot to push the chunk of wood against the door to keep it open and encourage a breeze to float through.

"What the..." came from Pete. Andre's head snapped up. There sat Elmer. Elmer was sitting in the sheriff's chair with his hat in his hands and his feet on the desk; he was snoring like a hibernating bear.

Surprised, Andre and Pete stood there for a minute just looking at him. Elmer's head was all the way back against the chair and his mouth was hanging wide open. As he sucked in a breath, his lips and cheeks went inside his mouth; when he exhaled, his cheeks filled with air, making him look like a chipmunk.

Wide grins spread across Andre and Pete's faces as they looked at each other. "Hey Elma," Andre said loudly.

Elmer didn't even twitch a muscle.

"Elma!" Andre shouted again. Elmer jerked his head up and stared glassy eyed at the sheriff and Pete. "Oh, sorry Sheriff, I must have dozed off there while I was waiting for ya. Sorry," Elmer said as he lurched up.

"No problem, Elma, what can ah do for ya today?" Andre drawled.

"Well," Elmer said as he stood there quickly turning his hat in his hands — as if he was way too nervous to stand still. His face was beet-red from being caught sleeping at the sheriff's desk.

"Uh, I need to talk to ya about something very important, and it should probably just be the two of us." Elmer's eyes were darting back and forth between Andre and Pete.

"It's alright, Elma, Pete here'ah is my new deputy. Anything ya say to me or Pete is strictly confidential. We cannot spread gossip or jeopardize the safety of anyone who comes to us in confidence. We have both taken the oath and cannot, by the laws of the State of Missouri, break it."

Elmer shuffled his feet around, still looking back and forth between Sheriff Andre and Deputy Pete. Andre wasn't sure if Elmer was completely convinced about Pete being his new deputy or not.

CHAPTER SIXTEEN: ELMER'S CONFESSION   191

Elmer kept right on turning his hat in his hands and looking as if, at any time, he was going to bolt for the door.

"Elma, here'ah, sit back down here'ah at my desk," Andre said as he pulled the chair further out for Elmer to sit in. "Make yourself comfortable. Let me get ya a cup of coffee and then we can all talk about whatev'ah ya have on yor'ah mind." Andre walked over to the coffee pot; hoping to make Elmer feel a little more at ease.

"As my deputy, Pete will uphold the law and be as trustworthy as Ah am. As yor'ah sheriff, Ah can guarantee that." Elmer stepped over and sat back down in the sheriff's chair. He still had his hat in his hands, but at least he had stopped turning it around and around.

"All right, Sheriff. I reckon I can trust Pete Turnkey."

"You surely can, Elmer, you surely can," Pete spoke up.

Elmer leaned forward in the sheriff's chair, picked up his coffee cup, took a long drink and spoke to them in a whisper, as if he was afraid someone outside might be listening.

"I think maybe we should shut the door Sheriff. I know it's getting a mite hot out, but what I have to tell you is for you and Pete's ears only. No one else should hear this."

"Okay," Pete said as he got up from his chair and moved the chunk of wood that was holding the door open. The door shut with a loud slam. Pete then walked over and grabbed two chairs, one for himself and one for the sheriff.

Pete and Andre sat down and looked at Elmer. "Okay," Andre said, "Start the telling."

"Well, let me tell you a tale you will both find unbelievable," Elmer said.

He took a deep breath and started in with the telling. "This here story started a long time ago. I was about fifteen years old and Miss Maude, a neighbor gal, was around sixteen or so. We both lived with our families in shacks down by the river, not too far from the very prosperous plantation of the Quinn family, down Natchez, Mississippi way. Growing up there was very little food for either of our families and our clothes were always pretty much rags. My eight brothers and sisters – and her eleven – never had shoes to wear. It didn't matter if it was winter or summer, we had no shoes. We wore hand-me-down clothes from the town church and wrapped in blankets during the cold days of winter. Both our lives were hard. After my youngest brother was born, Pa ran off and left Ma. She spent all but the last three years of her life washing clothes and selling summer vegetables to feed the nine of us.

Only when my older brothers were big enough to work did Ma get any rest; the boys made her stop working for other people and had her stay home and rest, but by that time, she was a woman much older than her years. After three years of rest, she passed away during a cold winter night. She had consumption and just couldn't fight it off.

I started working odd jobs and stealing everything I could get my hands on. It didn't matter who owned it or what it was, if something was loose and no one was looking, I figured I could sell it for money, so I took it.

One day old Mr. Henry D. Quinn or, Mr. H, as he was called, caught me stealing chickens from his plantation and twisted my ears. Then he offered me a job working for him. He was a grand old gentleman who was as honest as old Abe himself. He paid me some money and supplied me with warm clothes, socks and shoes. The Mrs. sent warm socks, coats and shoes home with me for the young'uns. Every day, Mrs. H cooked up a fine dinner for all the workers; if we had to work early, she would give us breakfast and if we were working late, she sent food home with us.

Well, about three years after I started working for Mr. H, I heard tell about Miss Maude's ma and eight of her brothers and sisters passing on from the influenza. Her pa took off with some gambling woman and left Maude and the last of her sisters to fend for themselves. Her sisters were a few years older than Miss Maude and both of them jumped right up and married two old men from town. The men were old enough to be their Granddaddy's, but the sisters knew they would have enough food to survive and a decent place to live. I guess they were only thinking about themselves since they didn't give a second thought about leaving their youngest sister alone.

So there Maude was, living by herself in that river shack with nothing to eat but the few vegetables she could scrap up from the garden or steal from other people.

Well, since I had known her since we were young'uns, I went to Mr. H and asked if there was any work Maude could do for them so she wouldn't set out there in that shack and just starve.

Well, Mr. and Mrs. H right away said that of course she could work for them, and in fact, she should come right on into the house and be a live-in companion for their daughter Birdie — since they were of the same age and all.

In the past, the Quinn's had hired on Maude's father and brothers from time to time. They had also helped Maude's family throughout the years with food and clothes and such."

Elmer leaned back and took another deep breath before he continued.

"Well, I felt mighty fine going out to that shack and telling Maude about me finding her a position with the Quinn's. I was as excited as a new born pup. But when I got to Maude's shack and knocked on the door, it was answered by this here big old burly man. He looked like a grizzly bear and smelled of sweat, whiskey and dirt. He slapped me with his huge paw of a hand and knocked me off the porch.

'Get out and stay out, boy!' he yelled at me. 'Maude is my woman and ain't no one else gonna have her.' So I picked myself up and took off running as fast as I could back to the plantation and goes right in and starts in telling the Mister what happened. Mr. H grabbed his gun and took off running toward the river, not even bothering to get himself a horse. And I was running right along behind him.

When we get to the shack we can hear Maude screaming at the man to get out of her house and leave her alone. We could hear the man laugh as he chased her around inside the shack. Things were being knocked over and it sounded as if everything in that shack was being thrown around. All of a sudden, out the front door comes Maude, running as fast as a rabbit. And right behind her was that grizzly-bear of a man.

But as soon as that giant came out the door at a full run, Mr. H stuck out his leg and trips him. He went down like a silo falling over. Well, he rolled over and looks up at Mr. H with murder in his eyes and Mr. H says, 'you make one move toward that young woman, mister, and I'll blow your head to New Orleans and feed your body to the snakes in the Mississippi and no one will ever find you. Stay down until I say you can get up. Elmer, get Maude and her things and run on back to the house, son.'

Well, I took off and did as he told me to do. We ran all the way back to the plantation without stopping. About half way there, we heard a shot. But we didn't slow down and we didn't look back.

Elmer closed his eyes as if remembering. "I can still remember that day as if it all happened this morning. Just as clear as the fine crystal bowls Mrs. H had in her parlor. Yes, sir, I'll never forget that day as long as I'm here on this here earth."

"We made it back to the plantation," Elmer continued, "and I told Mrs. H the whole story and she took Maude into the house and told me that everything would be okay and that I should go on back to work. Well, later that day I saw Mr. H walking back onto the plantation. I didn't say one thing to him because I figured it was none of my business. A few days later, Mr. H took me aside and told me not to worry about walking home after dark or coming to work before the sun came up; I didn't have to be on the lookout for the grizzly-bear of a man and that that feller would never again bother anyone. Well, I never asked him why and he never volunteered to tell me. And that was fine with me. The less I knew the less I could tell.

Well, that was the start of my knowing Maude Burbank so well. She was the companion for Miss Birdie and I was one of the farm hands. Eventually, Mr. H asked me if I would like to live on the plantation, seeing that I was there from daybreak till sundown, and sometimes later than that. Well, I right away accepted and that was the start of the many years I lived on that there beautiful plantation.

As the years went by, Miss Maude and I struck up a friendly relationship. There was nothing more to it. Only friends, mind you. After some years went by, old Mr. and Mrs. H both passed on at different times and young Mr. Henry Daniel Quinn took over the running of the plantation; with the help of his sister Birdie. By and by, young Mr. H was spending more and more time in Boston working with investors. That was where he met his pretty wife Molly. She was one fine woman. She was just as pleasant as a warm summer breeze. Miss Birdie and Miss Molly loved each other like sisters I do believe. They seemed to have the time of their lives around that big old plantation.

Mrs. Molly's family lived in Boston, so after she and Mr. H were married, she went with him every time he went east on business. After a short while, they all decided that it would be best if Mr. H and Molly just moved to Boston; seeing that Mr. H was spending more and more time there and traveling was getting difficult with their little Caitlin.

So Mr. H turned the running of the plantation over to Miss Birdie. That was what Miss Birdie always wanted and she was delighted. She begged him not to worry and assured them that she would miss them all, and that she really wanted to try her hand at running that plantation. So he made Miss Birdie the sole owner of that beautiful plantation, and he and Molly sat out to make a new life of their own.

Miss Birdie loved farming and she knew she could handle it. She was a capable owner and the working hands worked hard for her. Though the years the plantation made a great profit under Miss Birdie's guidance.

But, later on when Mr. and Mrs. H moved here to Caruthersville, she began to act a little strange. Finally one day, Maude told me that she had written Mr. H and told him about Miss Birdie's problem, and that he should not bring the children down to visit since Miss Birdie was violent at times. Mr. H came down pretty regularly to check on her, and sometimes Mrs. Molly would come with him. But mostly Mr. H came by himself. They never brought the children with them and I reckon it was because of the way Miss Birdie had changed.

I didn't see Miss Birdie much by that time, but Maude would tell me about her and how Miss Birdie wouldn't eat for days at a time and then she would start eating and wouldn't quit for a week or so. Strange things were going on and I just couldn't put my finger on it."

Elmer looked off into space as if he was in deep thought. "Just couldn't figure it out," he muttered to himself.

Andre and Pete sat there waiting with open mouths. Silence filled the room as Elmer stared past them. "Well," Elmer said, finally looked back at Andre. "I surely was befuddled by the whole thing. All those things together just kept on a'pickin' at my brain. And then the day came when the news of young Mr. and Mrs. H's passing. Miss Maude had just returned from a trip down to New Orleans for Miss Birdie and said she was told the news while waiting in Natchez for one of the farm hands to pick her up.

Miss Birdie was devastated. She took to her bed that night and that was the last I ever saw of her. The next day, Miss Maude called me into the house and told me Miss Birdie had passed on in her sleep. She said not to mention a word to any of the other farm hands and that Miss Birdie had spoken of her own passing and told Miss Maude just what she wanted to be done. Miss Birdie wanted to be buried in solitude the very next day and no one should be notified of her passing.

Now that sounded mighty strange to me since Miss Birdie had all sorts of friends in Natchez and the children here in Caruthersville. But I went along with it because it was Miss Birdie's final request."

Andre and Pete's eyes were bulged out; Andre's face was as white as snow and Pete looked as if he had seen a ghost.

"What the… Elma? What are you talking about?" Andre demanded. "You mean to tell me that the woman at the Quinn's farm isn't Birdie Quinn?"

"Now, hold on a minute Sheriff," Elmer said nervously as he stood to his feet, holding out his hands as if to defend himself. "Let me finish before you say anything."

"Okay, hurry it up, go on ahead," Andre spoke furiously.

"Well, about that time, Mr. Spivey, the Quinn's lawyer, arrived to read the will. Right off from the start, Mr. Spivey read the part about Miss Birdie's wishes to be buried the day after she passed, and then Miss Maude told me to leave. Well, I didn't leave the house. I walked on back to the back door, went out to the porch and slammed the door shut. I stomped around on the porch and down the steps for a bit before taking my boots off and creeping back into the house real quiet like and stood right next to the parlor door so I could hear what Mr. Spivey had to say to Miss Maude.

And this is exactly what the lawyer said. "If Miss Birdie passed on before young Mr. H, the plantation and everything with it would go to Mr. H, Molly and their children. But if Mr. H passed on first, it was to go to Mrs. H and her children. If both of them passed on, it would go to the children, Caitlin, Lily-Beth, Benjamin and Tessa Quinn.

But, this is the interesting part. If the children of Mr. and Mrs. Quinn were no longer alive, the entire plantation and everything in it would be sold and the money divided evenly between Mr. Spivey, Miss Maude and me. After the lawyer said that, both their voices got too low for me to understand.

Now sheriff," Elmer held up his hands again, "I never once thought a thing about getting any part of that plantation since I knew those children were all still alive. Well, after hearing those words, I snuck on out of there and sat down on the back porch steps as if I had been there all along. After a few minutes, I heard old Mr. Spivey leave by the front door and saw his buggy drive on down the way.

Well, about ten minutes go by and Miss Maude walks on out the back door and asks me to come on back into the parlor." Elmer hesitated and looked down and started twisting his hat around once again.

"Then she up and tells me the strangest thing ever." Elmer just sat there looking at Sheriff Andre and Pete.

Andre and Pete sat there looking at Elmer with anticipation.

"Well..." they both leaned forward and spoke at the same time. "What was it?"

"Well, it was a piece of paper. She wouldn't let me see it, but she acted like she was reading it. The paper was hand-written by Miss Birdie right before she passed on, or so Maude said, and in it Miss Birdie told Miss Maude that she wanted her to dress up as if she was Miss Birdie, go on up to Caruthersville and act like she was Miss Birdie. She was to take care of the Quinn children and be their mother. The letter went on and on about how Miss Maude was not to tell a living soul about the arrangement and Miss Birdie wanted Maude to talk me into joining her in this falsehood; seeing that it would be the best thing for the children with their ma and pa being gone and all. And we were to tell all the farm hands that Miss Birdie left the plantation during the night for New Orleans to catch a ship leaving for England because of the heavy heartache she was suffering from the loss of her brother.

Well, to tell you the truth, I didn't rightly know what to say. But, if Miss Birdie wanted it that way, I sure enough was going to go along with it. Miss Birdie always treated me with respect and kindness for as long as I had known her. There was no way I was going to deny her a death-bed wish.

So I packed up my things and when Miss Maude was ready to leave, so was I. I didn't question her at all, and I was ready and willing to do what Miss Birdie asked me to do."

Sheriff Andre and Deputy Pete just sat there waiting for Elmer to continue. When he didn't, Andre spoke up with an "and?"

"And here we are." Elmer replied.

"Is that it?" Andre asked.

"No, there's more."

Andre looked at him intensely. "What's the rest of it, my good man?"

CHAPTER SIXTEEN: ELMER'S CONFESSION

"Out with it Elmer, don't just stop talking, keep on going!" Pete broke in.

"I will, I will. Just hold on there, Deputy Pete."

"I'm a holding on so tight my fingers are hurting. So I suggest you start in talking right now," Pete responded sharply.

"Well, After me and Miss Maude arrived here in Caruthersville, I took a boat back down to Natchez to pick up a few things for Miss Maude, and while I was there, I heard about the death of Mr. Spivey. He was found dead in his study. He had been hit on the head with a heavy object. The authorities thought it was a surprise attack, since he was found sitting at his desk and he had been hit in the back of the head. The last I heard, no suspect has been found."

Elmer leaned forward and once again dropped his voice. "That there happening just kind of picked at my brain too."

He leaned back in his chair and continued. "I didn't start putting it all together like a young'un's puzzle until last night. And this here puzzle is much bigger than a young'un's puzzle."

Elmer stopped and loudly cleared his throat. "There I was sittin' at the kitchen table drinking coffee and just a wondering where Miss Maude had been for the last few days, and I see a box on the sidebar with the lid half open. Well, I get myself up and goes over to have a look-see. Mostly because I was just bored and kind of being nosey. Well, lo-and-behold, it's some of Miss Maude's paperwork and her diary.

Now Sheriff, I know it ain't rightly polite to read someone else's personal property, but I just couldn't help it. That diary just seemed to jump right into my hands and begged me to read it. So I did!"

Elmer once again stopped talking and stared at Andre and Pete. His hands were twirling his hat faster and faster and his foot was tapping the floor in rhythm with his twirling hat.

"And what did this diary say, Elma?" Andre sounded impatient.

Elmer sat there a few more seconds, just staring, twirling his hat and tapping his foot. Then he started rocking back and forth in his chair.

"Elmer!" Pete shouted, "Sit still, stop fidgeting and finish telling us about this dang diary. You're making me jumpy as a polecat with all the moving, foot tapping and the twirling of that damn hat."

Elmer stopped and looked at Pete as if he had just noticed him being there. He had a surprised look on his face at Pete's loud demands.

"Well fellas," Elmer finally said with a long slow sigh.

"It was for sure her diary. A diary of all the evils she has done during her many years at the Quinn plantation, including the time we have been here in Caruthersville. It has names, dates and each and every little thing she schemed. She wrote down which acts were completed and which acts were not. If something was not completed, she wrote down the reason why."

"Where'ah is this diary, Elma?"

"We need to see it, Elmer. It will just be your word against hers if you don't actually have the diary. We can't prove anything without it."

"Elma, I hope ya didn't put that diary back into that there'ah box of hers, did ya?"

"No, it's hidden. It's hidden in a place where no one will ever find it."

"And where'ah might that be, Elma?"

"Right here in this room, Sheriff."

With a frown on his face, Andre looked at Emer. "Here?"

"Right here, Sheriff, right here under the floorboards of your desk."

"How did ya get it in there'ah, Elma?"

"When I first came in and found you gone, I couldn't risk sitting here holding it. Someone else might have walked in and seen it, so I pulled up a board and stuck it down there and stomped on the nails to push the boards back down. It's safe and sound. Ain't anybody going to come in here and pull up the floorboards of a sheriff's office, now are they?"

"Well, I don't suppose so. Get on up from there'ah, Elma. Let's get it out and read it. Come on, what are ya waiting for?"

"Well, sheriff, let me just say this here one thing before you start in a'reading it. I'm not defending Miss Maude in her actions. But — she is not quite right in the head. She has done some terrible, dreadful things, but I think over the years she has lost her mind. Not one civilized proper woman I know could ever do the things she has done."

Elmer stood up and moved back from the desk as he pushed the chair out of the way and began to stomp the heel of his boot on one end of a board.

"Come on, Pete; help me get this here board up."

"Move on over Elmer, and let me get a hammer."

Pete walked to the back of the jail and returned with a hammer and began pounding on the end of the board until the opposite end of the board popped up.

Elmer reached down and pulled it the rest of the way up. Both Andre and Pete squatted there, staring as if they had never seen a book before.

"Well, pick it up Sheriff," Elmer spoke softly with a tremor of excitement in his voice. "You will not believe what is in it. You just won't believe it," he exclaimed.

Gingerly Andre picked up the book and walked back over to his chair. The book was quite thick, and some of the pages were tattered. He could tell that some of the last pages had not been used.

"Now sheriff, you may not be able to read the words real well; Miss Maude was taught to read and write by Miss Birdie, and I remember her whining about not needing to know how to read and write since she would never use it. She said it was a great waste of Miss Birdie's and my time. Miss Birdie also taught me to read and write, so I can read it pretty easily; seeing that I was the one who nagged at Maude to spell words for me, she never did take to it much. She can write some words, but she is a mighty poor speller. It isn't that she wasn't smart enough. She just didn't want to bother. But, go on ahead and start in reading. It will surprise you, it surely will."

Andre opened the book and started reading quietly so Pete could hear but no one walking by could.

May — I will kil her. I hate hre. I put som posin in hre watr. It wil kil hre lic it kilt Josie. She is a bad grl. jest lic Josie and Salie. Al she wants to do is lok at mi mr H. he is mi man. I wil hav hem an no bode else wil.

"Josie and Sally were two other house servants who worked in the house with Miss Maude," Elmer said. "They were both married and their husbands worked in the fields, but Miss Maude thought they were in love with Mr. H. I remember when Sally died. Everyone thought she died of consumption. She just kept on getting sicker and sicker. And the next year the same thing happened to Josie. Everyone was in a panic about it. They were worried it was some sort of influenza and we would all die.

Miss Birdie finally had the doc come out, and when she had gathered all the workers on the lawn, the doc told us that both women died of consumption and it could not be passed on to another person. He didn't know why both women had taken it on, but it must have been something they were both doing.

Now the woman she is talking about here is Anna Wallace," Elmer pointed out. "Anna was a friend of Miss Birdie's, and quite often she would come over and visit Miss Birdie and young Mr. H. They had known each other since they were all young'uns, seeing that Anna's family had a plantation not too far from the Quinn's. Luckily, Anna was not in love with Mr. H. She up and married a man from back east and moved to New York City. But when Anna would come to visit, Miss Maude would get all upset like and come out to the stable and go on and on about how she hated Miss Anna and she wished she would just up and die."

"I never thought she really meant it. I figured she was just talking the talk of a woman in love. I knew she was in love with young Mr. H, but not one time did I think it was something that would stay in her head and eat her soul," Elmer said.

Andre looked back down at the book and read the next entry.

May — That ugle Anna is gon. I em hapy. I did not want 2 kil hre but I wil if I can. She wantd mr H and that can not b.

Andre looked up at Elmer and spoke in a steely voice. "Elma, does this tell anythin about the disappearance of Caitlin Quinn?"

"Yes sir, it does."

"And just where'ah does it start in telling about that?"

"Turn to the last pages with writing, sir. Here, let me show you." Andre handed Elmer the diary.

"Right here, Sheriff. Start in reading right here on this page and it will tell you everything you want to know. But if you start out on back a couple pages, you will find out how Miss Birdie passed on and how young Mr. and Mrs. H died in that carriage accident."

Andrea looked up at Elmer again and frowned. He flipped to the back of the book and Elmer showed him where to start reading.

Febary- I did it! That terbel Molly is gone. But I lost mi tru love. He wood not com to me becas of that woman so he had to be takn out of mi lif. Ha! It wer so eze! No body wil evr gess I did it. Cutin that carage strap was eze! Ha! Ha! Now al I hav to do is get rid of Mis Birdie. I don't want to but I hav to. Notin can stop me now! I will use the same poton I usd with Jose and Salle.

Febary- I did it again! I kilt Miss Birdie. It wer not so bad. She died real quik like. Now I will go and kill thos off spring of mi man and that woman. It will be eze. I can do anything I want now. I wil tak this big plantaton and it wil be al mine. I wil kill Mr Spivey and Elmer. Ha! And I will get rid of them brats.

March- Mr. Spivey was eze. All I did was walk around behin him and hit him in the head. They will nevr find out. All anyone saw was a old man workin in Mr. Spiveys garden and Mr Spivey givin him a drenk of watr and the old man takin the cup bac in to the hous.

May- That Caitlin is goin to be gon in a few days. She is out at the farm with the stuped men. We wil sel her down in new Orlins as soon as we can.

May- Those brats ran a way. Oh wil it is ok. I hav alreade maid a lot of money sellin small childrin down the rivir. I wil get them brats bac and whin I do I wil sel them to.

I AM AMOST DONE!!!!!

May — Al I hav to do now is kil Elmer and get rid of thos brats! Kilin Elmer wil be eze. I wil jest posin him lic I did most of the othrs!

Andre and Pete looked back up at Elmer with disbelief. "She is one loco woman, Elmer," Pete said in a whisper. "You best be real careful until we find her."

"Oh, I will Deputy, I will. I'm not going back out to the farm until she is caught. At which time I will stay and help those young'uns until they tell me to leave. I've known that lil' Miss Caitlin since the day she was born. Mighty fine young woman is all I have to say about her. But for now, I'm staying right here in town. I can bed down over at the livery with the horses, they suit me just fine. I'm not rightly ready to meet my maker yet. I've got a lot of living to do before I check in."

"When was the last time you saw Miss Bir – ah, Maude?" Pete asked.

"A few days ago when she high-tailed it out from the farm in the carriage. She had me hitch up Caitlin's horse and off she went, likity-split. She hasn't been back since. I'm thinking she's out at the farm she mentioned. I have no idea what farm that might be. It's pretty unusual. She seldom leaves the house overnight. And if she does, she always tells me what time she will be back so I can be there to help her with the unhitching. She has been gone overnight before, but it's always out to some farm to take care of the sick. At least that's what she tells me.

She took off and left a few days after Miss Caitlin disappeared and I haven't seen her since. And I haven't heard a word from her since she left, either. Sometimes she will send in some farm hand to tell me to be at the farm at a certain time to help her.

Sheriff, I really don't know if she had anything to do with Miss Caitlin's disappearance, but now that I read this here diary of hers, I'm thinking mighty powerfully that Miss Maude had her taken."

Andre and Pete looked at each other as they stood up; Pete turned

CHAPTER SIXTEEN: ELMER'S CONFESSION

to Elmer and said, "Elmer, let's go find that gal before Miss Bir – Maude does something to her."

SLAM!

The door to the sheriff's office flew open, and in rushed Lily, Benny and the mountain man Mr. Bushman.

"Sheriff," Lily yelled. "Michael Thorne himself came to me last night as I was sleeping, and told me straight out that Caitlin is trying to make it home! We have to go RIGHT NOW and help her. Michael and that little gal Hannah came to me and told me she is out at that abandoned farm called Yoder's Place and she is trying to get home. Come on, come on let's go!"

CHAPTER SEVENTEEN

Home at Last

IN THE WILDERNESS, there is a window of time just before dawn when darkness is fleeing from the light of a new day and the day is just starting to open its eyes in the east. In the dense wilderness of all countries, that time span is often called a void of silence. Darkness is rapidly running to the west on its continuous flight from the sun, leaving only a few wispy tendrils of darkness scattered among the forest trees.

Before dawn makes her appearance, darkness feels her coming and starts to thin as it pulls its body from the light. Eventually, the only sign of night is its wispy tail as it is slowly dragged towards the west and then dawn slips her fingers into the forest and flicks away those last remaining wispy tendrils of night and replace them with her soothing warm smile.

At first, the thinning of the darkness is not visible to the human eye, but the animals of the night feel the air thinning and quietly start making their own rapid departure before the creatures of the day start their morning hunt.

So coins the phrase "void of silence". For neither night creatures nor day creatures are on the hunt.

And so, this was the hour in which Caitlin awoke from her deep sleep in the little shack in the wilderness.

She lay there listening to the silence as thoughts of the previous night played in her mind. The appearance of Michael and the little girl had been alarming. Now her heart felt crushed – she realized that the possibility of Michael returning, after all these years, was gone. The slight chance of him showing up alive was forever swept from her heart.

As she looked around the tiny little shack, she knew she had to get up, get back to town and wipe the past from her mind as she turned to the future.

Thump, thump. Caitlin heard Tabby bumping against the wall of the lean-to. "Okay, Tabby girl," Caitlin called out to the horse. "I'm coming, hold on a minute."

She pushed herself up from the floor and walked over to the door leading into the lean-to. As she pushing the door open, Tabby pushed her way through and headed for the outside door before Caitlin could get the lean-to door closed.

"Whoa, you must be hungry!" Caitlin laughed as she opened the door and let Tabby out. "There you go. Find your breakfast."

Caitlin went back inside and dug through the bag Katie Levi had packed for her. Inside she found more food. There was also a little milk left from the night before, along with plenty of leftovers, including biscuits and ham from the farmhouse. After eating, she packed up her meager belongings and sat them on the porch. She sat down on the front step trying to figure out how she could get into town without being seen or caught by Aunt Birdie and her band-o-rats.

Finally, Caitlin closed the front door of the shack and picked up her bag of belongings and slid the bridle over Tabby's head.

"Let's go girl," she spoke softly to her horse. "Let's go home." Caitlin led Tabby over to the porch and pulled herself onto Tabby's back.

Slowly they walked toward the road leading into town.

The sun was not fully up yet, and the tall meadow grasses were still covered with dew. It brushed her legs as they pushed through it, leaving the hem of her skirt wet and heavy. But Caitlin knew it would dry in no time at all once the morning sun came up.

They started out in a slow walk as Caitlin enjoyed the early morning. Gentle dove coos came from the forest and she watched as soft fingers of the early morning sun reached through the forest and caressed each tree with its warm embrace. The heady smell of wild flowers and sage began to softly drift up to her as the morning sun warmed the forest. Caitlin figured she had about four or five miles to go before she would reach town. She nudged Tabby into a gallop. Maybe she would make it into town without running into anyone else.

As she rode along the road, she looked down and noticed there were a lot of hoof prints on the road, so she pulled back on Tabby to get a closer look. It looked as if a lot of horses had traveled this road in the early morning hours. The prints were fresh and the grass was still pressed into the dirt. They were all going in the direction of the abandoned farmhouse.

All she could think about was that Aunt Birdie and those men must now have available horses. She and Tabby would have to make these last few miles in a hurry. Maybe they were already on their way back to town the same as she was. There was no way she was going to let them catch her and take her back to that farmhouse or the train.

Once again she gave Tabby a sharp nudge to get her going, and off they went in a full run. Every so often she would turn around and check the road behind her, but no one was in sight.

Quickly she and Tabby covered they ground as Tabby stayed in a full run. As they approached the outskirts of town, farms started to appear more frequently. Some of the farm families were up doing early morning chores and they stopped to wave at her. Others just looked at her as if wondering what she was doing out this far from town so early in the morning.

CHAPTER SEVENTEEN: HOME AT LAST

She and Tabby were approximately a mile or so from town when she saw them. They looked to be about a mile behind her, but they were quickly closing the gap. It looked as if Aunt Birdie was riding astride with every one of her men right beside her and Aunt Birdie was having no trouble staying on her horse.

"When did she learn to ride astride?" Caitlin wondered to herself as she turned around and gave Tabby a sharp nudge with her heels. "Come on, Tabby-girl!" she yelled out. "Let's get going!"

Caitlin knew if any of the men, or Aunt Birdie, had found and were now riding that big black horse, she and Tabby were goners. There was no way Tabby could out-run that horse. Tabby took off like a shot with Caitlin lying flat against her back. Caitlin hung on for dear life as she said all the prayers she had ever learned.

Suddenly she felt Tabby slowing down. "Land-o-Goshen," Caitlin said loudly. "What's wrong, girl?" Looking down, she noticed Tabby had lost a shoe and must have picked up a stone along the road.

Nervously, Caitlin looked back; her pursuers were still closing the gap. Panic took over as she tried to urge Tabby forward. The poor horse couldn't do it but Caitlin had not come this far just to be taken again!

From the side of the road came the sound of a large animal crashing through the brush. Out onto the road, right in front of her, burst the big black horse. The smaller black horse was right behind him. Slowly the horse walked over to Tabby and nudged Caitlin on the shoulder. It was as if the two black horses were intentionally there to help them.

"Alright boy," Caitlin whispered. "Come on over here and let me slide onto your back."

As if he understood what she had said, he walked over and stood alongside Tabby. Caitlin reached over and held onto his long beautiful mane and slid her body onto his back. "This is one giant horse," Caitlin said to herself. "Come on boy, let's get going!"

Just before the big black horse took off, she turned to look back. Aunt Birdie and her men was less than a half mile behind her. They were all yelling and a couple of them had their guns drawn. Caitlin gave the horse a nudge, and off he went in a flash. Leaning down, she buried her face in his mane and hung on. When she dared to look back, Tabby and the smaller black horse was nowhere to be seen and the big horse was pulling away from Aunt Birdie. But they continued to chase her.

"Let them come," she thought to herself. "That way, maybe they will be caught by the sheriff."

After a few seconds, she sat up a bit to see if she could tell how far they had to go to get into town. They were going to make it. There was only one more decision to make: should she go to the train depot and get Pete Turnkey, or should she just go to the sheriff's office and hope he's there?

Both places were on the other end of town so she guessed it wouldn't make a difference which one she ended up at, as long as she found help. By now, Caitlin and the big horse were in town and the sheriff's office was within sight.

The sheriff was just walking out the door of his office, followed by Lily, Benny, Pete, Elmer and Mr. Bushy. They all stopped and stood in front of the office as if discussing something.

Caitlin started to cry as she realized she was going to make it. Tears were streaming down her face as she yelled out Benny and Lily's names.

They all turned and stared at her until Lily and Benny took off running towards her. The sheriff, Pete, Elmer and Mr. Bushy stood there a few more seconds and then they also started running towards her.

All of a sudden, a loud whistle rent the air and her horse came to an instant stop. With that, Caitlin felt herself leaving the back of the big horse. In her mind's eye, she was moving in slow motion. Slowly her arms went out from her sides and her legs were being pulled straight out behind her. Leisurely, her whole body seemed to flip over and she could see the beautiful, blue morning sky. "What a pretty blue," she thought to herself.

There were white clouds floating against the robin's-egg blue sky, and small black birds were flying above the tree tops. In the distance she heard the familiar cooing of a Morning Dove. Once again, her body slowly flipped over and she could see the ground coming into view as she softly floated down. At least it felt like she was floating.

With a force she had never felt before, her body slammed into the ground and everything went black.

"Caitlin... Caitlin." Someone was shaking her. "Oh, don't shake me," she moaned. It felt as if every bone under her skin was shattered. It hurt to breathe, it hurt to move; it even hurt to think.

"Can ya open yor'ah eyes, Caitlin?" She forced her eyes open. She was staring into the beautiful black eyes of Sheriff Beaumont.

"Yes," she said, as she smiled up at him. "I can open my eyes.

"Good," said Sheriff Beaumont, with a smile", "I was thinking I would nev'ah be able to have ya sit on my desk."

Coming in 2015

Lily and the Ghost of Tillie Brown

CHAPTER ONE

IT WAS HOT! Just plain old sweltering southern Missouri hot. Lily's pillow was hot, her sheet was hot — even the breeze coming through the window was hot! It was so hot Lily's hair stuck to the back of her neck and the sides of her face. Sweat was seeping out of her body like a sieve; or so she imagined. She was quite sure even the bottoms of her feet were dripping moisture. Droplets of water from her head ran down behind her ears and soaked into the neckline of her nightshirt. The air was steamy and humid which in turn made it hard to breathe and the little bit of breeze coming through the window offered no relief.

Lily pushed herself up and leaned against the bedframe as she listened to the sound of a mosquito buzzing around her head. Finally she realized dampness was everywhere and the only way to get away from it was to climb out her window and go jump in the horse trough out between the house and the barn.

"Why are mosquitos so hard to slap when they are buzzing around my head?" Lily thought as she slapped wildly at a mosquito.

The mosquito had somehow managed to get through the new metal screen her brother-in-law, Andre, had just put across her bedroom window.

She was getting grumpier by the minute and was actually moving off the bed to go jump into the horse trough when…

Tap, tap, tap

"Lily"

Tap, tap, tap

"Lily…wake up, Lily!"

Lily's best friend, Ophelia, whisper/yelled through Lily's open window.

Lily's eyes darted to her window. The sky was crystal clear and the moon was full and bright as it illuminated the whole yard and its surroundings. Since the moon was behind Ophelia, her facial features were totally blocked out but Lily recognized her voice.

"Ophelia, not so loud, you're going to wake up the whole house." Lily whispered, "Pull the screen towards you and come on in through the window.

Ophelia pushed herself up and over the window sill: leaned into the room, fell through the window and landed on the floor with a loud "thud". Immediately she jumped right up, rubbed her backside and scrambled onto Lily's bed.

"We have to be very, very quiet" Ophelia nervously whispered to Lily. There was a long pause and then Ophelia leaned very close to Lily's ear and whispered: "I found a dead body! It's out in the woods between the levee and the river and…there is a great big dead parrot sitting right on top of the dead body!" Ophelia sat back and looked at Lily with wide eyes as she put a hand over her mouth; as if she had said something unspeakable

"Well," Ophelia continued, "the parrot was sitting on top of the body but now it's beside the dead body because I knocked it off when I stumbled over it. It's just lying there on its back with its bright orange feet sticking straight up in the air. Its wings are spread out like two big blue fans and it has a little crawfish net on its head like a hat. Its bright yellow beak is open and it's little round tongue is hanging out. That's all I saw before I took off running."

"That bird and that person are both dead, I tell ya. Just as dead as a body can get!" Ophelia was getting more frantic as each second passed. She jumped off Lily's bed and started pacing around the room. Suddenly she stopped and turned towards Lily as she said, "When I stumbled over them neither one of them moaned nor groaned or anything. They are dead for sure, and I've seen a lot of dead people so I should know."

Lily sat there with her mouth hanging open as she stared at Ophelia. Never before had Lily heard of a dead body being dumped in the woods between the levee and the river.

Ophelia continued talking without waiting for a comment from Lily, "I was on my way out to the river-bottom pond to cool off; since it was so hot and all in my bedroom, and when I got a short ways down the path, leading through the woods, I decided to take a short cut and just as I stepped off the path – BAM! THERE IT WAS! I stumbled right over that dead person and knocked that big ol' dead parrot right offa the top of that body. I purt near landed smack on top of them! At first I thought that parrot was still alive, since it had been sittin' up real straight-like on top of that body, but it was dead… just like that body! They are totally dead! There is no question about it. That person and that parrot are as dead as my pappy's old horse Penelope! But…I didn't even take a gander to see who the person was; I just jumped right up, without giving it a quick look-see, and took off running for your house! My skin was crawling right offa my bones I tell ya! I could feel their haints chasing me. It was like they were breathing down the neck of my nightshirt and, I tell ya, I really could feel their cold clammy hands getting closer and closer to the back of my neck. It was if they were just about to grab me. Every few seconds I could feel the cold breeze as their hands took a swipe at me, but I was runnin' just too fast for them to catch me. I kept on shaking my arms and rubbing the back of my neck to keep them from snatchin' me right up and taking me into the spirit world. I never ran so fast in my life. Gives me the willies, is what it does." Ophelia was talking fast and wringing her hands. "When I got to your window, I kept on looking back but I didn't see them so I must have gotten away in the nick of time."

Once again she stopped pacing but kept right on shaking her hands and wiping at her arms.

"I can't seem to get the feel of that dead bird off me!" she whispered loudly.

Ophelia's real name is Ophelia Corina Willamena Knudsen. When Ophelia was born her parents wanted to include the names of every important female member of their family. So, the name Ophelia comes from her Great-Great-Grandmother, Corina is her mother's name and Willamena is the name of her mother's great Aunt Willamena who, at the grand age of 90, still lives on Sugar Cane Island off the coast of South Carolina where she had once been an indentured servant and who, at one time, had been imprisoned for spitting on a military officer after he voiced his crude opinion about her mistress. Her mistress, Ms. Opal Ray, then proceeded to bribe the jailor and was able to convince him to release young Willamena into her care and after a lengthy lecture, the jailor reluctantly released Willamena into Ms. Opal's care along with a long written list of how Ms. Opal should control her servants. The list was pinned to Willamena's dress so as to make sure Ms. Opal would read it. Well, Ms. Opal never did beat any of her servants, as the jailor had instructed her to do. In fact, when Willamena turned eighteen Ms. Opal Ray, as a gift and "to show that haughty military officer and the ignorant jailor" (as Ms. Opal Ray put it), gave Willamena papers releasing her from her indentured servitude and made Willamena an official member of her paid staff. Ms. Opal also built Willamena a fine little house and deeded the land to her. When Ms. Opal passed on, she left Willamena a large sum of money. Local gossip amongst the servants and towns people always said that Willamena was really Ms. Opal's granddaughter; seeing that while Willamena was supposedly an indentured servant, she had no duties and never had a want for anything. But, not one person knows for certain, except for Willamena herself and she has never said yes or no to all the gossip.

Ophelia's last name, Knudsen was passed down from her Great-Great-Grandfather, Jansen George Knudsen, who, when he was a young boy had lived in Holland and was also an indentured servant for a family called Wijhe-Knudsen. When the Wijhe-Knudsens traveled from Holland to America to become Americans citizens, they brought Jansen George along and soon after their arrival in New York City; the Wijhe-Knudsens made Jansen George a free man by releasing him from his servitude. In honor of the family he had grown to love dearly, Jansen George took a part of their last name as his own. As a freed man, Jansen George traveled across America enjoying the sights and going-ons of his new country. When Jansen George arrived in Missouri he met and fell in love with Ophelia Belle Bogarie. The two of them married and settled in the Missouri Ozark mountain wilderness where they raised their fifteen children.

Ophelia's family now lives in the small settlement of Pinecone, MO, which was only about a half mile from Lily's house and Ophelia and Lily have been best friends since the very first day they met.

Ophelia is a year younger than Lily but she is a head taller. Her hair is white-blonde and her eyes are the same color as Tessa's eyes (Lily's little sister) are. Sometimes their eyes look like the lily pads in the pond behind Granny Tomason's house and other times they look like the moss growing on the trunk of a tree. Ophelia's legs are long and thin and she can "run like a deer" as Ophelia's mama always said. Ophelia can beat Lily in a foot race without even trying. In fact, Lily was quite positive Ophelia was the fastest runner in Caruthersville; and most people seemed to agree.

Lily lived with her oldest sister, Caitlin, Caitlin's husband Sheriff Andre Beaumont, her brother Benny and her little sister Tessa. Not too many months back, Caitlin had been kidnapped by their alleged Aunt Birdie who had planned on selling Caitlin down the river to New Orleans where she would be sold into the underground slave market.

Fortunately, Caitlin had escaped from the old abandoned farm house where she was being held captive and managed to make it back to Caruthersville with Aunt Birdie and her river rats in hot pursuit.

And, come to find out, Aunt Birdie wasn't their real Aunt Birdie after all. Her name had been Maude Burbank and she had killed their real Aunt Birdie along with Lily's parents and a few other people.

Sheriff Beaumont, who was now Lily's brother-in-law, had put Maude and her band of rats in the Caruthersville jail to wait until a judge could make it into town but Maude died from unknown causes while waiting for her trial to begin; or so Doc Pfeiffer said. There were a few questionable stories about Maude's death, but no one bothered to look into them. The band of rats, and all the others involved, had been sentenced to life in prison for their evil doings.

"You sure you want to go see it, Lily?" Ophelia whispered. "It's pretty scary, I tell you!"

"Yes, I want to see it," Lily quickly replied; as she jumped up to get dressed, "there's no doubt about it, I want to see it tonight!"

After hastily putting on her clothes and shoes, Lily whispered. "Ok, I'm ready; let's go see that dead body. Did you bring a lantern?"

"Yes." Ophelia replied wearily, "Its right outside the window. But maybe we should wake up Sheriff Beaumont and let him take care of it. That's what sheriffs do."

Lily looked at Ophelia with astonishment, "No way am I going to let Andre Beaumont take away that dead body before I get to see it. He'll make us stay right here in this room and then he'll wake Benny up to go help him cart it back to town! Nope, that is not going to happen. You ready to go?"

"Well," Ophelia sighed, "I guess I am...let's go and get this over with. But, I'm telling you, if a haint tries to snatch us, I'm out of there and even though you are my best friend, I will leave you behind."

"Okay," Lily nodded, "that's a fair bargain."

Lily and Ophelia climbed out the bedroom window and pushed the screen back into place; Lily sure didn't want more bugs getting into her room.

Since Lily's bedroom was the only bedroom on the first floor, it was easy for them to get outside without being heard.

The sky was still clear as they took off running towards the levee. The brightness of the full moon distorted and lengthened the shadows of the buildings and trees and both girls kept a keen eye on the buildings and trees as they watched for strange movements. There was a feeling of a disturbance in the air, as if something was amiss.

Lily pushed the feeling of unease out of her mind and made herself keep on running towards the levee.

It didn't take the girls long to reach the top of the levee where they stopped and looked towards the river. Most of the trees were too tall to see over, but through the open spaces they could see the river and the campfires burning along the edge of the river bank.

With the night being so sultry hot, critter noise along the levee was louder than usual; even the critters were complaining about the heat. Cicadas were buzzing loudly; bullfrogs and crickets were singing and the hoot owls were calling loudly to their mates. Off in the distance, on the other side of the woods; next to the riverbank, fires were burning brightly as small boats and rafts pulled up onto the shore for the night and built their fires high so they would smolder throughout the night in hopes that the smoke would chase the mosquitoes away.

Further out on the Mississippi River, four large steam-wheelers were anchored. Their lighted decks and windows created beautiful sparkling reflections on the face of the glassy river.

As Lily looked towards the tree line, fear started creeping up her body and into her throat. She kept swallowing in an attempt to push the fear down and calm her nerves.

Both girls continued to silently stand there, all the time staring at the land between the levee and the Mississippi river.

"We have to go see it now before someone else gets to it and maybe moves it. It's pretty scary I tell ya." Ophelia said again. "I don't know about you, but I don't like haints and I'm a'thinking that this person's haint is still hanging around; just waiting for the killer to come back so they can spook 'em."

"Yeah", Lily slowly whispered, keeping her voice low so it wouldn't carry across the forest and attract any stray haints that might be aimlessly floating about. "I hear-tell that sort of thing will happen every time a body passes-on but doesn't get a proper burial and all. They say those haints are floating around about all the time but we just can't be seeing 'em unless they want us to. One time I overheard two church-going ladies saying that haints are watching us all the time and are just waitin' around for a chance to spook us. Those ladies said that it's the law of heaven and earth that haints can't spook us unless we are doing something bad. Like robbing, stealing or killing, and then they can spook us as much as they want. But, if we are doing something good, like burying a body, they won't spook us. So you're probably right, Ophelia. I'm quite sure the haint is still hanging around, but if we go do them a good deed, I don't think they will spook us, and I'm thinking maybe it's our duty as good neighbors and all, to go make sure the body has a proper burial and such. That must be the reason why you couldn't sleep and wanted to go out to the pond. When you showed up at my window, I was just fixin' to go jump in the horse trough and cool off."

"Wellllll…I reckon that's true." Ophelia slowly whispered, "I suppose it is our duty, as good neighbors and all, but I would rather poke a fork in my eye than touch a dead body — so I'm not touching it! And, I sure do hope the good Lord gives us a lot of credit for doing this here good deed. I don't like it one little bit!"

Lily nodded in agreement. Even though they could see the familiar well-worn path leading down the levee and into the trees; they just kept right on standing there staring at the tree line.

"A whole lot of people use this path every day." Lily mumbled to Ophelia, "I'm kind of surprised the body was dumped so close to the path. So, I'm thinking it must have happened after dark."

"I reckon so." Ophelia groaned.

The trees between the levee and the river were thick with underbrush. Spring flooding encouraged small scrub-brush to grow thick in the woods; which in turn made it difficult to maneuver around the trees. There were mud bogs and sink holes everywhere amongst the trees in the river bottom —or the shoot, as it was locally called. It was called the "shoot" because during spring flooding, water rushing down from the north filled the Mississippi to its breaking point and it would overflow onto any low-laying path it could find, and since the land between the levee and the edge of the river was so low the river would shoot onto the lowland and then make a big swiping curve back into the main river where it would shoot down into the Gulf of Mexico.

Lily leaned close to Ophelia's ear and in a squeaky little voice whispered, "Well, let's go and have a look-see. Ya ready?"

Ophelia nervously looked at Lily and whispered, "I reckon so, if we have to. Should we light the lantern now or should we wait until we get to the tree line, what do you think Lily?"

"Well, let's wait until we get off the top of the levee and a little closer to the woods." Lily said, "We don't want any of those folks over on the river bank to come snooping around trying to find out what the light is, do we?"

"Right," Ophelia said as she nodded her head, "that's a good idea"

Lily took a deep breath and Ophelia shuddered.

After a couple false starts, they worked up their courage and started shuffling down the path. Just as they did, Lily caught a glimpse of two big lanterns being carried into the trees from the river side of the woods. Even though the river side of the woods was more than a half mile away, in the bright moonlight Lily was able to make out the shapes of what looked like two big men.

"Wait" Lily stopped and whispered to Ophelia, "look over there," Lily pointed in the direction of the river, "Someone else is going into the trees! Let's get on down to the tree line and see if we can tell where they're going."

"Land o' Goshen!" Ophelia muttered frantically, "Let's hurry before they catch sight of us."

As fast as they could run — without falling down the side of the levee — the girls made it down to the mouth of the path and stood behind one of the larger trees.

The woods down on the river bottom were always sinister. Tangled trees and brush grew in abundance on most of the land. Vegetation and dead fish from the run-off of flooding made the soil of the river bottom extremely fertile. Seeds from every kind of plant growing along the Mississippi was carried downriver and deposited in the river bottom soil. Folks would plant their crops in the fertile land every year, hoping it would not flood. Most years the crops grew in abundance, but then there were some years when the floods came and farmers lost everything to the rushing water as it carved through the shoot and washed all their efforts and hard work further down the Mississippi.

A couple hours before Lily and Ophelia got to the top of the levee; the fog from the river had rolled into the woods and was now hanging in misty clumps from the branches and vines. Half broken tree limbs made a canopy over the path leading through the woods. During the day, it kept out the heat along with the any sunlight. Some of the trees in the distance were so thickly covered by the fog only an outline of their shape was visible.

Peeking around the trees they were hiding behind, Lily and Ophelia tried to see the lights from the lanterns coming from the river side of the woods. Nothing was shining through the trees so the men with the lanterns must not be on their way to the dead body.

As Lily and Ophelia walked a little further into the woods, they realized the forest had taken on an eerie silence of fear and sadness. Goose bumps popped up on Lily's arms and legs and the back of her neck was tingling.

After going about twenty feet into the woods Ophelia stopped and whispered; "I think this is the spot".

Lily stopped and both of them looked off to the side of the path.

"Do you see any other lanterns coming?" Ophelia whispered.

Lily squinted her eyes as she strained to see any light coming through the woods.

"Nope, not yet," Lily said, "let's light our lantern."

Squatting down, Ophelia lifted the lantern globe as Lily reached into her own pocket and pulled out a match. Bending over, Lily used the side of the lantern to strike the match, and then she lit the wick. Carefully Ophelia replaced the globe and they both stood up.

Slowly, Ophelia took a step off the main path with Lily following close behind her. Suddenly Ophelia stopped and Lily bumped into her.

"Don't push me, Lily" Ophelia said in a sharp whisper.

"Sorry, I didn't mean to" Lily replied.

Ophelia whispered in a squeaky little voice; "Here they are"

Very slowly Lily stepped around to stand beside Ophelia and… there the body was. It was a dead woman with a big dead parrot lying beside her. The parrot had beautiful long blue and red tail feathers. On the parrots blue head was a small crawfish catch-net with its draw string hanging alongside the parrot's beak. Its huge beak was bright yellow and there were three lines of little black feathers swirled around the parrot's eyes. Short little green feathers were sticking through the crawfish net like tufts of grass.

"Some of those tail feathers must be two foot long." Lily mumble-whispered, "and look, Ophelia, the wings are bright blue and green."

"That's what I told you, Lily." Ophelia replied

It was a magnificent looking bird.

Holding the lantern a little higher so they could get a better look at the body, Ophelia leaned in a little closer. In the haziness of the forest, they could tell it was a small woman and she was dressed unlike any other woman they knew. She wore a bright red gypsy top and burlap bloomers. It looked as if she had worn the burlap bloomers as trousers since they were dirty and frayed around the edges. On her legs were black stockings and dirty brown men's boots. Her legs were so skinny the tops of the boots were not lanced tightly around her ankles. Her hair was black, long and bushy; as if she had never pulled a comb through it. On her head was an old holey floppy brown felt hat with five bright blue parrots feathers pushed into the dirty hat band. In her hand she was clutching an old smoke pipe. Her face and hands were dirty but her gypsy blouse looked new and fairly clean.

"Wow", Lily said as she bent down to have a closer look. "I know who this is – it's Tillie Brown! She lives over on the riverbank and is a gambling boat-hopper. She sneaks on board and they just let her stay until she takes too much money from the other gamblers; then they boot her off at their next stop. Sometimes, when the New Orleans Sirene passes by town, I see her on the deck leaning over the railing smoking her pipe; all the while laughing at the town folk as they gawk at the boat. Her parrot's name is Duck. Wow, wonder what happened to them?"

"Are ya shh…ure about that Lily." Ophelia stuttered as she squatted down to get a closer look. "I don't think so. It doesn't look like Tillie Brown to me.

"Of course it's me, you empty headed gal." a voice yelled from the trees, "Who do you think it is; the King of Persia maybe?"

The voice let out a loud laughing cackle and started coughing.

"Awk…awk…Tillie Brown is dead!"

"Awk…awk…Tillie Brown is dead!" a parrot screamed.

Lily and Ophelia jumped up and grabbed each other's arms as they looked up in the trees; trying to find where the voice and squawk was coming from.

No more than ten feet above them on a small branch sat the ghosts of Tillie Brown and her parrot, Duck.

"Awk…awk…Tillie Brown is dead" screamed Duck

SMACK!

"Shut-up, Duck" yelled Tillie Brown's ghost as she smacked the ghost-parrot's chest. Duck flopped back and spun around the tree branch three times before coming to a wobbly stop. He swayed a bit as he tried to stop himself from going around a fourth time.